The White Indian Series
Book XXVII

CREEK THUNDER

Donald Clayton Porter

 BCI Producers of **Children of the Lion,**
The Holts, and **The First Americans.**

Book Creations Inc., Canaan, NY • Lyle Kenyon Engel, Founder

BANTAM BOOKS
NEW YORK • TORONTO • LONDON • SYDNEY • AUCKLAND

CREEK THUNDER

A Bantam Book / published by arrangement with
Book Creations Inc.

Bantam edition / December 1995
Produced by Book Creations Inc.
Lyle Kenyon Engel, Founder

ISBN 0-553-56143-X

Published simultaneously in the United States and Canada

Bantam Books are published by Bantam Books, a division of Bantam
Doubleday Dell Publishing Group, Inc. Its trademark, consisting of the
words "Bantam Books" and the portrayal of a rooster, is Registered in
U.S. Patent and Trademark Office and in other countries. Marca
Registrada. Bantam Books, 1540 Broadway, New York, New York
10036.

PRINTED IN THE UNITED STATES OF AMERICA

RAD   0 9 8 7 6 5 4 3 2 1

WHITE INDIAN FAMILY TREE

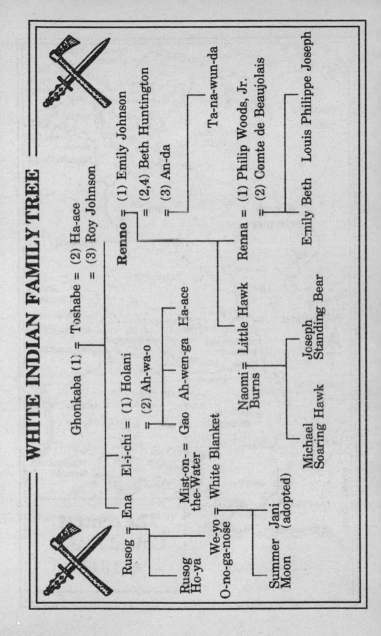

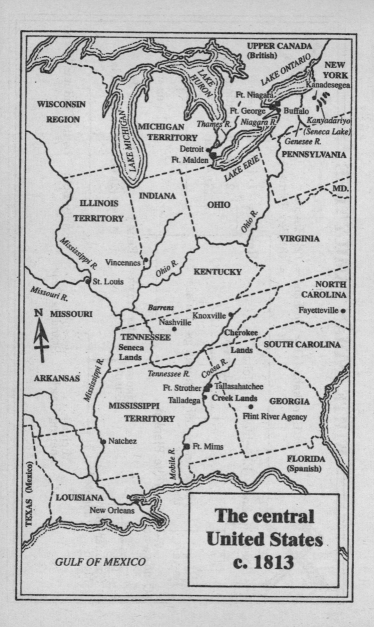

The central United States c. 1813

August 1813

"My son!"

Renno bolted upright in bed. He sat in the darkness, shaking his head.

"Are you all right?" his wife muttered, stirring beside him. When he did not reply, she touched his arm. "Renno, are you all right?"

"Yes, Beth. I'm fine." He patted her hand. "Just a dream."

"What about?"

"I . . . I don't remember."

"Lie down," she soothed. "Try to sleep."

He fell back against the pillows and lay staring into the blackness. His wife's breathing deepened, and when he was certain she was sleeping again, he rose and walked to the window.

Pulling the curtain aside, he stared into the night. Moonlight glinted across his broad, strong forehead, making his blond hair appear grayer than it was. At forty-nine, Renno was the fourth in a line of men known as the white Indian. His great-grandfather, for whom he was named, had been found as an infant by the sachem

Ghonka and raised as a Seneca. It was Renno's father, Ghonkaba, who had led some of their nation south to live with the Cherokee. Like his ancestors, Renno had been sachem of his people, but in recent years he had abdicated his position to his younger brother, the shaman El-i-chi. Still, Renno was given the honor and respect afforded a sachem.

This morning he did not feel like a sachem, for today he felt a strong measure of fear—something he invariably attributed to the white half of his blood.

It was only a dream, he told himself. Still, he could not shake the troubling images.

He understood that the best way to exorcise both the images and the fear was to confront them.

Alone. Like a sachem of the Seneca.

His feet and chest bare, Renno put on trousers and went outside, circled the house, and passed through the gardens. Leaping across a small creek, he started to run, guided by the pale light of the moon and his keen knowledge of the countryside. He entered the woods and quickened his speed until he was almost at a warrior's pace, his muscles tight with awareness as he raced along the path, dodging the trees that loomed up in front of him in the thin light.

The land gradually rose, and the trees grew sparser. Gaining the top of the ridge, he plunged down the other side into a broad, grassy meadow, then ran through another copse of trees and up a bluff that overlooked a broad stream. Here he came to a halt and stood with his hands on his hips, breathing hard, gazing across the valley to where the moon was settling into the west.

He knew that in the distance was the northward bend of the Tennessee River and beyond it the languid waters of the Mississippi. Farther still were lands seen only by their native tribes and by the few intrepid men who had dared the journey—among them his son Little Hawk, who had accompanied Meriwether Lewis and William Clark on their expedition to the Pacific Ocean.

Little Hawk was out there now, somewhere in the vast reaches of the Ozark Mountains of Missouri Territory. He was alone—and he was in trouble.

"Unless it was only a dream," Renno whispered.

But it had been a dream of such intensity that he could not shake the vision it had brought him:

Little Hawk writhing on the hard-packed earth. Clutching his side. Bleeding. . . . Three Creek warriors lying sprawled alongside him. Faces painted for war. Their eyes fixed in death. . . . A hand lifting Little Hawk's head. Caressing his long locks of yellow-gold hair. . . . A flash of steel. A whoop of victory. The scalping knife making its sharp, quick cut. . . .

Renno gasped and dropped to the ground. "No!" he blurted, pounding the earth, fighting the vision. "Not Little Hawk!"

"Who-o-o?" the wind seemed to call as it caressed his face and arms.

"I won't let you take Little Hawk!" he cried.

"No-o-o . . ." the wind replied.

Renno struggled to sit up, crossing his legs as he stared into the distance. Silently he called for them to come—the manitous of his ancestors.

They did not fail him. The first apparition was little more than a glimmer of light upon the white braids of an old man. Indistinct, floating in front of him, it spoke in the Seneca tongue of Renno's father, Chonkaba.

"No . . ." the manitou said, its voice one with the wind. "Little Hawk shall not die. The line of Renno and Ja-gonh and Ghonkaba shall continue."

"But the dream," Renno said, trying to focus on the face of the manitou, unable to see who it was. "What of the vision?"

"Do not be afraid. Os-sweh-ga-da-ah Ne-wa-ah"—it used Little Hawk's Seneca name—"walks the red path, though he does not see it. He will sit again at the council fire."

"But he has renounced the Seneca blood within him. He has turned his back on his ancestors."

"His ancestors do not turn their backs on him. And we will not turn our backs on Renno, son of Ghonkaba, grandson of Ja-gonh."

The manitou started to recede into the darkness.

"What must I do?" he called after it. "Why does this vision trouble my sleep?"

"Renno . . ." a soft voice, exceedingly sweet and familiar, whispered in reply.

"Emily!"

He struggled to see the face of his beloved first wife, but the moon had set, and all was darkness. Darkness and wind.

"Our son," the manitou said through the breeze. "Our son shall come home."

"Is he all right?" Renno asked. "Is he alive?"

"He shall come home. You shall see him again. Before you make the great journey."

"Is it me? Am I the one who will die?"

Something glimmered in front of him: hair as lustrous and golden as corn silk. "Be not concerned about the time or the place. You shall see your son again. You shall know who he is. The song shall be passed from father to son."

He sensed her withdrawing, and he reached toward her voice.

"That day, I shall be waiting," she promised, her voice caressing him as it faded into the night. "Then we shall journey beyond the river. Then I shall lead you home. . . ."

"Emily!" he called after her.

The wind echoed her name. And then she was gone.

Renno rose and took a step forward. To the west, the sky was pitch, but behind him he felt the stirrings of dawn. Turning, he faced the birthplace of the sun. It had not yet risen, but the blackness was giving way to streaks of blue. And low in the sky was a crimson glow, as if a council fire burned at the horizon.

"Home . . ." he breathed. "Little Hawk will come home."

Renno started down off the bluff. Heading east. Toward the sun.

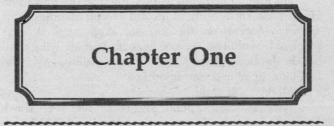

Chapter One

Hawk Harper hefted the long rifle once owned by his friend Meriwether Lewis. Lifting it to his shoulder, he sighted down the barrel and trained the gun at a point on the opposite side of the meadow. He held his breath, his finger tightening against the trigger.

Branches rustled, and the leaves parted at the precise spot he was aiming. Through the heavy mist he saw the animal emerge: a doe, almost as large as a buck. She hesitated, looking around the clearing, then took a few steps forward and nibbled at the grass.

Hawk chose a point on her midsection. As he pulled the trigger he saw a second animal, a young fawn, waddle into the meadow and stand behind its mother on gangly, unsteady legs. He tried to ease up on the trigger, but it was too late. The mechanism had already engaged, and the spring drove the hammer down onto the flashpan with a snapping *thunk*. The doe's ears rose. In the split second it took for the spark to ignite the powder and travel down the touchhole, Hawk threw the barrel skyward.

The explosion shattered the morning calm. Spinning

around, the doe leaped into the forest. The fawn hesitated, its body shaking with fear. And then it, too, was gone, racing into the underbrush after its mother.

Almost killed her, Hawk thought, shaking his head. Mother and child. Innocent. So close to death.

His eyes welled with tears as the memory took form. He saw the small body of his son Joseph Standing Bear sprawled lifeless on the ground, skull crushed, eyes plucked by vultures. He saw his wife, Naomi, lying dead beside the body of the Creek warrior Calling Owl, who had kidnapped and murdered her.

Mother and child.

They had died brutally, and brutal had been Hawk Harper's revenge. He had been known as Little Hawk then, but with their deaths he had disowned the one-quarter part of him that was Indian.

"Captain Hawk Harper," he whispered, trying to shut out the painful memories.

But he was not even Captain Harper any longer. He had resigned his Marine commission on the very eve of his appointment as President James Madison's military liaison officer. He had fully intended to report for duty after taking his surviving son, Michael Soaring Hawk, home to Huntington Castle. Months had passed since the deaths of his wife and son, and he had thought himself past mourning. But when the time came for him to set out for Washington, something had kept him from making the journey and had led him west instead, to live alone in these mountains and see if he could make some sense out of his great loss.

But he could not forget. He saw Naomi and Joseph in each change of season, in every living thing. Nor could he forgive, try as he might.

The weeks had become months. And still he did not know when he would be ready to return home, when he would be able to see his family and surviving son again.

Hawk Harper shivered and told himself it was from

the late-summer chill that had begun to settle each night over the Ozark Mountains. Leaning his rifle against a tree, he reached into the leather pack at his side for a sizable metal flask, uncorked it, and took a quick tug, feeling the warm whiskey burn the back of his throat. He started to replace the cork but raised the flask to his lips again and then again. Soon he was seated with his back against the trunk, his knees drawn up under his chin.

Hard drink did not agree with Hawk, but he no longer cared. He never bothered to shave anymore, and it had been more than a few weeks since he had last bathed in the creek near the cave that he called home.

"What does it matter?" he asked himself and took another gulp.

By the time he set out for home, his legs were as unsteady as that fawn's. He had managed with some effort to reload the rifle and hoist it over his shoulder, and now it balanced there precariously, the barrel swinging as he tottered along the narrow deer path. The forest grew quiet as he passed, birds and squirrels flitting for cover as if they knew the weapon might go off at any moment.

Usually Hawk moved silently through the woods—in the manner of the very ancestors he now rejected. This morning he didn't even try. Instead he burst into an old tavern song he had learned at West Point:

> "Bring 'round the whiskey, boys.
> Let all the maids be kissed.
> For when we march agin the king
> They surely shall be missed.

> "So raise high your flagons, lads,
> And to the maidens sing.
> For when the cocks have made their call
> We march agin the king."

Hawk downed the last of the whiskey and dropped the flask into his bag. It missed its mark and clattered to the ground, left forgotten alongside the trail.

He swung the rifle off his shoulder and clutched it against his chest. Throwing back his head, he laughed uproariously at some imagined fantasy, some remembered incident of his youth. His bellowing voice rose again:

> *"So raise high your flagons, lads,*
> *And to the maidens sing.*
> *For when the cocks have made their call*
> *We march agin the king!"*

The deer path widened, opening into a grassy clearing set against the base of a rocky escarpment. Stepping into the clearing, Hawk lowered the rifle butt to the ground and leaned against the barrel, steadying himself as his blurred vision adjusted to the glare of sunlight. With some effort, he focused on the jumble of rocks at the base of the escarpment and made out the entrance to the small cave he called home.

Assured that no one was about, he muttered, "All's well that ends well," then staggered across the clearing.

As he neared the cave a dark shape appeared among the boulders, and he stopped short, jerking up the barrel of his rifle.

What he thought might be a bear took human form as it stepped into the light: a man about thirty years old, wearing the distinctive paint of a Creek warrior. Two younger warriors came into view on either side of him, all three standing in front of the cave from which they had emerged—*his* cave.

Their appearance instantly cleared the fog from Hawk's mind. Gripping the rifle and swinging the barrel between them, he cursed himself for drinking too much and making such a commotion tramping through the trees. He noted that the two younger ones carried firearms—old trading muskets from the looks of them—while their leader had only a bow and arrow. None of them were making any move to bring their weapons into play.

Warily, Hawk lowered the barrel but kept his finger on the trigger, reasoning that if he handled things right, there wouldn't be any need for gunplay. Raising his other hand, he called out, "Welcome."

The warriors looked at one another. Then the leader raised his hand and repeated the English greeting, followed by a few words in his language. Hawk shook his head, indicating he did not understand, though in truth he knew a little Creek—enough to be a better listener than talker. With the odds so much against him, it was far better to listen than to speak.

The man repeated his question in passable English, and Hawk replied, "My name is Harper. I am a hunter, and this is my home." He waved the barrel, indicating the entire clearing. "By what name are you called?"

"Thunder Arrow." The man pointed to his companions and introduced them as Running Fox and Talks-with-Clouds.

"You are welcome to my home," Hawk said, trying to sound as sincere as possible. He took a cautious step forward, then halted. When they made no hostile gestures, he moved closer and asked, "Have you traveled far?"

"Many days." Thunder Arrow signed that they were coming from the north.

"Then you must rest awhile from your journeying." Lowering his rifle all the way, Hawk gestured at the cave. "You may share my meal."

The young man named Running Fox whispered something to Thunder Arrow, his tone curt and somewhat agitated. From the few words Hawk picked up, he guessed the man was suggesting they kill him and take whatever he had. But Thunder Arrow cut him off with a sharp glance.

Turning back to Hawk, the Creek warrior nodded and said, "We share your fire."

They followed Hawk into the cave. It was not much more than a deep cleft in the escarpment, and quite a bit of light spilled through fissures in the rock above.

As the warriors sat around the fire pit, Hawk stood his rifle near the entrance but kept the pair of ornately carved pistols tucked under his belt. He gathered dry branches from a pile inside the cave and added them to the hot coals. When they crackled and burst into flames, he placed several small logs on top.

Hawk took out some dried venison and handed it to the three men. As he sat among them he noticed they were closely examining the cave, as if looking for something. He did not doubt they had already searched the premises. Nor did he doubt what it was they desired.

It took only a few minutes before Thunder Arrow came to the point with a single questioning word: "Rum?" He made a sign of drinking from a bottle.

Hawk weighed his options. It was likely they were making no moves against him because they had not found his stash of liquor. And they would certainly assume he kept such a stash, given his recent inebriated state. But if he shared his supply, they would have little reason to let him live. Then again, it was equally possible it would make them forget their natural animosity toward him. The one thing of which he was certain was that turning them down would be a sure route to disaster.

"Rum. Yes, let's have something to drink."

He could feel their eyes upon him as he rose and crossed to the cave entrance. Heading outside, he made his way among the boulders strewn along the base of the escarpment until he found the one marking where he had hidden many of his supplies. Moving some of the loose rocks, he retrieved a jug and carried it back.

They just want a drink, Hawk told himself as he reentered the cave. The three men were seated where he had left them, and indeed they did not appear threaten-

ing. They were Creeks, to be sure, and as such his sworn
enemies. But those responsible for the deaths of his wife
and son had already met their fate at his hand. There was
no need for further bloodshed.

*Let them have their drink. Then they will be on their
way.*

Removing the cork from the jug, he handed it to
Thunder Arrow, who sniffed at it and nodded. Apparently he did not mind that it was whiskey instead of
rum—if he even knew the difference.

The jug was passed eagerly from hand to hand.
When it reached Talks-with-Clouds, who sat at Hawk's
left, he took a long swig, then hesitated. Finally he
grunted and thrust the jug at their host.

Hawk pretended to drink, then passed the whiskey
back around.

"Where are you traveling?" he asked after the jug
had made a third circuit.

Thunder Arrow said in the Creek tongue, "We are
on our way home to Cusseta, in the south."

Hawk knew perfectly well what had been spoken.
But guessing the man was testing his knowledge of their
language, he shook his head and shrugged, indicating
that he did not understand.

"We go home," the warrior said in English.

"Ah, yes. To your village?"

The man nodded. "Cusseta."

Hawk raised the jug. As the whiskey touched his
closed lips, he jerked the jug away. *Cusseta.* The name
came back to him in a flash—and with it bitter memories.

His eyes narrowed as he handed Thunder Arrow the
jug. "Cusseta," he repeated, forcing calm into his voice.
"Is that near the Flint River Agency?"

Thunder Arrow nodded and took a long pull at the
jug.

Hawk felt his back stiffen. He had found the body of
his beloved Naomi near Cusseta.

The jug continued its circuit, and Hawk could see

that the whiskey was having its effect. If he did not antagonize them and perhaps offered them a second jug for the trail, they likely would soon have their fill and be on their way. No need for bloodshed. No need for violence.

If he just did not push things.

Hawk passed the jug around yet another time, trying to remain silent, to let the matter rest. But then, before he realized what he had said, he had spoken the name aloud: "Calling Owl. Did you know Calling Owl?"

Thunder Arrow eyed him suspiciously. "You know of Calling Owl?"

"All of my people know the name Calling Owl."

Running Fox turned to Thunder Arrow and asked, "What does he say about Calling Owl?" Though he spoke in his own tongue and used Calling Owl's Creek name, he apparently understood what Hawk had been speaking about.

Paying no attention to his comrade, Thunder Arrow asked Hawk, "Why you speak of Calling Owl?"

Hawk shrugged as nonchalantly as possible. "Calling Owl was a great warrior. Yet we heard he was killed by a woman. Not just a woman but a white woman."

Talks-with-Clouds now pressed for an explanation of what was being discussed. Thunder Arrow turned to the warriors and said in Creek, "He has heard how Calling Owl was disgraced by that whore of a white devil."

Running Fox chuckled. "He took her like a dog, and she bit off his nose like a mountain lion."

"And cut off his manhood!" Talks-with-Clouds added, laughing loudly.

Thunder Arrow did not seem so amused. He looked back at Hawk and said in broken English, "You hear of Calling Owl so far away?"

Hawk's nod was solemn and threatening. "Calling Owl is known far and wide as a man who would spill the blood of a woman and child rather than face his enemy alone on the field of battle."

Thunder Arrow's hand eased toward the tomahawk

at his belt. Prodded by his comrades, he translated what
had been said.

"Tell him how the white woman squealed like a pig
as she died," Running Fox suggested, laughing even
harder.

"And how our warriors first passed her around and
tasted her pale flesh." Talks-with-Clouds snatched the
jug from his friend's hand and took a generous gulp.

"Calling Owl was great warrior," Thunder Arrow
said in English.

"He was a coward," Hawk Harper shot back. "A
coward and a skunk."

Thunder Arrow stood, gripping the handle of his
tomahawk. Hawk rose and faced him, his own hands not
far from the pistols in his belt. Still seated, the other
warriors stopped chuckling and stared up at the two men.

"Calling Owl was my friend," Thunder Arrow declared solemnly.

"As he was my enemy," Hawk replied. "Still, that is
no reason for us to be enemies. Unless you would speak
poorly of the woman he killed."

Sneering, Thunder Arrow spat out the words, "The
white whore."

Hawk kept his tone calm and even. "That woman
was my wife."

Thunder Arrow's eyes widened, and he whispered,
"Little Hawk . . ."

His companions asked what had been said, but before the warrior could reply, Hawk turned to them and
said in Creek, "My name is Hawk Harper, but Calling
Owl knew me as Little Hawk. It was my wife who cut off
his manhood and took from him the breath of the Master
of Life. And it was my own hand that struck down his
followers: New Man, Wild Wind, Eneah, Little Fox, Red
Runner, and Gator Toe. Of those who were with Calling
Owl when he kidnapped my wife, Stone Head alone still
walks the earth. He lives only because I had had enough
of killing."

Running Fox shot to his feet and exclaimed, "New Man was my cousin! You left him for the buzzards to devour!" He stood a bit unsteadily as he glowered at Hawk.

"What is in the past need not come between us," Hawk said in their tongue. "But you must not speak ill of the woman who was my wife."

Talks-with-Clouds rose also but with greater difficulty. His words slurred, he said, "Red Runner and Gator Toe were my friends."

"And the white woman was a whore!" Running Fox spat, drawing the knife from his belt.

Thunder Arrow alone remained calm. Letting go of his tomahawk, he raised his hand to restrain his companions. Fixing a cold eye on Hawk, he said in Creek, "You have shared your rum and your fire. We have no quarrel with you."

Turning, he motioned sharply for the others to leave the cave. Talks-with-Clouds complied, staggering out into the morning sun. Running Fox was more reluctant, but with a prod from his leader, he turned and stalked outside.

Thunder Arrow paused at the cave entrance. Looking back at Hawk Harper, he nodded and said in English, "Your wife brave woman. She honored your name."

Hawk returned the nod and stood motionless as the warrior disappeared into the glare of sunlight.

Realizing he was gripping the handles of his pistols, Hawk let go and rubbed his palms together. Walking to the cave entrance, he stepped into the light and watched the three men continue across the clearing. Running Fox and Talks-with-Clouds were talking to each other as they approached the trees. Thunder Arrow was farther behind and to their right.

As they gained the trees, Hawk started back into the cave. He was still turning when something slammed into his left side, followed by the sound of a gunshot. Thrown to the ground by the force of the slug, he spun around and caught sight of Running Fox at the edge of the trees, his musket smoking as he reloaded.

Even as Hawk jerked one of the pistols from his belt, he realized it was too long a shot. Dropping it, he crawled to his rifle, leaning against the entrance. He thumbed back the hammer and swung it around, praying the charge was still primed. Sighting down the barrel, he saw a puff of smoke from Running Fox's barrel, then heard the report a split second after the musket ball ricocheted off the rock wall beside Hawk's head.

Hawk held his breath and squeezed the trigger. The hammer snapped down, and there was a moment's hesitation as the spark set off the powder in the pan. Then the gun recoiled with an echoing boom, and Running Fox was thrown off his feet, the side of his face blown away.

As the acrid smoke cleared, Hawk spied Talks-with-Clouds racing toward him, musket at the ready. Close on his heels was Thunder Arrow, who looked as if he was trying to run down his companion.

Hawk drew the remaining pistol from his belt and in one smooth motion cocked, aimed, and squeezed the trigger. The hammer struck with a dull *thunk*. Thumbing it back, he pulled the trigger a second time, but the gun would not fire. Tossing it aside, he leaped for the pistol left lying by the entrance and heard the muffled boom of the musket and the whistle of the ball flying past his head.

Snatching up the pistol, he rolled and came up on his knees, firing at the warrior, now less than twenty yards away. But Talks-with-Clouds was prepared and dived to the ground as the gun fired. In horror, Hawk saw a spurt of red from the chest of Thunder Arrow, who was close behind. Thunder Arrow drew up short, staggered a few more steps, and fell to the ground.

Talks-with-Clouds was already on his feet. He sprinted the remaining yards between them, pulling a tomahawk from his belt as he came. With a terrifying yell he leaped at Hawk, raising the tomahawk above his head.

Hawk swung his pistol, slamming it into the man's hand as Talks-with-Clouds knocked him back into the cave. The young warrior managed to hold on to the weapon and viciously swept it down, just missing Hawk's head. Hawk smacked his pistol barrel into the man's cheek, knocking him to the side.

The two men went rolling. Talks-with-Clouds flailed away with the tomahawk, but Hawk managed to grab it and wrench it away. It spun through the air, landing at the edge of the fire pit.

The young warrior pulled himself free of Hawk and scrambled across the floor. His fingers were about to close around the tomahawk when Hawk landed on his back, shoving him aside. Talks-with-Clouds twisted around, throwing Hawk over him and onto the fire, but Hawk rolled clear. The warrior was instantly on him again, hands locked around his throat, thumbs pressing into his windpipe. Sputtering, Hawk tried to break the man's hold. But the grip tightened, and Hawk felt the heat of the flames only inches from his face.

Hawk's body went limp. His hands fell from the warrior's forearms to his sides.

Talks-with-Clouds continued to press, intent on choking the life out of his enemy. But his victim no longer struggled, and so he eased the pressure slightly.

Hawk struck with the speed of a snake. He drew the knife from his belt and drove it into the warrior's midsection, jerking it upward, through the stomach, the long blade piercing the heart. The Creek's body jerked; his nerveless fingers loosened, falling away.

There was a dull moan, then silence. Hawk rolled the body off and rose to his knees. Talks-with-Clouds's eyes were open, and for a moment Hawk thought he was making some sort of entreaty. Then the spirit passed from him, and his eyes glazed over.

Hawk pulled himself to his feet and thought he saw a shadow move out in the clearing. With that came the realization that one of the others might still be alive, and in a heartbeat he yanked the knife from the body at his feet and staggered toward the cave entrance.

He blinked, struggling to clear his vision as he came out into the glare of sunlight. Someone was kneeling at Thunder Arrow's side, but it was not Running Fox, whose body lay crumpled a dozen yards away. It was another warrior, and when he saw Hawk standing there, he jumped up and ran toward the forest.

Hawk cursed. The three men must have left a lookout in the woods—someone who might be on his way to summon other Creeks in the area. Forgetting his weakness and pain, Hawk took off at a run, his head still foggy and his vision a blur as he raced across the clearing and entered the woods only yards behind the warrior.

Branches slapped against his face as he closed in on his prey. He knew if he did not quickly overtake the Indian, his little remaining strength would be exhausted, and the man would get away. But he had the advantage of knowing these woods and was able to leap over fallen trees and other obstacles that slowed his quarry.

The underbrush thinned. He heard a cry and saw the shadowed figure only a few feet ahead. The fellow was shorter and slighter than his companions—possibly a young warrior on his first foray.

Hawk closed the distance between them, raising the knife in front of him. But when the man stumbled, Hawk barreled into him, the blade barely missing its mark as they tumbled to the ground. In an instant Hawk was up, spinning and lunging at the young warrior, who lay facedown a few feet away.

The Creek rolled over and gave a cry, hands raised to ward off the thrust of the knife, eyes open wide. Dark, frightened eyes—the eyes of a young woman.

Stabbing down with the knife, Hawk jerked his hand to the side at the last moment, and the blade sank into the soft earth beside the woman's head. She flailed at him, her fists smacking his shoulders and chest, her breath coming in ragged gasps that Hawk was surprised to find moved him. He managed to grab her wrists and pinned her to the ground.

"Stop!" he yelled, repeating it in the Creek tongue.

She stared up at him, her body rigid, her eyes filled with shock and fear.

"Don't move!" he ordered in Creek as he gingerly released first one hand, then the other.

She lay beneath him, her only movement the quick rise and fall of her chest and the darting of her eyes as she sought a path of escape.

Snatching the knife from the ground, Hawk held it in front of her as he rose to his feet. She wore the leggings and hunting shirt of a young warrior, but as he gazed down at her, he wondered how he had ever thought her a man. It did not surprise him that the three Creeks would not want such an attractive young woman to accompany them while they investigated the white man's cave.

Stepping back a few feet, Hawk tucked the knife under his belt. He felt strangely light-headed, and remembering the wound he had suffered, he ran his hand along his left side just under the armpit and felt the warm, sticky blood that was soaking through his buckskins.

"Get up," he told her, first in English and then Creek. He motioned with his hand, and at last she complied, standing up and brushing off her clothes. Finally he muttered, "Go on, get out of here," and gestured for her to leave.

She glanced toward the clearing where her friends lay dead and after a few moments of indecision set out in the opposite direction. When she hesitated again and looked over at Hawk, he waved her away, then turned his back on her and started toward the clearing.

Fog suddenly settled, closing around him. A cold, numbing fog. He shivered as he forced one leg in front of the other. His body was leaden, his head swirling like a leaf on a river.

He thought of his young son, his small skull crushed by Calling Owl's tomahawk. And of his wife's corn-silk hair matted with blood.

He had taken a musket ball, but he did not feel it. He did not even think about it. His mind's eye was focused on the faces of Joseph Standing Bear and Naomi. They called to him, and as his legs gave way beneath him, he went rushing toward their outstretched arms.

Chapter Two

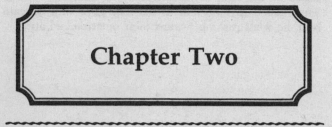 Ta-na-wun-da ran at a warrior's pace across the broad green meadow. Far to his right the waters of the Tennessee River glimmered a deep purple in the filtered afternoon light. Beyond it a bank of clouds eased across the grasslands, burnt-orange tendrils entwined around the sun.

The rifle tucked under his arm felt as heavy as a tree trunk, and he shifted it to his other side. His legs and lungs cried out for him to stop, to stand motionless in the middle of the field and embrace the final hours of what had been a perfect day. But he would not rest—not until he had crossed the ridge that loomed in the distance.

One more hill, he told himself. *Just one more.*

It felt good to be out on his own, running free, away from the Cherokee-Seneca village of Rusog's Town and the confines of Huntington Castle. Not that he spent all that much time at the home of his father, the sachem Renno. His father had seemed sullen and withdrawn this past year—ever since Ta-na's half brother, Little Hawk, had resigned his military commission and gone west into the Ozarks. Ever since Renno's eldest son. . . .

My son . . . he heard his father intoning. And Ta-na knew it was spoken for his brother.

"Little Hawk," he whispered between panting breaths.

In the months before departing, Little Hawk had stopped using that name, preferring to be called simply Hawk or even Harper, the family surname. And he had completely rejected his Seneca name, Os-sweh-ga-da-ah Ne-wa-ah, just as he had rejected his Indian blood.

The one-quarter part of him that is Indian, Ta-na-wun-da thought, shaking his head ruefully.

Ta-na, on the other hand, was three-quarters Seneca. He could not help but wonder if that was why his father did not seem to notice him.

"Little Hawk," he breathed. "Always Little Hawk."

Ta-na tried to shake loose the troubling thoughts. He was twenty years old—far too old for self-pity or regrets. If Renno favored his elder son over his younger, such was a father's right. Some would call it his duty. And Ta-na would do well to accept it as the will of the Master of Life.

If Little Hawk owned their father's heart, at least Ta-na possessed a full measure of the bloodline of the first white Indian, who had been named Renno like their father. In fact, Ta-na's grandmother, Toshabe, used to say that though Ta-na's hair and skin coloring had come from his full-blood Seneca mother, he had the features and physique of his great-grandfather, Ja-gonh, son of the first Renno.

Ta-na-wun-da shortened his stride but maintained his pace as he left the meadow and started up an incline toward the ridge. On the far side was a valley with a small stream running through it; he would rest there and take his evening meal. He might even make camp and return to Rusog's Town the next morning. He knew Renno would be annoyed if he stayed away the whole night—but his father would keep that anger to himself.

Not once during the past year had he questioned Ta-na's comings or goings. Not since Little Hawk went away.

Ta-na's own heart was heavy, though not from his brother's absence. True, he and Little Hawk had always gotten along well. But nine years separated them, and Ta-na had spent much of his childhood in the home of his uncle, El-i-chi. Though Little Hawk was his brother in the flesh, his cousin Gao, with whom he had been raised, was his brother in the spirit. In fact, he had suckled at the breast of his aunt, Ah-wa-o, alongside Gao, who was only a few months older.

Ta-na missed his cousin terribly, but more than distance had come between them. After marrying the young Potawatomi-French woman Mist-on-the-Water, Gao had joined the Pan-Indian movement led by Tecumseh, a prophet and war leader determined to drive the whites back across the great water of the Atlantic. To further those ends, Tecumseh had allied his forces with the British, who were battling the Americans in the frontier around Lake Erie. This placed Gao in opposition not only to the young nation but to his own family, who considered themselves Americans.

Ta-na had been thinking more and more about his friend in recent days. What had become of Gao? Was he well? Had he been injured in battle?

"He is fine," he declared, nodding. Of that he was certain, for they had been almost as close as twins, and Ta-na always felt Gao's suffering as if it were his own.

If something happened to him, I would know, he told himself.

Yet thoughts of his best friend were coming with marked frequency, leading Ta-na to suspect that something was about to happen—that some news of Gao's circumstances would reach him all the way here in the Cherokee Nation.

As Ta-na gained the ridge, he slowed his pace somewhat and sprinted down the slope toward the creek. A line of thin alders marked its banks, and he headed toward a broad bend where a calm pool had often provided him with fish. If he was lucky he would soon be roasting one over a campfire.

His luck held, and in less than an hour he had a low fire burning and several trout laid out on a hot stone. His pack contained a thin blanket, and he spread it in front of the fire and sat cross-legged upon it, stirring the coals with a stick.

Another hour passed. The sun was just touching the horizon when he heard people approaching from the south. Indians, he guessed from the sound of their moccasins.

Leaving the fire burning, he snatched his rifle and moved upstream, hiding in the underbrush from where he could see the campsite. A few minutes later the travelers emerged from the trees on the far side of the creek and waded across the water.

It appeared to be a Creek raiding party—an even half-dozen men, faces painted, muskets at the ready. They searched the campsite, emptying Ta-na's pack but making little effort to ferret him out.

Perhaps they will take what they want and leave, he told himself.

It would be readily apparent that this was the campsite of a lone person, and they might not waste time rousting him from his hiding place. Unless, of course, they were looking for a little entertainment.

Take what you want and go, he silently urged them. *Before it gets dark.*

But the sun had already dipped below the horizon, the light was growing thin, and they were making no effort to leave. In fact, three of them had seated themselves around the fire and were picking at the remaining scraps of trout. They appeared ready to settle in for the night, and they wouldn't want to leave a stranger—presumably armed—lurking somewhere among the trees. Ta-na was convinced they would soon search the area.

As he knelt in the bushes, rifle shouldered and

cocked, one of the men moved away from his companions and started toward him. The fellow was about Ta-na's age and size, his features obscured by paint, his head half hidden by a plait of feathers that cascaded down the left side of his face. He looked somewhat different from the others in both dress and physique, and for a moment Ta-na assumed he was their leader. But as he drew closer, Ta-na decided he must be from some allied tribe.

Even as Ta-na trained the rifle barrel on the stranger's chest, he knew resistance would be futile. His only hope was to make a run for it and pray they were poor shots. He would wait as long as possible; each second he delayed was another moment for the darkness to close in and assist his escape.

Stay calm, he told himself. *Let this fellow pass.*

But the warrior wasn't moving on. In fact, he seemed to possess an uncanny sense for where Ta-na was hiding. He walked to within a few yards of the bushes and stood gazing at them, trying to peer into their shadowed recesses. Beyond him, the Creek warriors began beating the underbrush closer to the campfire in an attempt to roust him out.

The Indian with the plait of feathers moved a few steps closer, held his palms forward as if to show he came in peace, and intoned, "Ta-na-wun-da."

An electric bolt shot up the young Seneca's spine. The voice was so familiar, yet almost unreal.

"Ta-na-wun-da," the warrior repeated.

Dropping his rifle, Ta-na leaped from the bushes and raced toward the man, arms wide in greeting as he shouted, "Gao! You've come home, Gao!"

As the cousins embraced, Gao's companions gathered around him, grinning and clapping him on the back.

Ta-na sat in front of the fire, listening as his cousin explained how he had been sent by Tecumseh on a mission to Creek country south of Tennessee. Gao and the Creeks had been on their way back north when he decided to visit his parents in Rusog's Town. Leaving his companions some distance from the village, he had gone in alone and spent a few hours—long enough to assure his family he was all right and to learn where Ta-na had gone.

"I still cannot believe you found me," Ta-na marveled when Gao finished his story.

"It really was quite easy," Gao professed. "When your father told me you were on a run, I knew I must either wait for you to return or go looking. My friends were eager to push on, so I decided to hunt you down. And where else would you be but along this trail, where we spent so many hours of our youth? When I saw this reckless fire, I knew it had to be my little cousin." He gave a teasing grin.

"This region has been at peace since Tecumseh went north," Ta-na replied, his look almost accusatory. "A man can make a fire without fear of losing his scalp." He gazed at Gao's companions, his jaw tightening.

Gao glanced over his shoulder at the Creeks, who were contentedly eating chunks of venison. "It's a good thing I am with them, cousin. If not, that beautiful long hair of yours might be gracing a Creek musket barrel."

"I suspect that without you, they never would have passed through Cherokee lands or Tennessee."

Gao nodded. "There is truth to what you say. The Creek have learned to avoid Andrew Jackson's country. When they must journey north, they travel on the far side of the Father of Waters." He used the Indian name for the Mississippi River.

Ta-na stared at his cousin for a long moment, then shook his head in amazement. "I would have loved to see your father's expression when you showed up in Rusog's Town."

Gao looked down at his outfit. "I was not dressed like this. And I did not have my Creek friends with me."

Ta-na chuckled. "I can only imagine what El-i-chi would have thought if you walked in like that." He leaned over and smudged his cousin's face paint with his thumb.

Gao slapped his hand away, then grinned sheepishly. "To be truthful, this was mostly for your benefit."

"You thought to put a scare in me, yes? And what if instead I had put a bullet in you?"

Gao chuckled. "Ah, so you learned to fire a rifle since I left." His eyes narrowed thoughtfully. "I knew you would do no such thing. Ta-na is far too cautious."

"You don't know that. Many moons have crossed the sky since we parted company."

"And in that time you have begun to soar free? Like a little hawk?"

Ta-na knew the comparison to his elder half-brother, in whose shadow he had always been, was intentional. He chose not to respond to the comment but instead declared, "I choose my own path."

"Then why are you still under the wings of our fathers? You can fly higher than a hawk. As high and swift as a ball of fire that streaks across the sky."

"You want me to fly on the tail of the Panther Passing Across," Ta-na said solemnly. He spoke of Tecumseh, who had been given the name Panther Passing Across because of the flaming ball of green fire that had lit the sky on the night of his birth.

"It is a good life in the Canadas. There we are not Seneca or Shawnee or Creek. We are one people, and we will have our land and our honor back." Gao leaned forward and grasped his cousin's forearm. "Come with me, Ta-na. It is our destiny."

Ta-na frowned but did not pull his arm away. "Is it our destiny to be slaves to the British? Since when have they cared what becomes of us? Their coats may be red, but their skin is as white as the Americans they fight."

"The British are less than nothing," Gao spat, sneering with contempt.

"Yet you fight at their side."

"Their guns will help us drive the Americans from

our land. And when that is finished, we shall send the redcoats scurrying back to their ships."

"No, Gao, you will not. The British lost this land; they will not reclaim it. The only thing Tecumseh's war will accomplish is to harden the hearts of the Americans against all of our people."

"Their hearts are already hard." Gao smacked fist against palm.

"You speak of my father's people."

"Renno is a sachem of the Seneca. His blood may be mixed, but his spirit is red."

"And what of my blood . . . and yours? Do we not have a portion white?"

"The red has long since drowned out the white," Gao declared.

"And you would have me drown the oath my family has taken to the Americans?"

"The Americans do not keep the many promises they have made to our people," Gao argued.

"We are speaking of *my* word—no one else's. Would you also have me turn against my father? And what of your father? Does El-i-chi's heart not ache to see you join arms with Tecumseh?"

Gao's gaze lowered, and he shook his head. "We did not speak of Tecumseh. He saw from my eyes that my path was set. He did not try to talk me from it."

"Then do not try to talk me from mine."

Gao looked up, his eyes entreating. "Is it truly your path, Ta-na? Are you certain this is so?"

Ta-na hesitated. "I know only this: It is not my path to take up arms against the people of my father and my grandfather and his father before him."

"Are you so sure?"

He folded his arms over his chest. "If such is my path, let the manitous tell me it is so."

"So now Ta-na-wun-da speaks to the manitous?"

Ta-na allowed himself a small grin. "I have always

spoken to the manitous. They just do not choose to reply."

Gao smiled as well. "Nor to me. That is why I put my faith in a prophet with a human voice."

"I am pleased for you, Gao. Pleased that you are so certain of your path."

The two men fell silent. When at last they spoke again it was of more pleasant topics. Ta-na described the things he had done during the past year—and the young Cherokee and Seneca women he had wooed. Gao told of his life with Mist-on-the-Water and how his heart ached for her while he was gone.

It grew late, and they settled in for the night. As they spread their blankets and prepared to sleep, Gao made one final entreaty.

"Ta-na-wun-da, in the morning I return to where Tecumseh is gathering warriors in the north. I want us to part as brothers and friends, so when the sun rises I will trouble you no more about this matter. But tonight I must ask one last time if you will reconsider and take the red path. If it is your family that concerns you, know that Tecumseh assures us that when the Americans begin to retreat, our families and our people will see that this is the will of the Master of Life. They will know that Tecumseh speaks the truth, as he did when he warned that the earth would shake."

Gao referred to the great New Madrid earthquake of January 1812, an event foretold by Tecumseh as a sign for the Indian nations to unite against the white invaders.

"When they see the truth of the Panther's words," he continued, "then we shall walk the red path together."

"I am already upon that path," Ta-na declared. "But it does not lead me to the north or to Tecumseh."

"Then I shall wait until our paths meet. And I shall pray that the Master of Life brings that day soon." Gao rolled over and pulled the blanket around him. "Good night, Ta-na-wun-da."

"Good night, my cousin . . . my friend."

* * *

The next day, Ta-na-wun-da walked briskly up the broad, straight lane that led to Huntington Castle, the home of his father, Renno, and stepmother, Beth Huntington Harper. The lane, just outside Rusog's Town in the Cherokee Nation, was lined with pecan trees, with split-rail fences enclosing the surrounding pastureland. The white clapboard house at the end of the lane was more correctly called a mansion. Since there were no brick-making kilns in the Cherokee Nation, it had been constructed of native timber and sported a pillared front veranda. Craftsmen hired in Knoxville and Nashville had done the interior work, and furnishings had been brought from as far away as England to fill the twenty spacious rooms.

Ta-na halted at the end of the lane. He had only been away for a day, yet now as he looked up at the building, gleaming white in the early afternoon sun, he realized how out of place it was here in Cherokee country. Somehow that seemed appropriate, for the owner was not Cherokee but half Seneca and half white. Like this house, Renno did not always look as if he fit into his surroundings. Yet he moved effortlessly between the dual worlds of his ancestors.

Things were not so clear-cut for Renno's younger son. He often wore white men's clothing, although it made him feel ill at ease. Yet Ta-na was sometimes accused of not thinking like an Indian, and he had to admit there were moments when he simply did not know what to think.

He stared down at his buckskins—not Seneca or Cherokee or even white. Then he gazed back up at his father's home and shook his head ruefully. Truly he did not belong here in Huntington Castle. But where was his home? In what world did he fit?

"Ta-na!" a voice shouted, and he turned to see his father rounding the corner of the house. "You are home!"

The young man felt awkward and self-conscious as

Renno hurried over and clasped his forearms. Ta-na covered his feelings by asking, "Did you see Gao?"

Renno's smile faded. "He was here yesterday. I fear he has broken his father's heart."

"Gao must walk his own path."

"That boy had better come to his senses. Anyone who believes Tecumseh can overcome the westward march of white settlers is a fool. Their numbers are too great . . . like the stars in the night sky."

"I think in his heart Gao knows this to be so."

"Then why does he fight alongside Tecumseh? To take up arms against the United States is to die. It is that simple."

"There are those who would rather die free than live as slaves."

"Are we slaves?" Renno asked, waving a hand to indicate their home and the land surrounding it.

"I fear the day will come when even this will be taken from our people," Ta-na replied. "We will be forced to walk a bitter trail beyond the Father of Waters to an unknown home and an uncertain future . . . whether we are full-blooded or only one half."

"Were you off on a run or a vision quest?" Renno asked, his tone tinged with scorn. When Ta-na did not reply, he took a step back and looked his son up and down. "Or perhaps it was your cousin who put such dark visions in your head. Did he convince you to take up arms against your own people?"

Ta-na hesitated a long moment before finally shaking his head. "I do not choose Gao's path of blood. But I understand it. And I suppose a part of me even envies it."

"Things are not as simple as Tecumseh would have us believe. He would defeat the Americans by siding with the British. Even should he succeed, it would not reduce the number of whites any more than my plucking a single strand of hair would make me bald. It would only place a less sympathetic ruler in Washington."

Ta-na sighed. "I know that you speak the truth. But still my heart is troubled."

Renno came up beside Ta-na and wrapped an arm around his shoulder. "I know just the thing for a troubled heart. One of Beth's hot meals."

"Yes. I'd like that."

"Then we will speak no more of Tecumseh. And if we mention Gao, it will be to wonder how he is handling that young wife of his. From what he told us, she is quite a beauty."

"A spirited one," Ta-na added, remembering the last time he had seen her at Vincennes.

Renno led his son toward the veranda. "And what of Ta-na-wun-da? Is there a spirited beauty in his future?"

Ta-na grinned. "Many. There will be many."

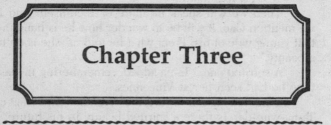

Chapter Three

Hawk Harper lay on his side and gazed down a long, dark tunnel toward a distant point of light. It drew closer, larger, blazing and dancing with all-consuming radiance.

Such is death, he thought and felt strangely at peace.

A figure moved in the light and stood haloed by it. A manitou of his father's people? he wondered. An angel of his mother's? A friend?

Naomi . . . he breathed, his voice no more than a faint rush of wind.

The face of the angel was shrouded in darkness, so great was the flaming halo of light at her back. But he saw her long, flowing hair and imagined it as golden as the sun. He gazed upon her lush, graceful figure and knew that soon he would be in her arms.

Naomi! he called again as he tried to reach out to her. He wanted to run to her, hold her close, breathe the aroma of her, and know that he was home. At last.

But he could not move—could not even raise his arms. And with a shock of fear he knew he would have to leave her again. It was not yet time.

And with that thought his beloved turned away from him. She turned to face the light.

"No!" Hawk shouted, railing against the angels, the manitous, the Maker of Life. Raging against God.

He felt heat at his back, as if another light was ablaze close behind him, drawing him back. Away from Naomi, away from God.

"No! No! No!" he screamed, struggling to hold on to her, afraid to let her go.

She heard his desperate cry, for she turned toward him again. She moved away from the light and came closer, down the long tunnel, until she was hovering in front of him, kneeling at his side.

"Naomi!" he cried, his eyes flooding with tears as he tried to make out her features through the shadows.

"Shh . . ." she whispered, placing a hand on his lips. Then she spoke something in a language he did not understand.

The language of the angels? he wondered.

The light flickered at Hawk's back. It danced across her face: skin soft and coppery, features delicate yet sharp, long hair that gleamed like a raven's wing.

She spoke again, and now he recognized the language as she told him, "Lie still."

It was the language of the Creek.

Hawk lay there, afraid to speak, unable to move. The young Creek woman rose and moved passed him. He heard her stirring the embers of a fire and felt its heat as it flared up behind him. As it cast a warm, shimmering glow on the walls of the cave.

The woman returned to his side and knelt in front of him, her touch gentle but her expression exceedingly sad, almost lifeless. She said, "Do not move," then stood again and started back down the tunnel through which she had come—the tunnel formed by the cave entrance.

Outside, the great light continued to rage. She walked to it, then disappeared off to the side. When she came back into view, she was dragging something along the ground. Hawk watched as she hoisted it with great effort and dropped it onto the blazing light.

It was indeed the light of death. It was a funeral pyre, and she stood framed by its glow as it consumed the bodies of her Creek companions.

"My brother . . ." Ma-ton-ga whispered, gazing up as streamers of smoke curled into the blackness above. "Be on your way, Thunder Arrow. May Running Fox and Talks-with-Clouds walk always at your side."

The pyre flared brighter, branches crackling with heat, hair and flesh and sinew hissing as they singed and charred. When she could bear the sound and smell no longer, Ma-ton-ga backed toward the cave. Turning, she ducked through the entrance and approached the white man. The one who had killed her brother.

He was in the other world again, eyes closed, breath shallow, completely unaware of her presence.

It is better this way, she told herself. She would not have to imagine him looking at her. She would not have to wonder what he was thinking or see the image of her brother reflected in those terribly cold, terribly blue eyes.

She had observed enough from the shelter of the forest to know that this white man had not drawn the first blood. Before the gunfire had erupted, she had thrilled to see her brother and his companions leaving the cave and coming to where they had left her. She had told them that they did not need anything the white man had to offer. They only needed to be on their way to the Creek lands in the south.

But Running Fox had been greedy. No sooner had they entered the woods than he had called out that he would not let the white man live another day. Then his musket had spoken, and it was answered by gunshots from the cave. And soon they all were lying dead: Running Fox, Talks-with-Clouds, and her beloved Thunder

Arrow. All but the white man, who hovered between the worlds of shadow and light.

He must be a great warrior among his people, to best three Creek warriors, she mused as she stared down at him. But a great man did not hide himself away in a hole in the mountainside. Perhaps he had the yellow-metal fever, though there were no signs that he had been digging in the earth or fishing rocks from streambeds.

He must suffer from the firewater madness, she told herself. Had they not heard him singing like a crazy one when he first appeared?

The young woman knelt beside the unconscious man and touched a lock of his hair. Never had she seen hair so golden or a face so strong and mysterious. It was true that he had the pale skin of his people, but it had been bronzed and toughened by the sun until it was almost as richly colored as her own. There was something familiar about him—something she could not identify. It was as if a part of him had come from the same source as her people.

Ma-ton-ga slowly drew forth the knife, which she had painstakingly cleaned and oiled after removing it from the white man's belt. She ran her thumb sideways across the blade. It was the sharpest edge she had ever felt; it could sever a man's throat as easily as a blade of grass.

She leaned over and held the knife close to his neck, watching the reflected firelight dance along his skin. She thought of how it had sliced open Talks-with-Clouds, spilling his blood upon the ground. She thought of the blood of her brother and Running Fox soaking into the earth.

Ma-ton-ga gently pressed the blade against the white man's throat. As her pressure increased, a trickle of blood oozed up along the edge of the metal. The man stirred but did not awaken, his head turning slightly, away from the knife.

"Thunder Arrow," she breathed. "Guide my hand. Steady my arm."

Again she placed the blade against his throat. She imagined his blood running free, his body being torn by vultures or joining her brother upon the pyre.

She wanted to cry, but she had forgotten how. Thunder Arrow was dead. And with him had gone all her feelings, all her tears.

She drew the knife upward under his chin, then along his cheek. Long, steady strokes, taking care not to break the skin as she scraped away the heavy stubble of beard, exposing the smooth flesh underneath.

She worked slowly and meticulously until his beard was gone. Then she stood and gazed down at her handi-work. Shaking her head, she circled the cave and rum-maged in her leather travel pack for a strip of beaded cloth. She returned to where the man was lying and tied it around his head, smoothing his hair into place.

Clean shaven and wearing a woven headband, he looked like the warriors of her tribe. A warrior with sun-bronzed skin and long, golden hair. A white Indian.

Hawk Harper parted his lips, felt the steam of the dandelion broth as the Creek woman spooned it into his mouth. He tried to swallow, gagged some of it back up, then managed to down a mouthful. When she tried to press the spoon back between his lips, he turned his head to the side. Even that small movement sent a wave of dizziness through him.

He had lost a lot of blood, but he would live. He was not certain such a prospect pleased him.

"What . . . what is your name?" he muttered in her language, glancing up at her.

It was not the first time he had asked, and again she did not reply. Instead she rose, crossed to the fire, and poured the broth back into the iron kettle.

When she looked back at him, he thumped his chest and said, "Hawk. Hawk Harper."

Seeming totally disinterested, she turned away and busied herself tending the fire.

The routine was the same since he had regained consciousness the night before. She would prepare broth and feed him, taking almost no nourishment herself. Then she would dress his wound and tend to any other chores—including emptying and cleaning the small pot in which he was forced to relieve himself. Hawk, in turn, would try without success to get the woman to speak. What little communication she offered was in the form of signs, though he knew she understood what he was saying. The only information he had managed to pry out of her was he had been unconscious for a day and a half.

"Enough of this," he told himself, jerking aside the blanket that covered him.

With a supreme effort of will, he pulled himself to a sitting position, then pushed up onto his knees. By the time the woman saw what he was doing, he had managed to get up off the floor and was standing on extremely wobbly legs, clutching his side.

"No!" she cried out in English as she rushed over to him.

"So you *do* speak," he exclaimed, his grimace giving way to a smile.

She tugged his arm to make him lie back down. When he did not cooperate, she turned her attention to the bandage—a poultice of crushed and boiled herbs held in place by a strip of cloth tied around his chest. Satisfied the wound had not opened, she frowned at him and walked outside. When she returned, she handed him a long stick, gesturing that he should steady himself with it. Then she went back about her business.

Hawk's first foray from the cave was only a few steps into the clearing—far enough to see that she had cleaned up all signs of the pyre. Then he hobbled back in and tried to sit down. He almost fell over, and the woman had to come over and grip his arm as he lowered himself onto the blanket.

At the end of the day, the woman slept on the far side of the fire. In truth, she hardly slept at all, for every time Hawk glanced over at her, he saw her looking back at him. Her expression was hard to decipher. He could see she was concerned about his health, much as a doctor might be for a patient. But there was something else—a mixture of anger and fear. It made him wonder why she had stayed and helped him. He had taken the lives of her companions; the spirits would not have blamed her if she had left him lying where he fell.

Every now and then he saw something in her eyes that suggested a more sinister motive—that she worked so hard to heal him so he would be fully conscious when she exacted revenge.

Hawk shook off the thought. It was a preposterous notion, and he was ashamed it had even occurred to him.

The next two days passed in much the same fashion: The Creek woman took care of the chores, while Hawk Harper grew steadily stronger. Soon he was able to tend the fire and cook his own meals. He no longer had to use the makeshift chamber pot and was even able to wash in the small stream at one end of the clearing.

Just before dawn five days after he was shot, Hawk was awakened by the Creek woman poking at his arm. She had already built up the cooking fire, and the walls of the cave seemed to dance in its glow. As his eyes adjusted to the light, he realized she had prodded him with the barrel of one of the Indian muskets.

For an instant he thought his time of reckoning had come. But then she raised the barrel and slung the weapon across her back, tightening the beaded strap so that it would not slip off her shoulder. Reaching down, she placed Hawk's knife on the ground beside him. Then she circled the fire and hoisted a leather pack over her other shoulder.

Picking up his knife, Hawk tossed aside his blanket

and stood. He watched her walk toward the cave entrance and tried to think of something appropriate to say.

"Thank you," he called, following her outside. He repeated the words in Creek.

She turned to him and nodded, then started across the clearing.

"Wait!" He moved toward her as quickly as he could manage.

She waited but kept her eyes lowered.

"I . . . I am sorry," he said in her language when he stood in front of her. "I did not want it to end that way."

She nodded but still did not look up.

"I want you to have this." He held out his knife. When she shook her head, he said, "It is yours."

He reached for her hand and placed the knife handle in her palm. Her fingers closed around it, and she gazed at it a long moment. Finally she looked up at him. There were tears in her eyes.

"Thunder Arrow was my brother," she said in Creek.

"I am sorry. Truly I am."

"Yes. I know."

She tucked the knife beneath her belt and started to walk away. But then she hesitated. Turning back around, she clapped her hand against her chest and intoned, "Ma-ton-ga."

Hawk smiled. "Thank you, Ma-ton-ga."

She returned his smile. Then she continued across the clearing and disappeared into the forest.

"Ma-ton-ga," he whispered after she was gone. Then he repeated her name in English: "Place-Where-the-Sun-Sleeps."

He thought of his beloved Naomi. She and little Joseph had gone ahead to that place where the sun sleeps, leaving him alone in this land beneath the sky. Though he wanted to follow, he was not brave enough for such a path. Instead of defending himself against Ma-ton-ga's warriors, he could have accepted their bullets and tomahawks as a fulfillment, a grace. Instead of struggling against death, he could have taken that final journey.

Was it Ma-ton-ga who had saved him? he wondered. Or was he simply too much of a coward to die?

A warm breeze poured from the cave at Hawk's back. He could almost see it as it swirled around him and followed Ma-ton-ga's path into the woods.

"You are the breath of the Master of Life," Hawk whispered. "Carry away my anger and pain. And carry my love to that place where the sun sleeps. To Naomi."

Chapter Four

 Renno joined his younger brother, El-i-chi, on the veranda of Huntington Castle. Dropping into his favorite bentwood rocker, he took out a pipe that had been carved from a gnarled root by his Cherokee friend Se-quo-i and filled it with tobacco. Resting his moccasined feet on the porch rail, he lit the pipe and turned to his brother.

"Ta-na-wun-da did not come?"

"He has gone on a hunt with friends," El-i-chi told him. "He has had enough of war and does not wish to see another man in uniform—even a friend of General Jackson's."

Renno nodded and drew on the pipe.

El-i-chi tapped the ashes from his own pipe and started to refill it. Glancing over at his older brother, he commented, "Your son has seemed ill at ease these few weeks."

"It will pass," Renno replied. He could feel his brother's eyes upon him, but he stared straight ahead, down the rows of pecan trees that lined the road leading up to the house.

"Has he spoken to you?"

"I have not seen him for several days." Renno's lips quirked into a smile. "Ta-na has always preferred a simple log cabin to . . . this." His hand indicated Huntington Castle.

"He was raised in a longhouse," El-i-chi pointed out.

Renno nodded. "*Your* longhouse."

"You do not regret—"

"No, no, El-i-chi," Renno cut him off. "I will always be grateful that you and Ah-wa-o taught him the ways of our people. But there are times I wish I could have been with him more when he was growing up."

"Ta-na understands."

Renno shook his head. "A child never understands the absence of a father."

"You were a good father, Renno. You *are* a good father."

Renno took a long draw on the pipe and released the smoke slowly, watching it curl overhead. When he finally spoke, his words had a quiet sadness. "A good father has his sons at his side. Ta-na-wun-da prefers to live in his uncle's house. And Little Hawk . . ."

"You've had no word of him?"

"We know where he lives, but he has asked that we not go there."

"He'll be back," El-i-chi declared. "When the time is right, he will return."

Renno was about to speak, but then he lowered his feet and leaned forward in the rocker. "They are coming," he said, waggling the stem of the pipe in the direction of the lane. "Ten of them. A captain rides at the head."

El-i-chi grinned. "You see fairly well . . . for an old man. But there are eleven: ten militiamen plus their captain."

"That's what I said."

"Ah, that's what you *meant*, perhaps. But you said

ten. Many a battle has been lost because of poor communication."

Renno turned to his brother and frowned, then chuckled. "That's why you are the sachem instead of me."

"No, big brother. I may wear the headdress now, but you will always be a sachem of our people."

"Come, El-i-chi." Renno stood and clapped his brother on the back. "Let us meet these fellows and find out what Andy Jackson wants of two old sachems like us."

The riders halted their horses in front of the veranda. With a great flourish, the captain removed his hat and swept it in front of him.

"Captain Scott Ridgley at your service. Might one of you be the Seneca sachem known as Renno?"

"I am Renno, but I am no longer sachem of the Seneca." He came down the steps and turned to his brother. "May I present my brother, the sachem El-i-chi."

Captain Ridgley dismounted and approached. "Yes, General Jackson mentioned your brother." He gave El-i-chi a perfunctory nod, then grinned smugly at Renno. "And you are the white Indian. A most curious appellation, I must say."

Renno chose to overlook the man's condescending tone for the sake of his old friend Andrew Jackson.

"To friends—Indian and white alike—I am simply Renno," he remarked matter-of-factly.

"Pleased to make your acquaintance," Ridgley said, adding to El-i-chi, "and yours, sir."

Renno was glad the officer made no effort to shake hands. He decided to come straight to the point. "You carry a letter from General Jackson, do you not?"

"Why, yes, I do." The captain looked both surprised and impressed that Renno had guessed his business there. In fact, Renno had been informed of the captain's mission by a Cherokee runner, who had been in Nashville when the militiamen set out. "How did you know?"

"The manitous told me you were coming," Renno replied. Out of the corner of his eye he could see that El-i-chi was struggling to keep from laughing.

"I've heard of them," Ridgley acknowledged, nodding enthusiastically. "Did they tell you what is in the letter?"

"I am afraid they cannot read English. But I can, so if you would be so kind . . ." Renno held out his hand.

"Why, yes, of course."

The captain gestured to an aide, who slid down off his mount and hurried over, handing Ridgley a letter from a leather pouch at his waist.

"Here it is." He extended the letter.

"Thank you," Renno said, taking it. Reading the inscription on the front, he recognized Andrew Jackson's handwriting.

When Renno did not immediately open the letter, Captain Ridgley told him, "The general asked me to await your reply."

"Of course. If you'll excuse me a moment . . ."

Renno climbed the steps and sat back down in his rocker. Turning over the letter, he broke the wax seal, pressed it open, and quickly perused the contents. Jackson began with the usual pleasantries, then shifted to more pressing matters:

> As you well know, these are troubling times for our young United States. As we approach our fortieth year of independence, we are again threatened on all sides. The British oppose us along the Canada frontier and impress our sailors on the high seas. To the south, the Creeks provide their share of trouble (though I need not tell you, whose family has lost so much at their hands, about the endless vexations they have caused us). And Tecumseh

and his lot are doing their best to stir the natives all along our borders.

Though I am presently without an army, I have maintained my commission in the Tennessee militia. I have been lobbying Washington for a more active role, but they seem content to let me live out my remaining days in oblivion at my beloved Hermitage. What they do believe suitable for this aging frontier fighter is to pester my friends for information with which they may send younger men into battle to gain the glory and the day.

I hope you will forgive me for not making my entreaty in person. As you know, I sustained a shoulder wound during a recent unpleasantness with Colonel Thomas Hart Benton and his damnable brother, Jesse. You'd think a man of Benton's reputation could take a horse-whipping without resorting to a pistol. I must therefore rely upon this letter and the good Captain Ridgley, who carries it to Huntington Castle.

Let me get to the heart of the matter. It has come to the attention of our military that your nephew Gao has been serving with Tecumseh in the north. It was not long ago that I had the honor of entertaining Cao and your son Ta-na-wun-da. At the time both were as stalwart in their opposition to Tecumseh as you have been. If Gao has indeed now joined that bunch, it must be quite vexing to you and to El-i-chi.

What I must ask is simple, though I understand if it is not so simple for you to reply. Our nation is at war with the British and with their ally, Tecumseh. If, through your nephew or any other source, you have learned something about Tecumseh's whereabouts or plans, it would greatly help our nation's cause if you share that information with us.

I will say no more. I know you realize I would not ask if this matter were not of grave importance to all of us.

I will close with far more pleasant news. My friends in Washington (of which there are still a handful) have informed me that the court of Napoleon is sending a new emissary, who is charged with seeking ways in which our mutual interests in the matter of Great Britain may be served. Though the identity of the emissary is not yet public knowledge, I have it on good authority that it is none other than your son-in-law, the comte de Beaujolais. He has already set sail from France, and accompanying him are your daughter, Renna, and her two children.

I know that you will search your heart on the matter of which I have spoken and will smoke on it. Captain Ridgley will remain at Rusog's Town until you are ready to send your reply.

The signature of Major-General Andrew Jackson was written in bold letters across the bottom.

Renno beamed as he handed the letter to El-i-chi. Already forgotten was the request for information about Gao and Tecumseh. All he could think about was his daughter setting sail from France.

Renna was coming home at last.

That evening, Renno was troubled as he sat at the big mahogany desk in his library. He had started and restarted a letter to Andrew Jackson but found himself torn by what to say. Though he disapproved of Gao's decision to fight with Tecumseh, he did not want to do or say anything that might jeopardize his nephew. Yet he did not want to lie to Jackson, who had always been scrupulously honest in their dealings.

He started on a fresh piece of paper, but after a few sentences he crumpled it up and tossed it onto the floor with the others. Standing, he walked over to the window and looked toward Rusog's Town. He could see the lights of the Cherokee-Seneca village and even thought he heard the sounds of people enjoying the warm summer night. Halfway between the town and Huntington Castle were other lights—the fires of the militia detachment encamped in a meadow near the edge of Renno's land. The two officers, Captain Scott Ridgley and a medical officer named Lieutenant Jameson, had accepted Renno's invitation of accommodations in his house. Tired from their long day of riding, they had already gone to bed and would start for home in the morning, carrying Renno's return letter to Jackson at the Hermitage, his six-hundred-forty-acre farm just outside Nashville.

"That is, if I ever finish the damn thing," he muttered, shaking his head and walking back to the desk.

"Is something wrong?" a voice asked.

He looked up to see his wife standing in the doorway. She held a candle lamp, which enveloped her in a warm glow and accentuated her fiery-red hair.

"I was working on the letter to General Jackson. That's all." He forced a smile.

Beth came across the room and held the lamp low over the scatterings of paper on the floor.

"The words aren't coming, are they?"

Sighing, he dropped down into his desk chair. "I cannot tell him of Gao's visit, nor do I wish to help the Americans find Tecumseh, for then Gao would be at risk."

"Gao has placed himself at risk by siding with that . . . that false prophet."

"That may be so, but I cannot deny that some of Tecumseh's teachings have the voice of truth. It is his methods I deplore."

Moving closer, Beth laid a gentle hand on his shoulder. "Then what will you say to General Jackson?"

Renno picked up the quill pen, held it over the bottle of ink, then shook his head and put the quill back down. "I have no idea. None whatsoever."

"Why not ask your brother?" Beth suggested. "After all, Gao is his son."

Renno was silent a long moment, and then a slight grin spread across his face. Turning to his wife, he wrapped an arm around her waist and pulled her close. "A wonderful idea," he declared. "Now I know why I married you."

Leaning down, she kissed his forehead. "Just don't stay out too late. Go speak with El-i-chi, then write your letter while the words are still fresh."

Renno rose to kiss Beth tenderly on the lips. "I'll return before you've fallen asleep."

"I expect you to keep that promise," she said, stepping back and waggling a finger at him.

His gaze swept the length of her dressing gown. "It would take the combined forces of General Jackson and Tecumseh to make me break that promise." He leaned close and kissed her again, then hurried from the room.

"Don't go out there," Ah-wa-o urged, coming up beside her husband.

"I just want to see what all the commotion is about." El-i-chi slipped a beaded white shirt over his head.

"You know what is going on. It is those soldiers."

"And our boys as well," El-i-chi noted, referring to the young men of Rusog's Town.

"They are just having some fun."

"They are drinking; I want to be sure they don't drink too much."

Ah-wa-o tugged gently at his arm. "Let them be. Come back to bed."

"I will be right back," he promised, pulling away and heading to the door.

"Why must *you* go?"

"I don't want them waking Ah-wen-ga and Ha-ace." He gestured toward the room where his seven-year-old daughter and five-year-old son were sleeping.

"Don't be silly. Nothing will awaken those two."

El-i-chi sighed. "Ah-wa-o, I must go."

"Those soldiers came to see your brother, not you," his wife said with a frown. "If anyone should go—"

"Renno is no longer the sachem. *I* am. It is for me to do, no one else."

"I know . . ." Ah-wa-o forced a smile as she padded across the cabin floor and leaned close to kiss him on the cheek. "Just don't do anything foolish," she told him.

"Foolish?" His eyes widened in mock disbelief. "I am also a shaman, am I not? A shaman never does anything foolish."

"No?" Ah-wa-o said teasingly. "You let your brother make you the sachem. If he hadn't, we could be curled up under our blankets right now."

He chuckled. "And miss all the excitement outside?"

"El-i-chi!" Ah-wa-o exclaimed. "You just want to join in the fun!"

El-i-chi furrowed his brow and declared with righteous indignation, "A sachem never has fun."

"See that you don't!"

He kissed her, then strode from the cabin.

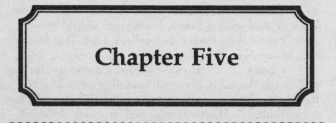

Chapter Five

 El-i-chi stood in front of his home, looking across Rusog's Town. The moon had risen, and it cast a soft blue glow upon the buildings of the village. A harsher light shimmered to his left, where a small bonfire had been built in an open area near the edge of town. From the sounds of shouting and laughter, he guessed a couple of dozen people—Seneca, Cherokee, and white—were gathered around the fire.

He started walking toward the bonfire, and as he approached it, he recognized some of the celebrants. The warriors were mostly Seneca, numbering almost a dozen. The half-dozen militiamen were easy to pick out, even though their uniforms were an assortment of colors and styles. A few young women were on hand as well, and he was distressed to see them partaking of the several jugs being handed around the circle.

"Little Flower, does your father know you are here?" El-i-chi asked in the Seneca language as he walked over to a girl in her midteens, sitting at the edge of the group. The girl looked up at him, and her face filled with fright. Jumping to her feet, she disappeared in the direction of the lodges, longhouses, and log cabins that comprised the village.

The gatherers were mostly seated, with a few standing behind the others, laughing and prodding one another as they told jokes and sang songs. There was a blend of English, Cherokee, and Seneca, and it was apparent the white soldiers did not know much of what was being said—but it did not dampen their enthusiasm.

However, El-i-chi's presence dampened things a bit. He noticed a pair of young women stand and slip away into the shadows when they caught sight of him. And a Cherokee boy, not more than twelve years old, also took the opportunity to scurry home.

He almost hated interfering in the celebration. It was good to see these young people of three nations sitting in a circle of brotherhood. But much of the camaraderie was the product of whiskey and rum, and El-i-chi had watched too many such gatherings disintegrate into misunderstandings, even violence. He especially did not want to see the firewater disease spread among his people.

"Is that you, Ho-ta-kwa?" he called to one young man—a friend of his older son's—who was crouching near the fire and using ashes and saliva to paint streaks of black lightning down his cheeks.

The young man was one of the leaders of his generation, and El-i-chi knew the others would follow his actions. When Ho-ta-kwa looked up, El-i-chi continued his address in English, so the soldiers would understand.

"Your father would not wish to see you painted up like that. Are we taking to the warpath tonight?"

"Leave the poor fella alone," one of the militiamen mumbled, waving El-i-chi away with one hand and thrusting a jug into Ho-ta-kwa's chest with the other.

The Seneca warrior smiled sheepishly at the sachem and passed the jug to his right without taking a sip.

"It's all right to have a little fun," El-i-chi acknowledged. "But I'd say enough of that whiskey has gone around."

A soldier rose and held out one of the jugs. "Here, old man. Try a little yourself. It'll make a real friendly Injun o' you."

"Not tonight," El-i-chi replied, stepping aside when the inebriated man almost barreled into him.

El-i-chi turned to Ho-ta-kwa and saw in the young man's eyes that he was embarrassed at how the soldier had addressed the Seneca sachem—and ashamed that he and his friends had been partly responsible.

The soldier tried to force the whiskey on El-i-chi, raising it toward the older man's lips and accidentally spilling some down the front of his shirt. Laughing, he wiped at the wet stain, his shaky hand pawing at El-i-chi's chest.

The sachem stood his ground, not reacting, his eyes fixed on Ho-ta-kwa.

The young Seneca glanced around the circle and saw his friends all watching him. Finally he rose, grabbed the jug from the warrior beside him, and carried it to where El-i-chi and the soldier were standing.

"Thank you for your hospitality," he said to the soldier, speaking the words slowly and carefully, as he had heard El-i-chi and Renno say them in the past. "We will go now." He handed the jug to the man, who stood trying to balance both jugs and himself.

Ho-ta-kwa turned from the fire and started back toward the center of the village. One by one, the other Senecas and Cherokees rose and followed.

The sachem nodded, proud of Ho-ta-kwa and the others. The soldier, meanwhile, staggered over to his friends and handed them one of the jugs, keeping the other for himself.

El-i-chi was just starting back to his cabin when he heard a short, high-pitched cry. It came from beyond the fire—in the shadowed trees that marked the edge of the village. He listened carefully, heard the sound again, and knew it was one of the young women who had left the group when he first appeared on the scene.

El-i-chi hurried around the circle and approached the trees. With the fire at his back, he could make out two people. A woman—she was little more than a girl—was struggling as a man pinioned her against a tree and awkwardly tried to kiss and fondle her. As El-i-chi drew closer he confirmed what he had suspected: It was one of the militiamen, who must have slipped away from the group and followed the young woman.

"Enough of that!" El-i-chi exclaimed, striding briskly toward the soldier.

The man glanced over at the Seneca elder and sneered.

"Let her go!"

"G'way," the man muttered, waving him off.

"Release her, I said!" He grasped the man's shoulder and pulled him off the girl. She tried to run, but the soldier grabbed her blouse, tearing it further, and dragged her back.

"Enough!" El-i-chi shouted. He threw the man backward, knocking him to the ground. Turning to the Seneca girl, he said in their language, "Go home. Quickly."

Tears spilled from her eyes. Clutching her tattered blouse to her chest and stammering words of thanks, she raced off toward the village.

El-i-chi turned to the drunken soldier, who was trying to stand up. Shaking his head in dismay, the sachem approached and held out a hand. "Come on—let's get you back to your camp."

The soldier slapped his hand away and tried to rise on his own. He fell onto his side.

Hearing the others behind him, El-i-chi glanced over his shoulder and saw that the militiamen had come to see what was happening. So had some of the warriors, who must have seen the girl go running from the trees.

Signaling for them to assist, El-i-chi reached for the

soldier again. He found himself looking down the barrel of a military pistol, which the man had jerked from beneath his belt.

El-i-chi stared at him in silence, the only sound the harsh rasp of metal as the soldier thumbed back the hammer.

"This what you want?" the man muttered, his lips pulling into a smirk. He struggled to his feet and stood wavering in front of the Seneca.

"I have no quarrel with you," El-i-chi said, raising his hands to show they were empty.

"No quarrel, eh? Well, maybe I got one with you." The man stepped forward, jabbing the gun barrel at El-i-chi.

"Hey, Nate, put that down!" one of his companions called. "It's over. Let's go."

"It ain't over," the man named Nate declared as he waggled the gun. "Is it, old man?"

"You have had too much to drink. That's all," El-i-chi said in a calm, almost soothing voice.

"I had me just the right amount. And I'm fixin' t'have some more. And if it weren't for you, I'd be havin' more'n whiskey right now. A damn sight more!"

"Come on, Nate," said the other soldier, who was coming up beside El-i-chi. Apparently he could hold his liquor better, for he pointed a steady hand at the gun. "Put that away. Let's not cause any more trouble."

"'Tweren't me caused the trouble. This fool Injun did that all by hisself."

"You were out of line, Nate. We all saw. This man was just watching out for that girl. If the captain knew what you were up to—"

"Damn the captain!" Nate blared, swinging the pistol toward the other soldier. "And damn you, Murphy!"

With the drunken man's attention elsewhere, El-i-chi was able to strike. He did so with remarkable speed, his clasped hands slamming Nate's pistol to the ground. Mercifully it did not fire.

El-i-chi was about to fell the man with an uppercut, but before he could unleash the blow, the fellow staggered backward and lost his footing, coming down hard on his rump. He howled in pain and grabbed at his twisted ankle.

El-i-chi watched him until certain the danger was past. In the background, several of the soldiers and warriors could be heard tittering and clapping their hands with delight.

"Thank you, Mr. Murphy," El-i-chi said to the soldier who had assisted him.

"Just Murphy," the man said, nodding. "We'll get him back to the camp. He won't cause any more trouble."

El-i-chi gestured at Nate's pistol, which lay still cocked on the ground. "I'd wait until he's sobered up before giving him that."

The sachem bent to pick up the gun, then stiffened as something struck him from behind. Dropping to his knees, he twisted around, vainly trying to yank what felt like a hot poker from his back. Ten feet away he saw Nate on his knees, arm extended as if it had just thrown something—like a knife.

El-i-chi drew in a sharp breath and heard the blood rush and gurgle in his lungs. He forced himself to his feet and staggered toward the fire, toward the stunned faces of soldiers and Indians.

"*El-i-chi!*" cried Ho-ta-kwa, rushing forward with arms outstretched.

"My son!" gasped the sachem of the Seneca as he fell forward into Ho-ta-kwa's arms, and drifted into the abyss.

"*El-i-chi!*"

Renno heard the shout and broke into a run across the field, angling away from his brother's cabin and toward the bonfire near the edge of the village. A small crowd was gathered between the fire and the trees beyond.

There had been no warning vision, but the moment Renno had heard that pained cry, he knew. When he saw the young Seneca Ho-ta-kwa kneeling on the ground, cradling a man in his arms, he cried out his brother's name.

The big hunting knife still protruded from El-i-chi's upper back. Renno pulled it free, releasing a gush of blood. Seeing that, he realized the knife had pierced his brother's heart—that his brother's heart had already stilled.

"El-i-chi!" he cried over and over as he folded his brother into his arms, caressing his cheek, trying to will the spirit back into him. The sachem's eyes were open and still seemed to hold a glimmer of light. Then the flicker of life passed from his body, the only remaining light being the reflection of the bonfire.

Renno's eyes filled with tears, with rage, as he looked around the group and demanded, "Who? Who?"

All eyes turned toward a single man—a soldier kneeling ten feet away.

Renno lowered his brother onto the ground and gently ran a hand along his face, closing the eyelids. He crouched there a moment, looking shrunken, frail. But as he rose, the power seemed to flow back into him—the power not only of himself but of the sachem of the Seneca.

Turning, he faced the soldier and held out his hands. "Why?" he implored, his voice steady and firm.

"Nate didn't mean t'do nothin'," one of the militiamen offered, his speech and movements slurred by the effects of hard drink as he took a few steps toward the man on the ground.

Renno fixed the speaker with an incredulous stare. "He threw a knife into another man's back but did not mean it?"

The militiaman seemed to realize how ridiculous the notion was. He lowered his eyes and shrugged. "'Twas the whiskey, I guess."

"Whiskey . . ." Renno muttered with a sneer. "It's always whiskey."

Angrily shaking his head, he strode over to the drunken soldier and jerked the kneeling man to his feet. Gripping his shirtfront with one hand, he pulled back his other arm, hand balled into a fist. Nate's bloodshot eyes were wide with fear, and his body shook uncontrollably. His legs went rubbery, and he slunk low in Renno's grip, his head turning to avoid the coming blow.

Renno glared at him a long moment. Slowly his fist unclenched, and he shook his head in disgust. He shoved the man away, knocking him onto his back on the ground.

"The man you killed was a great sachem among our people," Renno intoned, standing over the murderer. "He should have died in battle or as an old man with his medicine shield and robes wrapped around him. But to be struck down by a knife in the back? By a . . . an *insect* like you?"

Turning away, he approached a soldier who seemed more clearheaded than the others and said, "Put him under arrest."

"Arrest? But we can't—"

"You had better do as I say. If not, there are many here who will see that justice is swift and sure."

The soldier glanced around at the Senecas and Cherokees, who greatly outnumbered the whites. Nodding feebly, he signaled for a couple of the other militiamen to assist him. Nearing the murderer, he said, "We're gonna have to arrest you, Nate."

"No one's gonna arrest me!"

The soldiers came to an abrupt halt.

"Put it down!" one of the soldiers exclaimed.

Renno spun around. The man named Nate was holding a pistol—the same pistol that El-i-chi had knocked from his hand. It was cocked, and he was waving it between the approaching militiamen and Renno.

"Don't do anything crazy," the lead soldier said.

"No one's takin' me!" Nate shouted. "No one!"

The soldiers eyed the growing crowd of Indian warriors. Most were armed with knives, and a few had pistols tucked beneath their belts.

"Put the pistol down, Nate," the soldier said in as calm a voice as he could muster. "You're gonna get us all killed."

The Indians fanned out, forming a semicircle around the militiamen and Renno. Nate could see they were getting ready to rush him, and he swung the pistol toward Renno and declared, "Make 'em move back! Get 'em away from here!"

"Lower the pistol, and no one will hurt you," Renno told him.

"All right, all right. Just make 'em move back!"

The man retreated a step, sweat beading his forehead, his pistol still trained on Renno. His shoulders slumped slightly, and he reached up with his left hand to uncock the hammer. But his fingers slipped on the metal, and the hammer slammed down with a *thunk*.

Renno saw the flash of sparks as flint struck frizzen, and he dived to the ground. There was a thunderous boom and flash of light, and he felt the stab of a bullet tearing into the top of his shoulder.

He could hear the shouts of the warriors as they fell upon the man who had shot him and killed El-i-chi. Renno tried to get up, but his body did not respond, and he feared he might be paralyzed. But he could still feel, though he was not sure that was such a blessing, for already the initial shock and numbness were wearing off, replaced by a sharp, excruciating pain that ran from his shoulder to the small of his back.

Hands tugged at the fallen Seneca, turning him over, and he found himself in Ho-ta-kwa's arms.

"I am . . . all right," he grunted in the Seneca tongue. "Just my shoulder."

Ho-ta-kwa pulled open Renno's shirt and grimaced at the sight. "It looks bad."

"I've had worse." He glanced to the side. The man who had shot him was being beaten and probably worse. "Stop them," he muttered. "Don't let them kill him."

"Forget about him," Ho-ta-kwa said as he tore a strip from Renno's shirt and pressed it against the wound.

"Stop them, Ho-ta-kwa," Renno repeated, staring up into the young man's eyes.

Ho-ta-kwa held Renno's gaze a long moment, then nodded. He gestured for someone to take his place, then ran over and started pulling men off the soldier.

"Renno!" a voice wailed, and Ah-wa-o dropped down at his side.

He tried to reach out to his sister-in-law, but his hands would not move.

"What have they done to you?" she cried, tears in her eyes. She grabbed the cloth compress and pressed it hard against his wound to stanch the flow of blood.

"Ah-wa-o . . ."

"Shh, Renno. Lie still."

"El-i-chi . . ."

Suddenly remembering why she had come, she glanced around. "Where is he? I heard the gunshot and came running. But I didn't see him."

"Ah-wa-o . . ." His lips quivered, and tears flowed down his cheeks. "El-i-chi . . . he . . . he is . . ."

She looked at Renno curiously, still not comprehending.

"El-i-chi tried to stop him," Renno whispered. "The man had a knife. He . . ." His words trailed off. His eyes squeezed shut from the pain in his heart.

"Renno, what are you saying to me?" Ah-wa-o muttered, more a statement than a question. Her expression darkened as terrible fear touched her eyes.

Some of the Indians standing nearby realized what was happening and moved to either side. Ah-wa-o looked between them and gasped.

There, less than ten feet away, lay the body of El-i-chi, sachem of the Seneca, husband of Ah-wa-o.

"Ai-eee!"

Ah-wa-o's keening pierced Renno more deeply than the militiaman's bullet. It soared up over the village, over the Cherokee Nation, an ululating cry that shook the earth more forcefully than Tecumseh's great earthquake.

Renno felt as if his heart would break. Until that instant the full impact of what had happened had not dawned upon him. Now it came like a flood, pouring through him like the blood from his wounds.

The sachem of the Seneca was no more. His brother, El-i-chi, was gone.

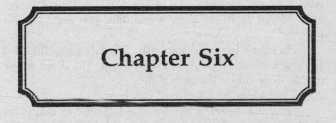

Chapter Six

 Renno was brought to Ah-wa-o's cabin and placed in the bed she had shared with El-i-chi. Though a medical officer was accompanying the militia, Renno asked to be attended by a Seneca healer, since Indians had much better success treating gunshot wounds. Meanwhile, Beth and Captain Ridgley were sent for at Huntington Castle.

When Beth arrived, Renno was weak but lucid. He had lost quite a bit of blood, but the medicine man had effectively stopped the bleeding at both the entrance and exit wounds. Beth sat with her husband for a while, then consulted with Ridgley's medical officer after he had examined the healer's work.

"The fellow did a fine job," Lieutenant Jameson acknowledged with some surprise as they stood outside the room where Renno was lying. "Your husband must have been bending forward when he was struck. The bullet entered the top of his shoulder and angled downward, exiting through his lower back."

"Is that bad?" Beth's lower lip trembled slightly as she struggled to maintain her composure.

"Fortunately the bullet passed through and did not have to be probed."

"Thank heavens." Looking up into his eyes, she read a note of concern. She gripped the lieutenant's forearm. "What is it? Is there something you are not telling me?"

He shook his head somberly. "Nothing specific. But the track of the bullet was very long. We don't know exactly how much damage it did."

"You mean in his chest? His heart?"

"No, the heart is not involved. And I'm confident the lungs were missed as well. If not, I'd hear blood. But the exit wound was very low—just above the small of his back. If the bullet stayed near the surface, everything should be fine. If not . . ."

"What?" she pressed. "What are you saying?"

"Well, organs may have been involved. There could be internal bleeding. We just won't know for a while."

"He's going to be all right," Beth whispered.

"Mrs. Harper, you must understand that your husband already has lost a lot of blood. And if there is internal bleeding—"

"Renno will be fine," she stated emphatically.

"I hope so. We all do."

Beth started back to her husband's room, then turned to the officer. "Is it all right for me to stay with him tonight?"

"By all means, Mrs. Harper. That is probably just what he needs right now."

Beth thanked the lieutenant, then consulted with friends and relatives on hand. Ah-wa-o and her children, Ah-wen-ga and Ha-ace, had been taken to the home of El-i-chi and Renno's older sister, Ena, and her husband, the Cherokee chief Rusog. Ah-wa-o was still in shock over the death of her husband, leaving Ena and Rusog to explain as best they could to the young children what had happened to their father.

A bed was carried from the children's room to where Renno was lying so that Beth could spend the night near him. Beth then went in to see if he was comfortable and if she could do anything for him.

Renno was drifting in and out of sleep. At one point he opened his eyes and noticed Beth in the chair beside the bed. "You are still here," he whispered with a faint smile.

"Of course I am, Renno. I wouldn't leave you." She reached over and took his hand.

"I will be fine."

"I know. But *I* will feel better if I'm near."

Renno squeezed her hand, and his eyes brightened. "There, did you feel that?"

"Of course, my dear."

"I can move my feet, too."

"You'll soon be running all over the countryside like the warrior that you are."

His smile faded, and he closed his eyes. "I may never run again."

"Don't talk like that," she urged, lifting his hand to her lips. "You are going to be fine. You will regain your strength, and then—"

"I don't think I can run again without him."

"El-i-chi . . ." she breathed, clutching her husband's hand to her face as tears ran down her cheeks.

For a long time they did not speak. Beth thought Renno had fallen asleep, but then he said in the faintest of voices, "Take me home. . . ."

She smiled at him. His eyes were half closed, and his eyelids fluttered slightly, as if he were straining to see something in the distance.

"You have to stay here until you are better," she told him.

"Home . . ." he repeated. "I . . . I am ready."

"But the doctor said . . ."

Her voice trailed off as she gazed down at Renno. There was something curious about his expression, something in the faraway look in his eyes. She realized he was not speaking to her.

"Renno . . ." she whispered, caressing his hand.

"El-i-chi!" he proclaimed, his head rising slightly from the pillow.

"Renno!" she called, vigorously rubbing his hands and arms. "Don't go!"

"El-i-chi . . ." he sighed, falling back onto the pillow. His eyes closed, and he lay without moving, without breathing.

Beth patted his cheeks and shook him as she called his name. Jumping up, she ran to the door and yelled for help. Lieutenant Jameson responded first, and he raced over to the bed and checked Renno's pulse, then put an ear close to his mouth.

"Don't let him die!" Beth blurted as others rushed into the room. "Dear God, don't let him die!"

Jameson concluded his examination, then looked up at her. "He's still breathing." When she did not immediately calm down, he grasped her arms. "He's alive, Mrs. Harper. But I think he may be slipping into a coma."

"C-coma?" she stammered.

"He has lost a lot of blood."

"Will he . . . ?" She could barely say the word, but she forced it out. "Will he die?"

"His pulse is weak but steady. Only time will tell." Jameson started for the door, then looked back at her. "He'll probably be like this for some time. When he awakens . . . then we shall know." Turning, he strode from the room.

Beth sat back down. Gently rubbing and caressing her husband's hands, she whispered, "Don't leave me, Renno. Not yet." She glanced around to make sure they were alone. Then she raised her eyes toward the ceiling and called out quietly, "Don't take him, El-i-chi. Please, dear El-i-chi, as you make this journey, leave your brother behind." She choked back her tears. "His people need him, El-i-chi. *I* need him."

She fell forward onto the edge of the bed, her arms draped protectively over her husband.

"Please, dear God, don't let him die. . . ."

Captain Scott Ridgley stood alone outside the cabin where Renno was lying. He gazed out upon Rusog's Town, seeing the lights of several large fires and hearing drums and chanting. He hoped the Indians were praying for the spirit of their fallen sachem and not beating the drums of war.

"Damn fool," he spat, shaking his head as he debated what to do about Private Nathan Horigan. The soldier's recklessness had put them all in peril. If Ridgley did not assuage the anger of the Indians, there could be a major uprising that might sweep across the territory. But if he remained in the area much longer, he risked having his men massacred. Either way, he would receive the blame, all thanks to the actions of one drunken soldier.

"Captain," a voice called, and one of the militiamen emerged from the darkness.

"What did you find out, Carpenter?"

"They're praying over that dead Indian, like you thought."

"Could you hear what was being said?"

"My Seneca isn't that good, but I heard some."

"And?" Ridgley said impatiently.

"Most of it was the usual chants. But a few of the younger bucks spoke up, and they want blood. *Our* blood."

"They damn near killed Horigan already. Isn't that enough?"

"Not hardly, from what I seen. Most of 'em are carrying pistols now, and they probably would've used 'em on me if I hadn't gotten the hell out of there."

Ridgley swore. "It was bad enough he killed that sachem. But did he have to shoot Renno? We had a chance with Renno around to stand up for us. But now . . ."

The captain walked a few feet away and stood with his hands on his hips, weighing the decision he had to make.

"We gotta get Nate out of here," Carpenter said, coming up beside the captain. "We're no match for those Seneca and their Cherokee friends. They outnumber us twenty to one."

Ridgley cursed again, then turned back around. "I could care less about Horigan, but there are the rest of the men to think about. Tell them to get ready to pull out. And whatever you do, keep Horigan out of sight."

"Yes, sir. And you?"

"I'll get Jameson out of there"—he indicated the cabin—"and be along presently. Prepare to leave in fifteen minutes."

"We'll be ready in ten."

"Fine. When I get there we'll ride."

Ridgley watched the soldier walk off into the darkness, then briefly eyed the bonfires of Rusog's Town before looking across the fields that led to Huntington Castle. The soldiers had wisely doused their own fire, but they were right out in the open—an easy target for any Indian seeking revenge. Hopefully they would be packed and on the trail long before the Senecas concluded their ceremonies for the dead and turned their attention from salvation to retribution.

Turning on his heels, Ridgley strode toward Eli-chi's cabin, calling for Lieutenant Jameson as he jerked open the front door.

Five minutes later the captain and medical officer were nearing the encampment in the field on Renno's property. A few torches provided light as the militiamen loaded supplies onto the backs of their packhorses and mules. The last item that would be packed was the tent that served as headquarters and provided shelter for the officers while on the trail. It was here Nathan Horigan was being held.

"Bring him out and strike that tent," Captain Ridgley called as he approached.

"Yes, sir," one militiaman replied.

A pair of soldiers ducked inside and dragged Horigan out. His hands were tied in front of him, but there was little need for such precautions. He could barely stand, let alone take off on his own, having been severely beaten before Ho-ta-kwa prevailed and got his enraged comrades to stop.

Ridgley did not know of the role played by Ho-ta-kwa or Renno in ending the beating, nor would it have made any difference to him. He did not much care that one Seneca had been killed and another gravely wounded—half-breed or not. What did bother him was that that reckless action had placed him and his men in danger. For that, Nathan Horigan would have to pay when they got back to Nashville.

A few weeks in the guardhouse ought to teach him to be less careless, Ridgley thought with a smug grin.

There was also the matter of the man they called the white Indian. As far as Ridgley was concerned, Renno was no different from a full-blood. But he was a friend of Andrew Jackson's, and though Jackson had lost most of his influence in Washington, he still had many friends in Tennessee and could make trouble for Ridgley if he chose.

I'd better make it a few months—at hard labor, Ridgley told himself as he approached Nathan Horigan.

The militiaman half stood, half slumped in the arms of the two soldiers who had brought him forth. One of his eyes was swollen shut, the other puffed up but still visible behind the purplish welts.

"What do you say, Nate?" Ridgley asked, halting in front of him. "Think you can ride?"

Horigan's reply was an unintelligible grunt as he strained feebly against the rope binding his wrists.

"If you'd prefer, we can leave you behind. Do you hear those drums? They're drumming for you. For your head, I should say."

"I . . . I c-can ride," the man mumbled, closing his one good eye.

"That's what I thought." Ridgley addressed the man on Horigan's right. "Get him onto his horse. And cut away that rope." He indicated the wrist binding. "He'll have a hard enough time just keeping his mount."

The soldiers led Horigan over to where the horses were being saddled.

Ridgley noticed that the tent was about to be struck. "Wait a moment," he told the men, striding over to pull back the flap. Snatching a torch from one of them, he thrust it inside and looked around the interior, satisfying himself it was empty. Then he stepped back and watched as the stakes were pulled and the canvas dropped to the ground. A minute later the men had it rolled and were muscling it onto the back of a mule.

"Captain!" the soldier named Carpenter shouted as he ran up to the officer. "Over there!"

Ridgley looked where Carpenter was pointing and saw a line of flickering lights approaching from the trees that separated Renno's fields from the Indian village.

"Damn!" Ridgley exclaimed. "Let's get out of here. Now!"

Carpenter shouted the order, and the militiamen began untying their horses.

Ridgley strode to where a soldier was holding his mount. Taking the reins, he was about to climb into the saddle when he glanced in the opposite direction from Rusog's Town. A line of torches was coming up over the nearby rise. The Indians had sent some of their men around the encampment and were closing in on both sides.

"Mount up!" he ordered, jabbing his foot into the stirrup and hoisting himself into the saddle. "Let's get the hell out of here!"

The air was split by a piercing, thunderous cry as more than a hundred Seneca and Cherokee warriors closed in on the small company of militiamen. Several horses spooked and reared up, dumping their riders. Ridgley spun around, searching for the best route of escape. But there was none, for as the two lines of Indians drew closer, their flanks converged, until they completely encircled the soldiers.

Ridgley jerked at the reins, turning his horse left and then right. He yanked the pistol from his belt, but some voice of reason told him that pulling the trigger would bring certain death upon all of them. The other soldiers had also drawn their weapons, and he rode up and down among them, ordering them to hold fire.

The Indians halted about twenty yards away and fell silent. Some held torches. The rest were armed with muskets, pistols, lances, or bows. They stood motionless, their weapons trained on the militiamen, ready to unleash a deadly cross fire at their leader's command.

Ridgley twisted in the saddle to see who was leading this group, praying it was not some hothead thirsty for a scalp. Then a man walked forward from the rest, a long lance in one hand, a brightly decorated shield in the other. He was not a young warrior but an older chieftain, with a headdress of eagle feathers.

The Indian pointed his lance at the sky and called in heavily accented English, "I am Rusog, chief of the Cherokee, brother by marriage to the Seneca sachems El-i-chi and Renno. I would speak with your leader."

Ridgley kneed his mount forward. Tucking his pistol beneath his belt, he raised his hand. "I am Captain

Scott Ridgley. Why do you come here with weapons in hand?"

"Would it not be better to ask why you would sneak off into the night?" Rusog replied.

"We have finished our mission here and must return to Nashville."

"Was it your mission to kill my Seneca brother El-i-chi? Was it your mission to leave the sachem Renno near death with a bullet through the back?"

"I did none of those things. They were the actions of a single man, who now will face military justice."

"White man's justice," Rusog declared with contempt. "And what would that justice be?"

"He will stand trial and receive the sentence of the court."

"And at that trial, who will speak for El-i-chi? Who will be Renno's voice?"

"We have witnesses who saw what happened. They will speak the truth."

"Whose truth? Yours? Or that of El-i-chi and Renno?"

Ridgley held his horse steady as he looked left and right at the circle of warriors, all eager for the command to commence firing. Grabbing his saddle horn, he slid off the horse and let the reins drop to the ground. Walking forward, he said loud enough for all to hear, "There is a single truth, the truth of the one God of our people. To take a life—any life—is to violate the laws of our God. I promise that this man will pay for having broken God's law."

"This crime was done on Cherokee land. The murderer must face Cherokee justice."

"I promise you this crime will not go unpunished," Ridgley declared, trying to reassure the chief.

As if in reply, Rusog pounded the butt of the lance upon the ground. In unison, the hammers of a hundred rifles and pistols were cocked, the sound shuddering like a clap of thunder through the small ranks of the militia.

"Your sachem Renno would not have you do this," Ridgley cried out, his voice quavering.

"Our Seneca brother lies at the edge of the next world; he may not walk again among us."

"But he knows a soldier must stand trial and receive military justice. We cannot turn him over to the justice of a mob."

"We are no mob," Rusog declared. "He will be brought before our council, and if he is shown to have done this deed, his death will be swift and certain. There will be no torture on Cherokee land."

The captain looked back at his men and read the fear in their eyes. He caught a glimpse of Nathan Horigan, who was slouched forward over the saddle and only seemed vaguely aware of what was going on.

"Chief Rusog," Ridgley said, taking a step closer, "I am a captain in the Tennessee militia. It is my duty to uphold military law. I ask that you allow me to hold a trial, here and now, so that I may hear from all witnesses —American, Seneca, and Cherokee. If I am convinced that this man committed the crimes of which he is accused, and that he acted without provocation, my judgment shall be as swift and certain as any from a Cherokee council."

Rusog hesitated a moment, then asked, "And this judgment will be carried out upon Cherokee land?"

"Let me hold my trial. If you do not approve of the outcome, you have lost nothing but a few hours."

Rusog lowered the tip of the lance until it touched the ground. In response, his Seneca and Cherokee warriors put up their weapons and uncocked their firearms.

"Hold your trial," the chief told the captain. "But we will not move from this spot until the judgment is made and carried out."

* * *

The trial was something of a formality. It was held there in the middle of the field, under the glare of torches. Witnesses were called from among the Indians and whites who had been on hand at the bonfire, with the most damning evidence coming from Nathan Horigan's fellow militiamen, who confirmed that he killed El-i-chi when the sachem's back was turned. By now Horigan had recovered his senses enough to realize what was going on. When offered a chance to speak in his own defense, he claimed he had no memory of the incident and, if indeed it had happened, his actions were unintentional and the result of too much whiskey.

Lieutenant Jameson faithfully recorded the proceedings so that Captain Ridgley could justify what was, in fact, a predetermined verdict. When all the statements had been made and Ridgley had finished with his questioning, he addressed Horigan. His speech was short and direct, given more for the benefit of Chief Rusog and his warriors than for the prisoner.

"Private Nathan Horigan of the Tennessee militia, it is our finding that you willfully and without justification took the life of El-i-chi Harper and gravely wounded his brother, Renno Harper. The sentence of this court is that you pay with your life for the life that you took, that sentence to be carried out immediately. Do you have anything to say?"

Horigan dropped to his knees, begging for mercy. Ridgley listened to his sobbing for a moment, then turned and walked away.

Nathan Horigan's hands were tied behind his back. The circle of warriors parted as he was dragged through their midst to a small tree in the middle of the field. Two militiamen secured him to the trunk, while six others were chosen for the firing squad. The medical officer, Lieutenant Jameson, who was the closest they had to a minister, said a few words. Then a makeshift hood was placed over the condemned man's head, and the sentence of the court was carried out.

As the echoing blasts faded and the acrid gun smoke rose into the darkness, Chief Rusog took up his lance and shield and led his warriors back to the village. Five minutes later the militia pulled out, the body of Nathan Horigan wrapped in a blanket and tied across his saddle.

Chapter Seven

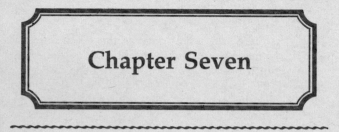 Gao pushed the blanket off his shoulders as he strode through the village of tepees. It was a brisk, late-summer night, with a cool breeze that blew down through the Canadas and picked up moisture as it crossed the lake the whites called Huron. It would be an early and hard winter, he told himself. And for a moment he wished he was back home in the Cherokee lands far to the south.

But then he saw the small tepee near the edge of the village. He had cut the poles himself, and Mist-on-the-Water had sewn the skins and painted them with symbols of their people, the Seneca and Potawatomi. Forgetting the warm nights in the village of his parents, he hurried forward, eager for the warmth of his young wife's arms.

Gao pushed aside the fringed buckskin flap and ducked through the opening. Inside, three women sat around a low fire. They looked up at his entrance. There was a moment's hesitation, and then the youngest of the women dropped the buckskin she was beading and leaped to her feet.

"Gao!" she exclaimed, running into his arms.

"Mist-on-the-Water, I am home." He pulled her to him and held her close. As they stood there, savoring each other's embrace, the other women smiled knowingly, gathered up their work, and departed.

"Oh, Gao, my dear Gao," Mist-on-the-Water whispered as she held and caressed her husband.

"I told you I would return before you finished beading that shirt."

"That one?" she said. "That is the third warrior's shirt I have made since you went south." She grinned up at him. "But it does not matter. Now you are home."

"Let me look at you." Gao held her hands and stepped back, his eyes wandering up and down her slim, youthful figure.

At seventeen, Mist-on-the-Water was three years younger than Gao. When they met, she had seemed so innocent and young, despite the hard life she had lived and the tragedies she had endured. Now, returning after so many months on the trail, Gao saw her for the woman she had become. The woman he had longed for so terribly.

Gao lifted her into his arms and carried her around the fire to a sleeping mat at the far end of the tepee. As he lowered her onto the bearskin robe, her hands were already untying the sash belting his waist, reaching for the thongs that held his breechclout and buckskin leggings in place.

"Gao . . ." she breathed, raising her skirt and drawing him to her. Drawing him home.

Gao lay on his side and stared into the glowing embers of the fire pit. Mist-on-the-Water lay snuggled against his back, a bearskin robe pulled over both of them. Looking into the simmering coals, he thought of home—the home of his childhood.

While he had made a new home here with Mist-on-the-Water, it was a temporary one, for they had to be ready to strike their tepees and move on at a moment's notice. This was a way of life for the tribes to the west, many of whom were represented among Tecumseh's forces. But Gao had lived a more settled existence at Rusog's Town, and a part of him yearned for the long-houses, hearths, and cornfields of his people. He knew that his half-French, half-Potawatomi wife also desired a place she could call home.

It will come in time, he told himself. *When we have driven the whites to the sea and reclaimed our land.*

It troubled him that his path had diverged so far from that of his family—especially his cousin Ta-na-wun-da.

But Tecumseh promises us that all our people will join us on the red path. All will share our vision, and we will live again in peace.

The coals flared up. His eyes widened as he peered into the brilliant red glow.

That day will come soon. Very soon. . . .

And then he would return home. He would be re-united with his father and mother and brother and sister. He would walk again beside Ta-na-wun-da, his brother in spirit.

Home . . . Soon you will journey home. . . .

The words seemed to come from outside of him, from within the embers of the fire pit. They had a famil-iar tone, as if a friend were speaking to him.

Home . . .

Not a friend, he thought with a start. It was his father, with a voice as youthful and strong as when Gao had been a child and El-i-chi a young warrior among the Seneca.

Soon you will journey home. And then we shall walk the red path together. . . .

"El-i-chi?" he called in the faintest of whispers. "Are you speaking to me?"

We shall walk the red path and lead our people, one by one, to a new land. . . .

"El-i-chi . . ." he breathed again as the voice faded into the embers.

Side by side, we shall walk . . . we shall walk . . . we shall live again. . . .

Gao wanted to reach out to the voice, to the embers, and call his father back. But the only sound now was the crackle of the coals. Gao smiled, feeling a rush of peace, not needing to go anywhere, knowing he was on the red path of his people and soon it would lead him home.

Many days' journey to the south, Renno lay in his own bed, carried there from El-i-chi's cabin by his family and friends so that death, should it claim him, would find him at his beloved Huntington Castle. There was little the medicine men could do for him. He had lost much blood, not only from the gunshot wound but from continued internal bleeding, which they were helpless to stop. Within hours of the shooting, he had fallen into a coma, and little by little they watched him slip ever further into that deepest of sleeps.

Beth remained where she had been ever since the tragic accident, at his side. She had sent to Nashville for a physician and had also dispatched runners to find Ta-na-wun-da and bring him home. She wished Little Hawk could be there as well and prayed that at least one of Renno's sons would be with him if the worst happened.

Two days after the shooting, Ta-na-wun-da came running into the house. The moment he saw his father's ashen skin and heard his faint breath, he knew that Renno was far away, at the border of the next world, and likely would not come back. He dropped to his knees beside the bed, clasping his father's hand, calling for him to come home.

"Ta-na-wun-da," Beth whispered, placing a gentle hand on his shoulder.

"How?" he asked, looking up at her, his face expressing his agony. "How did this thing happen?"

She recounted the death of El-i-chi and the shooting

of Renno. Seeing the desire for vengeance in her step-son's eyes, she told him of the trial and execution of the white soldier who had pulled the trigger.

"You must not hate them all," she said, squeezing his arm. "Renno would not want you to seek revenge."

Ta-na rose and looked down at his father. "He has fought so many battles, overcome death so many times. And now he is brought down by a drunkard's hand?" His muscles tightened with rage as he shook his head. "No! I will not let him die!"

"There is nothing we can do," she said, standing beside him and wrapping her arms around his shoulders. "We can only wait and pray that his body heals itself. We can only—" Her words caught, and she began to cry, softly at first; then deep sobs shook through her.

Ta-na took her in his arms. "I am sorry," he whispered, holding her close. "So very sorry."

He buried his face against her shoulder and broke down in tears.

They stood for a long time without moving. Finally, when she had calmed somewhat, Beth pulled back slightly and lifted her stepson's chin until he was looking at her.

"There is a great favor I must ask of you, Ta-na-wun-da."

"What is it? I will do anything."

"This you may not wish to do."

"Whatever it is, I will carry it out," he promised.

Her eyes lowered. "Ta-na, I want you to go west—to the mountains beyond the Mississippi. I want—"

"Little Hawk," he said, completing her thought.

She nodded. "I want Little Hawk here, should the worst . . ." Her shoulders slumped.

Ta-na-wun-da fell quiet as he looked down at his father. He could not bear the thought of leaving Renno now. Even on horseback, it would take as much as two weeks to find his older brother and bring him home. And if Renno did not survive until they returned, Ta-na would lose the last chance to receive the blessing of his father that he had so long desired.

Ta-na-wun-da opened his mouth to speak—to tell his stepmother why he could not accede to her request. Instead he heard himself say, "I will leave at once. I will bring Little Hawk home to his father."

He felt a cold hand close around his heart and feared that all was lost. But he was the son of Renno, sachem of the Seneca. He would do his duty and honor his father's name, even if it meant standing in the shadows as Little Hawk received the final blessing of their father.

Ta-na did not even spend the night at home. Less than an hour later, he had packed two horses and was ready for the journey. He said a final good-bye to his father, then took leave of his stepmother and headed for Rusog's Town. He would visit Ah-wa-o, the aunt who had raised him, and try to ease the burden of her heart at the loss of her husband. Then he would set out for the Ozarks.

Riding toward the Cherokee-Seneca village, Ta-na steeled himself against the pain that threatened to overcome him. He would not allow himself to consider that Renno, the father of his flesh, was hovering near death. Or that El-i-chi, the father who had raised him, had already gone beyond. He would not let himself feel the pain. Not yet.

As Renno walked in the land of shimmering light that lies between this world and the one beyond, he was visited by the manitous of his ancestors. They took him to the forest lands in the north, where his Seneca fathers once hunted deer and brought home the skins of bears. They took him to the blazing lands to the south, where brothers and sisters were taking up arms against the white invaders who pushed them ever west. They took him to the west, beyond the Father of Waters, where he saw the great plains of buffalo, the hunters on their fleet steeds, the sacred hills where the people of the red path would make a final stand.

Renno saw all this and was unafraid. He yearned to walk through those tall grasses, to be free once again to roam wherever he chose until the wind no longer blew and the buffalo were no more.

He was shown all these things by the manitous of his ancestors. And he was not afraid.

Until he heard the voice of his brother.

El-i-chi rode up to him on the back of a spotted pony, a white buffalo robe over his shoulders, a lance and medicine shield at his side. He looked down at Renno, his eyes dark and impenetrable, his smile as gentle as the breeze through the prairie grass.

"I have come to tell you that you may not follow." The sachem spoke through lips that did not move.

"But why?" Renno asked, moving toward him yet getting no closer. "I must make the journey to the place where the sun sleeps at night. I will hunt at your side, as we hunted in the forests of our youth."

"I will hunt at your side," El-i-chi repeated. "But first you must make a final journey."

"I am ready for that journey. I have my bow and quiver of arrows. I will follow wherever my brother leads."

"You are the white Indian, sachem of the Seneca," El-i-chi declared, lowering his lance until the sharp stone tip hovered in front of Renno's chest. "You were sachem before me, and you are now sachem once more. You will make a final journey—not in the land of the manitous but on the hard, red earth of your children. Only then may you place the white robe over your shoulders. Only then may we ride together on the hunt."

"What is this journey I must take?" Renno asked. "Where must I go?"

"You must find them," El-i-chi intoned. "You must bring them together. Little Hawk, Ta-na-wun-da, and

Gao. And then you must pass the sachem's headdress to your son."

"To Little Hawk?"

"Look into your son's eyes. When you see in them the path of the sachem, show him his destiny. Only then may we ride to the longhouse of our mother and father. Only then may we hunt at each other's side. First you must find Gao and Ta-na-wun-da and Little Hawk. First you must bring them together."

"Together? But I don't know where—"

"Go back now!" El-i-chi proclaimed. "Our people mourn for their sachem. Our sons wait for you on the red path. And one of them awaits the rainbow path that lies beyond." He thrust the lance forward, piercing Renno's heart.

Renno felt himself hurtling back through the darkness, through the night. He felt the track of the bullet, blood surging and seeping, deep within his body. Pain seized him, and he struggled against it as it wrenched him from the land of shimmering light back to the land of his children.

He heard the chanting of his people as they called home the white Indian, sachem of the Seneca.

The pain deepened. It tightened around his shoulders, his chest, his heart. He tried to fight it, to hold back, to keep from being dragged from that place of light. But it broke him, and as it flooded through him, he screamed for his brother to take him back.

"*El-i-chi!*"

His head jerked off the pillow, sweat dripping down his face. Pain lay deep within him, deep within every muscle and bone of his body. And with the pain came the awareness that he was alive. That he had come back.

"El-i-chi . . ." he whispered, trying not to forget the vision of his brother as it faded into the mist.

"Renno!" a voice exclaimed, and he opened his eyes to see his wife's joyful, teary face. She threw her arms around him, caressing him, kissing his cheeks and lips and eyes.

"B-Beth, I . . ." His voice trailed off as he fell back against the pillow, weak, smiling.

"El-i-chi!"

The keening cry shook the tepee as Gao bolted upright from beneath the bearskin robe. He was cold and shaking all over. Naked, he pulled the robe around him. The scream still rang in his ears, vibrated in his throat. It had been his scream. It had been his cry.

"What is it?" Mist-on-the-Water asked, concerned, as she sat up behind her husband and wrapped her arms around his heaving chest. "Did you hear something?"

"I . . . I . . ." He tried to speak, but the words caught in his throat. He shook his head and lay back down on his side, clutching his wife's hands as she lay behind him and pulled him close.

"You screamed," she whispered. "Are you all right?"

He nodded but did not reply. *How can I?* he thought. *What would I say?*

He felt her body tight against him, fingers pressing his chest. Her smooth, muscular leg draped over his hip. The swell of her breasts. The intense heat of her loins pouring through him at the small of his back.

He wanted her more than he could bear. He wanted to be lost deep within her. To forget the nightmare. . . .

I grip the mane of a spotted pony. Riding into battle alongside me is Tecumseh, seated upon a powerful red steed. The enemy marches toward us in a row that reaches from the land of frozen water to the land of burning sand. We draw back our bowstrings and release our golden arrows. The first line of the enemy falls to the ground, but another line of white demons replaces them. Another, still, comes marching.

They keep coming, rolling like thunder

across our land. Wave upon wave of white de-
mons, trampling our sacred ground.

   Our quivers are empty, and still they come.
Their bullets tear open our flesh. Their boots
crush fields of grass and corn. They roll over us,
stomping us into the ground. Our blood paints
the earth dark red.

   Still they keep coming. They devour our
women and children. They lay waste to our
land.

   I turn to Tecumseh. I beg him to save us.
But I alone am standing. Where are you? I call.
But the Panther is silent. The Panther does not
hear my cry.

   I walk out among the dead and dying. I see
the hollow face of my mother, the lifeless eyes of
my brother of the spirit, the ravaged body of my
wife. I search for my father and find him
facedown on the hard earth, a knife protruding
from his back. He looks up at me and asks,
"Why did you leave me, my son? Why have you
killed me, my son?"

   He is gone. I stand alone among the bodies
of my people. And then I see him, the Panther,
lying upon the ground. A soldier's bullet has
claimed him, and the blood pours like a river
from his chest. A river that flows among his peo-
ple—and gives them life.

   I cannot bear to walk alone upon the bones
of our nation. I clutch my knife and draw it
across my chest. Across my throat.

   But the blood that pours from me is not
red. It is white. It flows among my people. And
when it touches them, I hear them cry. . . .

"I won't let it happen," Gao whispered to himself. "I
won't let them die. Not my mother and father. Not Ta-na-
wun-da or Tecumseh. Not—"

He was again aware of Mist-on-the-Water, curled close behind him. He wanted her more than he could bear. To be lost deep within her. To forget . . .

Turning over, he grabbed his young wife and rolled her onto her belly. His fingers groped at her flesh, urgent, desperate, as he lifted her hips off the bed of robes. Lunging forward, he pushed into her and heard a gasp of pain and surprise. Her thighs stiffened, then softened, and she pressed against him, meeting each thrust, drawing him ever inward.

Deeper and harder he plunged. He cried out for her to take him. To release him. To remove the nightmare from his heart.

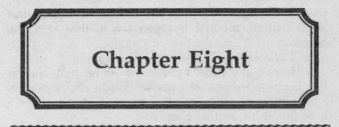

Chapter Eight

Ta-na-wun-da slid off the bare back of the pinto and patted its muzzle, then brought up the gray gelding that was trailing behind. Securing both to a tree, he took his rifle and powder horn and slipped into the forest alongside the trail. He moved as silently and effortlessly as a deer as he headed up the gentle incline to where he remembered the escarpment to be.

Ta-na had been through the region once before and had even spent a night in the cave that his older brother now called home. But the last of Little Hawk's letters to find its way back to Huntington Castle had arrived four months ago, and it was possible he had picked up and moved on. Until Ta-na was sure his brother was on hand and alone, he thought it would be best to keep to the woods at the edge of the clearing.

Hearing what sounded like an ax, he halted and listened. Someone was indeed cutting wood, but it sounded more like chopping kindling than felling a tree or splitting logs.

Approaching the clearing, Ta-na crouched low and

peered through the underbrush. A man stood near the entrance of the cave, hacking branches off a sapling to make another pole like the several others that lay nearby. His rolled-up sleeves revealed the corded muscles of his arms. His hair hung long and loose, as golden as an ear of corn. Though he did not have a beard, he had gone several days without shaving. He looked far leaner than Ta-na had remembered, but there was no mistaking who he was.

"Little Hawk," Ta-na whispered, smiling.

Hawk had a pistol tucked beneath his belt, and his rifle lay propped against a nearby boulder. Ta-na considered announcing his presence, then decided to have a little fun at his brother's expense.

Cupping his hand to his mouth, Ta-na gave the soft coo of a mourning dove. When he repeated it a second time, Hawk paused briefly and looked toward the trees. Then he went back to working on the sapling.

Ta-na made another call, this one of a thrush, repeating it until his brother again paused and listened. When Hawk resumed working, Ta-na made a new sound. After several more calls, Hawk grew noticeably suspicious. He moved closer to his rifle and checked the charge in his pistol. When Ta-na made the sound of a wild turkey, Hawk snatched up the rifle and cocked the hammer, retreating to the safety of the boulders at the base of the escarpment as he prepared to bring his weapon into play.

Ta-na stayed well hidden behind a large tree, in case his brother became reckless and fired, then concluded his impromptu concert by repeating all of the bird sounds, one after the other. He ended with the call of a particular owl with a strange screech. It had annoyed him as a child back at Rusog's Town, until his older brother felled it with an arrow and made him a gift of its feathers.

"Ta-na-wun-da?" Hawk called.

Glancing around the edge of the tree, Ta-na saw his brother rise up from behind the boulders.

"Is that you, Ta-na?"

"No," Ta-na called back. "It is the ghost of Owl-That-Does-Not-Sleep." He stepped from behind the tree and into the sunlight, his arms folded over his chest.

"Ta-na!" Hawk exclaimed, putting down his rifle and running across the clearing.

Ta-na threw his arms around Little Hawk, then stood back and looked him up and down.

Hawk was also appraising his brother, and with a chuckle, he declared, "You have grown. Eating too much from Beth's table, I'd wager."

"I am no bigger," Ta-na told him. "It is you who have shrunk. I can see your bones through that shirt." He poked Hawk in the ribs. "You must be living on locusts and honey. Did you forget how to hunt?"

"Forget? Why, I am so good a hunter that when the deer hear me coming, they figure there is no point in trying to get away and simply drop in their tracks."

"They *hear* you coming?" Ta-na gave a disappointed frown. "That is your problem. A true Seneca can only be heard when he chooses to be." He had meant the comment in jest, but he saw his brother's expression darken.

"I have not been a Seneca these many months."

"And neither are you white." Ta-na pointed to the poles Hawk had been cutting, two of which were lashed together. "You are making an Indian travois, are you not?"

Hawk's grin returned. "I may be white, but I still remember the things our father taught us."

"Are you going somewhere?"

"In fact, I am."

"But that travois is for a man on foot." Ta-na glanced around. "Where is your horse?"

"She died this past spring. I'm afraid I've been reduced to walking."

Ta-na nodded. "Is it getting too crowded around here? Are you headed west—perhaps somewhere the animals don't know the sound of your approach?"

Hawk gripped his younger brother's forearm. "Come inside. I'll tell you all about it."

Ta-na followed him into the cave. Sitting cross-legged on a blanket, he looked around and saw that most everything had been packed. Along with some personal supplies, there was a large bundle of pelts, which Little Hawk undoubtedly planned to pull on the travois.

"You must be headed to rendezvous," Ta-na commented. The rendezvous was a gathering place where trappers traded pelts for goods from the East.

"Not this season." Hawk sat beside his brother. "I plan to sell the pelts in Nashville."

Ta-na's eyes widened. "Nashville?"

"Yes. I thought it was about time I returned home. I miss little Michael terribly. Hell, I miss all of you."

Ta-na grinned broadly. "Then you will not mind if I accompany you?"

"Mind? I'm counting on it, little brother. I just hope you can keep up with my pace."

"Oh, I do not expect I will have much trouble. That is, if my horse is willing to walk so slow."

"You have a horse?" Hawk's expression brightened. "Has it ever pulled a travois?"

"Why should it? I'll let your horse do that."

"My horse?"

Ta-na slapped his brother's knee. "I would not come all this way without bringing a horse for you. I suspected you might have killed that old mare of yours by now."

Hawk eyed his brother closely. "You knew I would come back with you?"

Ta-na knew he could wait no longer. "I did not come only to visit," he began cautiously. "Or to tease you about your hunting. I am afraid I bring sad news."

"What is it?"

"Our uncle El-i-chi died at Rusog's Town just over a week ago."

Hawk's mouth dropped open. "Dead?"

"Some Tennessee militiamen visited Huntington

Castle. One of them got drunk and started molesting a Seneca girl. El-i-chi stepped in and took a knife in the back."

Hawk lowered his head, and Ta-na could see that he was choking back tears.

"So you see, Little Hawk, it is not only Indians who kill without cause." He regretted the words even as he said them.

But Hawk either had not heard the comment or did not care. Instead, he looked up and asked, "How are Ah-wa-o and the children?"

"I saw Ah-wa-o only briefly before I left. She has taken it hard, but she is Seneca. The children do not yet understand what happened. They think their father has gone on a hunt and will return."

Hawk nodded. "And what of Father? He and El-i-chi were more than brothers."

Leaning closer, Ta-na gripped Hawk's arm. "It is about our father that I have come."

Hawk stared at his brother in confusion. Then deep, desperate fear showed in his eyes. "Renno! Is he also—?"

"No, Father is alive. But he was shot by the same man who killed El-i-chi and was still unconscious when I left."

"Where was he shot?"

"In the shoulder, but the bullet angled down his back. Though the wound was repaired, he lost a great deal of blood."

Hawk stood and paced across the cave. "A week ago?" He shook his head in dismay. "It will take another week to get back. By then . . ." He could not complete the thought.

Ta-na nodded his understanding. "The sooner we get started, the better. We have a few hours until dark. We can make a travois large enough for the horse to pull and—"

"Forget the travois," Hawk snapped. "Forget the damn pelts. We can put ten miles behind us before dark."

"That is what I hoped you would say." Ta-na-wun-da rose. "I left the horses down the trail. I will get them."

As Ta-na headed from the cave, Hawk rummaged through his packs, removing anything he could spare. A few minutes later Ta-na returned to the clearing, horses in hand. Together they distributed their packs on the animals, some hanging from Hawk's saddle, others slung over the blanket that served as a saddle for Ta-na. Then they mounted up and rode toward the east.

The brothers traveled well into the night, guided by a bright moon and Hawk's knowledge of the mountains. They made camp in a copse of trees beside a creek, then started out again at first light. Ta-na carefully watched his brother's movements as they rode. No one specific thing alerted him to Hawk's condition, but subtle movements led him to an inevitable conclusion, which was reinforced by Hawk's seeming reluctance to remove his shirt, despite the heat of the day. Finally, when they had slowed to a walk to rest the horses, he broached what he sensed might be a delicate topic.

"You were injured, were you not? And not many weeks ago."

"Injured?" Hawk replied, feigning ignorance.

"It is your side, I would venture. The left one."

"Oh, this," Hawk muttered offhandedly as he touched the spot where he had taken the bullet. "Just an accident."

"An accident that came from the barrel of a gun?" Ta-na pressed.

"I'm fine," Hawk insisted.

"Has the bullet been removed?"

"It only grazed me. It won't slow me down."

Ta-na eyed him suspiciously. "I do not think it was only a graze. But if you prefer, I will not speak of it."

"I prefer."

Ta-na nodded, and they rode on in silence. But a few

minutes later he glanced over at his brother and asked, "Was he white or red, the one who shot you?"

Hawk turned in the saddle and fixed Ta-na with a withering gaze. "You promised not to speak of it."

"Of the bullet. And I am not speaking of that." Ta-na's lips quirked into a smile. "I am asking about the one who *fired* the bullet."

Hawk gave an exasperated sigh and faced forward. "If you must know, he was Creek. But he is Creek no longer."

"Ah, then the bullet he tasted in return was more than a graze."

"Oh, it was more than a graze, all right. It took off half his face."

"Your path and the Creeks' have crossed many times," Ta-na said somberly. "You came here to find a new path. Did you?"

"No, I have not."

"Is that why you were preparing to return?"

Hawk took his time before responding. When he did, his words were cautious and measured. "I was about to leave for Washington, but something kept me from going. I think now that I could not face so many people —their kind words about Naomi and little Joseph . . . their pity. It was more than I thought I could bear. And my son . . ."

Ta-na-wun-da waited for him to continue. When he did not, Ta-na said, "Michael Soaring Hawk is well. But a son needs to be with his father."

"I know."

"And that is why you are coming home?"

"I miss him terribly. But there is something else I miss." He again faced his younger brother. "I miss all those people I was so afraid to face."

"In Washington?"

"In Washington, in Tennessee, in the Cherokee Nation. People . . . I miss people."

Ta-na chuckled. "And this took you more than a year to discover?"

Hawk laughed as well. "No, not that long. I only discovered it these past few weeks. Ever since . . ." He touched the spot where he had taken the Creek bullet.

"Were you near death?"

Hawk thought a long moment, then said assuredly, "No, I was near life. One day, I will tell you about it."

Ta-na stared at his brother and wondered what had brought him to this simple discovery. The death of the Creek warrior, perhaps? Or was it something—or some-one—else? He examined Hawk's expression. He had seen it before—not only on Hawk but on Gao and other young men of the village. And usually it had to do with a woman.

Ta-na-wun-da rode on in silence, confident that Little Hawk's long period of mourning had finally come to an end.

The brothers reached Huntington Castle early on a Saturday afternoon, two weeks after Renno had been shot. As they rode up the lane through the rows of pecan trees, they spied a figure wrapped in a blanket on one of the veranda chairs. Ta-na-wun-da recognized who it was, and his heart soared. He was about to call out their fa-ther's name when Little Hawk slapped his horse into a gallop and shouted, "Renno!"

Ta-na kicked his horse in pursuit, and the brothers arrived at the veranda almost simultaneously. Hawk leaped from his saddle, taking the steps two at a time as he left Ta-na to tether the animals.

Renno was a bit pale but hardly looked like a man who had been so close to death. He beamed as he opened his arms and embraced his son. A moment later Ta-na joined him on the veranda, and they, too, em-braced.

"You look wonderful, Little Hawk!" Renno exclaimed, shaking his head in wonder. "Doesn't he, Ta-na?" he added, his eyes never leaving his elder son.

"So do you, Father," Ta-na told him. "I feared we might not find you looking so well."

Renno waved off the concern. "A pistol ball was not about to take me so easily. Especially not before I saw my Little Hawk again."

"Well, I'm here," Hawk commented: "But that doesn't mean you can now let that bullet get the best of you."

"A flesh wound, that's all it is."

The front door pushed open, and a young boy stepped onto the veranda and looked around cautiously. He stared at the man with the long blond hair and hesitated a moment. Then he blurted, "Father!" and raced into Hawk's outstretched arms.

Hawk twirled his son around and around. Setting him back on his feet, he stepped back a few paces and declared, "Is this my son? Can this possibly be Michael? Why, you've grown so big! You're no longer a boy!"

Michael stood up as tall as he could and puffed himself up proudly. "I am almost six. I have my own rifle, and I can load and fire it."

"With help from your uncle and grandfather," Renno put in, waggling a finger at the boy. "You know you aren't to be using it by yourself."

Michael grabbed hold of Hawk's hand. "Will you take me hunting, Father? Will you take me with you when you go back to the forest?"

"Actually, I figure to be spending some time right here, Michael." He turned to Renno. "That is, if you have room for me."

"Why, you can have any room you want."

"You can stay in my room," Michael declared, pulling him toward the front door. "I have an extra bed."

"Yes, I would like that."

"Come! Let me show it to you!"

"Go on," Renno said, waving a hand and smiling.

"That boy has been in a state ever since Ta-na went to get you."

Hawk looked over at his father and nodded. "I'll just take my packs up, then come back." He turned to Michael. "Just a minute, son." Scooping him up, he carried him down the steps to the horses. Plunking him in the saddle, he untied his packs from the two horses, then set Michael back down again. With Michael lugging one of the smaller packs and Hawk hoisting the others, they made their way back up into the house.

"Beth is likely in the kitchen," Renno called after them. "I know she's eager to see you, too."

Renno heard Hawk calling out his stepmother's name as he disappeared inside. Nodding in satisfaction, he turned back to his younger son.

"When I awoke from the coma, Beth told me where you had gone. I am grateful to you, Ta-na-wun-da."

"It is what any son would do."

"Not just any son."

"Any son of Renno Harper," Ta-na replied.

"Come . . . sit with me." Renno gestured at the chair beside his. "Tell me how you found him. Was he still at the cave? Did he come willingly?"

Sitting, Ta-na recounted his journey to the Ozarks. His description of sneaking up on his older brother, complete with samples of the birdcalls, started Renno chuckling. Renno was particularly interested to learn that Little Hawk was already preparing to come home when Ta-na found him.

"Perhaps he heard me," Renno commented.

"Heard you?"

"I called to him many times. Before I awakened."

Ta-na nodded in understanding.

"The bond between a father and his son is very powerful," Renno added.

Ta-na wanted to say "elder son" but refrained.

"He looks good, don't you think?" Renno mused.

Ta-na chose not to mention the gunshot wound his

brother had suffered. Instead he commented, "A bit thin, perhaps. A few meals at Huntington Castle will set that right."

Renno turned to Ta-na, his eyes narrowing in concern. "Did he say anything of his plans? Will he put on his uniform again and return to Washington?"

"I believe he wishes to stay here."

"Good," Renno said, though his tone betrayed his doubt. "Michael has lost his mother and brother; to lose his father yet again is more than any boy should have to endure."

"I believe he will stay," Ta-na said with conviction. "At least for a time."

"Well, I have a little surprise that just might keep him around a bit longer."

"What surprise is that?" Ta-na asked, eyeing his father suspiciously.

"His sister is on her way home."

"Renna!" Ta-na exclaimed eagerly. He had always felt a particular fondness for his older half sister.

"She has already sailed from France. Her husband is to be Napoleon's representative in Washington."

"And she will come to Huntington Castle?"

"If not, I shall have her kidnapped and spirited here," Renno declared with a jovial smile. "Come, Ta-na," he added, throwing off the blanket. "Help me into the house. My son has come home."

The words were like a cold hand seizing Ta-na's heart. Masking his sadness, he rose and took Renno's hands, lifting him from the chair. He saw his father grimace slightly but knew the pain of his wound mattered little now that his elder son had come home.

Ta-na-wun-da could only wonder if Renno would feel as much joy if his younger son were lost and then found.

Later that evening, Hawk Harper and his father sat alone in the parlor. Renno did not ask his son about his time in the mountains, nor did he press for a decision about his immediate future. In fact, Renno mostly related the many events that had occurred in Washington and along the frontier during the previous year. Hawk was especially interested in the war with England and why Renna's husband, Beau—the comte de Beaujolais—was coming to America.

"That Napoleon is a devious one," Renno said, filling his pipe. "General Jackson wrote only that Beau is to seek ways to serve our mutual interests against the British."

"No doubt Napoleon is eager to avoid war on two fronts."

Renno nodded. "Yes, he has his hands full with the British. Perhaps he finally realizes it is better to have us as friends than enemies."

"And how is the war going?" Hawk asked, leaning forward in his chair. "Is Tecumseh tipping the balance against us?"

Renno shrugged. "It's hard to say. That cowardly General Hull sacrificed the opportunity to defeat the British at Fort Malden largely because he so feared Tecumseh," he said, referring to the British fort near the eastern end of Lake Erie, across the river from Detroit. "We far outnumbered the British and Tecumseh's forces combined, but when Hull heard a few war whoops, he scurried back to Detroit."

"I heard about his surrender of Detroit last summer. Is it still in British hands?"

"Yes, and along with it, the entire Northwest Territory beyond the Ohio settlements. Much of it is Tecumseh's doing." Renno paused to light his pipe, then continued. "Tecumseh has been running free all along the frontier, whipping up support among the Winnebago, Potawatomi, Ottawa, and Creek. Even a few of our Cherokee friends have joined him. And a handful of Seneca, I am sorry to say."

Renno's expression was particularly somber, and

Hawk nodded in understanding, well aware that his cousin Gao was among their number.

"I believe the tide is turning, however," Renno went on. "Each of our defeats on the frontier—each new atrocity—only fans the flames of patriotism. In the past few months, thousands have joined the state militias. General Jackson is chomping at the bit to get back into action."

"Ta-na told me he was wounded."

"A nasty bit of business," Renno muttered, scowling. "Early this year he took his Tennessee Volunteers to defend New Orleans, only to be sent home upon reaching Natchez. You can imagine his foul temper at being forced to the sidelines again. Well, things got a bit out of hand in a Nashville tavern, and he found himself in a gunfight with his old enemy, Colonel Benton. Took a bullet in the shoulder from Benton's brother." He grinned sardonically. "But I daresay he's on the mend and itching for another fight. If the Benton boys are lucky, he'll make that fight with the British or Tecumseh instead of them."

Hawk rose from his chair and walked over to the fireplace. Hands on the mantle, he stared down into the flames.

"What is it?" Renno asked. "Do you miss the uniform?"

"No. It isn't that."

Hawk crossed the room to a sideboard that held a crystal decanter of brandy and several glasses. He held up the decanter, offering some to his father, who declined with a wave of the hand. Pouring himself a glass, he quickly downed it, then refilled the glass and returned to his chair.

"I thought I would miss the military, but I don't," Hawk said with a shrug. "Yet I feel I've let people down."

"Who?"

"Michael, for one. And President Madison."

"He had plenty of fine men to replace you," Renno pointed out. "And war had not yet been declared when you resigned your commission."

"But we knew it was coming. We just weren't sure whom we'd be fighting—England, France, or both." He gave a half smile. "With a first name like mine, you can be sure I was counted among the war hawks. Many an eyebrow must have risen when I chose not to return to Washington."

"No one judged or thought ill of you."

"Perhaps I did." Hawk fell silent.

Renno watched his son a few moments. Then with some effort he lifted himself from his chair, commenting, "I think I will have that drink now."

Hawk jumped up. "Let me—"

"No," Renno told him. "I need to be moving around. That good woman of mine will have me an old man if I'm not careful."

"She just wants you to take it easy."

"I know, I know. But there will be time to rest soon enough." Reaching the sideboard, he poured a glass of brandy and returned with it. Dropping into his chair, he took a sip, then looked at his son. "What do you plan to do?" he asked.

Hawk started hoisting his own glass, then lowered it to his lap. "I haven't decided. I want to be with Michael as much as possible. But I also want to do my part in the war effort."

"Then you'll return to Washington?"

"I don't know, Father. I just don't know." He downed the rest of the brandy.

"Well, there is plenty of time to make up your mind," Renno declared. "You have only just returned." He took a draw on his pipe and followed it with a healthy swallow of brandy. "And I'm mighty pleased to have you home."

Chapter Nine

At the beginning of September, news of a massacre in the Mississippi Territory traveled up the entire East Coast almost as quickly as the shock waves of Tecumseh's earthquake the previous year. Indian runners carried it north through the lands bordering the Mississippi River. Military couriers rode day and night, bringing reports to Atlanta, Richmond, and Washington, D.C. Newspapers spread the word from city to city, until almost everyone from New Orleans to Boston had heard of the slaughter at Fort Mims.

The people of Rusog's Town received word of the August thirtieth massacre only a few days later. At first all they knew was that Fort Mims, on the Mobile River, had been overrun by a superior force of Creek warriors, resulting in the deaths of almost all the settlers who had sought refuge there. Additional news then filtered in, and more detailed accounts arrived with the newspapers from Knoxville and Nashville.

Hawk Harper was eager to learn all he could about the massacre. He had served as military liaison to the

Creek Nation, and following the deaths of his wife and son at Creek hands, he had personal reasons for being interested in their affairs. Trouble had been steadily brewing the previous year, and he knew this latest incident would result in widespread public support for a full-scale action against the Creek.

Hawk journeyed to Nashville, ostensibly to purchase supplies but in reality to learn more about the situation. Accompanying him was Ta-na-wun-da, who, given the growing anti-Indian sentiment in the wake of the massacre, took the precaution of dressing like a white. They rode into town and immediately made for a familiar tavern, where they sequestered themselves in the corner with mugs of ale and the latest issue of the *Gazette*.

The massacre continued to dominate the front page. The banner headline proclaimed, "Shocking Reports of Indian Savagery." Below it was the subhead "260 Perish in the Flames of War."

Hawk angled the newspaper toward an oil lamp on the wall and read the story aloud to his younger brother:

> "On August thirtieth occurred one of the most shocking massacres that can be found in the annals of our Indian troubles. An overwhelming force of Creek savages laid siege to Fort Mims on the Mobile River in Mississippi Territory, setting fire to the fortifications and buildings and killing upwards of two hundred and sixty men, women, and children. The following is drawn from eyewitness accounts to the atrocity.
>
> "The settlers in the region were so alarmed during the course of the summer by the hostile deportment of the Creeks, that the greater part abandoned their plantations and sought refuge in the different forts along the various branches of the river.
>
> "These settlers, from an imperfect idea of

their danger, adopted an erroneous mode of defense by throwing themselves into small forts or stations, at great distances from each other. Early in August, it was ascertained that the Indians intended to make an attack upon all these stations and destroy them in detail.

"Toward the latter part of August, information was brought that the Indians were about to make an attack on Fort Mims, in which the greatest number of families had been collected, but unfortunately too little attention was paid to the warning. The fort was commanded by Major Beasley of the Mississippi Territory (a brave officer and highly respected), with about a hundred volunteers under his command. By some fatality, notwithstanding the warnings he had received, he was not sufficiently on his guard and suffered himself to be surprised on the thirtieth at noonday.

"The sentinel had scarcely time to notify the approach of the Indians, when they rushed with a dreadful yell toward the gate, which was wide open. The garrison was instantly under arms, and the major flew toward the gate, with some of his men, in order to close it and expel the enemy; but he soon after fell mortally wounded.

"The gate was at length closed, after great slaughter on both sides. But a number of the Indians had taken possession of a blockhouse, from which they were removed after a bloody contest. The assault continued for an hour on the outside of the pickets; the portholes were several times carried by the assailants and retaken by those within the fort.

"The Indians for the moment withdrew, apparently disheartened by their loss. But on being harangued by their chief, they returned

with augmented fury to the assault. Having
procured axes, they cut down the gate and
made a breach in the pickets, and possessing
themselves of the area of the fort, they compelled the besieged to take refuge in the
houses.

"Here the defenders made a gallant resistance. But the Indians at length set fire to the
roofs, making the situation of these unfortunate
people altogether hopeless. The agonizing
shrieks of the unfortunate women and children
at their unhappy fate would have awakened
pity in the breasts of tigers; it is only by those
who have some faint idea of the nature of Indian warfare, that the horror of their situation
can be conceived.

"Not a soul was spared by these monsters.
From the most aged person to the youngest infant, they became the victims of indiscriminate
butchery; and some, to avoid a worse fate, even
rushed into the flames. A few, only, escaped by
leaping over the pickets while the Indians were
engaged in the work of massacre. It is from
them that we have the benefit of this account.

"About two hundred and sixty persons, of
all ages and sexes, thus perished, including
some friendly Indians, and about one hundred
Negroes.

"The panic caused at the other forts and
stations by this dreadful catastrophe can
scarcely be described. The wretched inhabitants, fearing a similar fate, abandoned their re-
treats of fancied security in the middle of the
night, and in their endeavors to escape to Mobile, encountered every species of suffering.
The dwellings of these settlers (who were probably as numerous as the whole tribe of Creeks)

were burnt, and their crops and cattle destroyed.

"Everywhere upon the streets of Mobile can be heard the clamor for an accounting to be made. That the Creeks will be read a lesson of the severest magnitude for this latest act of butchery is a tenet of faith among the citizenry. They look to their brothers and sisters in the neighboring states to help them put an end to Creek savagery."

"Aye, 'twas a nasty bit o' business," a voice rang out, and the brothers looked up to see a burly, red-haired farmer. He stood rather unsteadily, waving the mug in front of him, obviously having consumed quite a bit of ale.

"The Creek can be a dangerous lot," Hawk commented in something of an undertone, not wishing to engage the stranger in conversation.

"*Can* be?" the fellow declared. "They are *the* most dangerous o' the whole lot o' them savages." He gestured with the mug as if taking in the entire Indian race. The frothy brew spilled over the sides and ran down his hand.

Hawk merely nodded. Ta-na-wun-da, however, seemed less sympathetic and, looking up at the drunkard with barely disguised distaste, said, "I don't much commend their actions, but it is to be expected when we adopt a policy of pushing people off their ancestral lands."

The big man stared at him curiously, as if having trouble determining exactly what position Ta-na was advocating. Finally he said, "Are you takin' up for them savages?"

"I am only pointing out that certain actions lead to inevitable reactions." He would have said more, but Hawk laid a restraining hand on his forearm.

"No," the farmer said, pointing the mug at Hawk. "Let the fellow speak his mind." He took a few steps toward Ta-na, narrowing his eyes as he examined him. "You don't sound like a savage, but you sure as hell talk like one. Look like one, too."

Hawk's grip tightened on his brother's arm, and Ta-na reluctantly turned away from the farmer. Doing so revealed the long braid of hair down his back.

"I'll be damned! You *are* one o' them!" He spun around and called to the barman, "Fitzpatrick! You've got a damned savage drinkin' in here!"

The barman looked up from clearing the counter. "Leave him be, Giles. He's just one of Rusog's Cherokees." He returned to his chore.

"A smart little Cherokee, too." Giles turned back to the table. "A damned smart one, I'd say. Knows all about how we should take care of our Indians. Right, boy?" He thrust the mug forward, nearly sloshing some of the liquid on Ta-na's back. "Let a few hundred o' them keep all the land for huntin' rather than turn it into good farmland t'feed thousands. That what you want, squaw boy?"

Seeing that Ta-na was on the verge of reacting, Hawk jumped up and jabbed a thumb toward the farmer. "Go on about your business. My brother and I want no quarrel with you."

"Brother?" the burly man muttered, clearly flabbergasted at the concept. He cocked his head as he looked back and forth between the two men, one raven-haired and the other blond. "You a damn Cherokee, too?"

The tavern had only a half-dozen patrons, all of whom fell silent as they turned to see what was going on in the corner of the room.

"Seneca," Hawk corrected, surprising himself by acknowledging his Indian heritage. "Now, let's just leave things be."

"Seneca!" the farmer blurted, looking back at the small audience of onlookers. "And I'm one o' them savage scalp-liftin' Scots!" He chortled at his feeble humor.

It was Ta-na who had to restrain his brother now.

With some effort, Hawk sat back down and busied himself folding the newspaper.

Giles tottered closer to their table. He swung his hand, as if to clap Hawk on the shoulder, but missed his mark and ended up clutching the mug in two fists. "If you're really the brother o' this heathen, then your mammy must've been one o' them squaws that warmed the Irish missionaries under their robes."

Hawk leaped from the seat, hurtling into the man and knocking him back onto an empty table. One of the legs collapsed, and the men tumbled to the floor amid splintering wood. Giles was stunned at first, but when he finally reacted, it was with fury. He smacked a fist against Hawk's cheek, stunning him and rolling him to the side. Giles tried to follow with the mug but hit the edge of the table, spraying them both with shattered glass.

Ta-na-wun-da entered the fray, grabbing hold of the big man and pulling him away from Hawk. But the farmer shrugged him off, and before Ta-na could lunge at him again, several pairs of hands grabbed him and threw him backward. His head smacked the wall with a thud, and he slid to the floor. After a moment he struggled to his feet, shaking his head to clear it, and found himself confronting three patrons, who proceeded to pummel him with fists and boots.

Across the room, Hawk was having a better time of it. He had finally gotten the advantage and knocked the farmer off his feet with a staggering uppercut to the jaw. He waited a moment to make sure Giles would not be getting back up anytime soon; then he spun around and went for the nearest man attacking Ta-na. He had just grabbed the fellow around the neck when a flash of movement caught his eye, and he glanced to the right in time to see the bartender swinging some sort of club. It connected with the back of Hawk's head. His body shuddered and went numb, and he felt himself falling forward through darkness.

* * *

Hawk Harper awoke to find his brother cradling his head and speaking softly to him. At first he could not make out Ta-na-wun-da's words. As things grew clearer, he saw that his brother's face was bruised and bloody, and he recognized the words as a Seneca chant.

"How is he?" another voice asked, and Hawk saw the shadowed figure of someone looking down on them.

"He is coming around," Ta-na told the man.

"Good. Then let's get him out of here."

"Hawk, can you stand?" Ta-na asked.

He nodded and felt a stab of pain shoot through his head. "H-help me up," he mumbled, raising his arms.

Ta-na and the other man each took an arm and lifted him from the floor. He leaned against his brother and looked around the murky room, wondering where all the lights had gone. It was chilly, the air close and damp. His vision cleared, and he realized he was not in the tavern but in a small room with a single bench.

"Wh-where—?"

Ta-na grinned at him. "The guardhouse, big brother. We're in the militia guardhouse."

"Damn," Hawk muttered, pushing away from Ta-na and straightening up. "How long—?"

"A couple of hours. I was beginning to think you were not going to wake up."

Hawk rubbed the back of his head and winced as he touched the lump. "I . . . I think I wish I hadn't." He turned to the other man, who was still in shadow but seemed somehow familiar. "Are we under arrest?"

"Not any longer, Captain Harper."

This time Hawk recognized the distinctive voice and blinked his eyes to confirm his suspicion. The man was tall and dignified, with graying hair and with his left arm in a sling. "General?" he said in disbelief. "General Jackson?"

"I hardly expected us to meet again under such circumstances." Andrew Jackson was grinning jovially. "Why don't we get you boys out of this place."

Hawk allowed himself to be assisted from the small room that served as a cell. He felt somewhat less dizzy as they made their way down a long corridor and outside into the courtyard. Raising a hand against the glare of afternoon sun, he glanced around the yard. The guard-house was the smallest building in a circle of rather meager wood structures that served as Nashville head-quarters for the Tennessee militia.

Ta-na started to take his brother's arm again, but then he waved him off and walked on his own across the yard, following Jackson into another building. It was a bare-bones office, with one militiaman on duty. Jackson dismissed the soldier, who saluted and headed outside.

"Please, sit down," Jackson said, showing them to a pair of hard-backed chairs while he took the seat behind the desk.

"We weren't doing anything wrong," Hawk began, but the general interrupted with an impatient gesture.

"Forget that," he said, shaking his head. "A tavern squabble, nothing more. With the trouble down at Fort Mims, it doesn't take much to set off some of these folks." He gestured at Ta-na-wun-da. "Most of them don't know the difference between a Creek, a Cherokee, or a Seneca. They see someone who looks even the least bit Indian and think he's to blame for every massacre of the past twenty years."

"Even those carried out by the Americans?" Ta-na said pointedly.

Hawk wondered if Jackson would take offense at the comment, but after a moment the general leaned back in his chair and gave a hearty chuckle.

"You certainly don't mince words, Ta-na-wun-da. I'd say you have more than your share of Renno's blood. But has it been bathed in the poison of the Panther Passing Across?"

"Tecumseh?" Ta-na's lips curled into a sneer. "He has taken too much from our people. His dreams will be the end of us."

"Then you don't stand with your cousin Gao?"

Hawk wondered how Andrew Jackson knew of Gao's activities. He was also wondered how his brother would respond. Ta-na had spoken little about Tecumseh's campaign other than to say he did not believe Indians should ally themselves with the British.

Rather than answering directly, Ta-na eyed Jackson suspiciously and asked, "What do you know of my cousin?"

"Only that he fights alongside Tecumseh. And that you two were raised almost as brothers."

"We *are* brothers," Ta-na stated emphatically. "Nothing the Panther Passing Across may say or do will ever change that."

Hawk noticed Ta-na's furtive glance and suspected he was gauging his real brother's reaction to the comment. Hawk tried to reassure him with a nod.

"Then you do not agree with Gao . . . or with Tecumseh?" Jackson pressed.

"I see truth in much of what they say. But I see nothing but darkness in what they do."

"And you are a man who believes in truth," Jackson stated as if it were fact.

"I do not appreciate a man saying one thing and doing another. In that regard, there is much to appreciate in Tecumseh, for he does exactly what he promises. I only wish the voices in Washington would speak with such honesty. Perhaps then there would not be so much trouble with Tecumseh or the Creek."

Jackson turned to Hawk. "I take it you would agree with your brother?"

Hawk leaned forward in his chair. "If you don't mind my asking, why do you care what we think of Tecumseh? If this has something to do with the tavern, I assure you we were doing nothing when that fight broke out."

"Believe me, Captain Harper, I care very little

about tavern brawls. But I care very much about the attitude and allegiance of the men I take into battle."

"Yes, but we're not . . ." Hawk's words trailed off as the impact of the statement sank in. "Just what are you suggesting, General Jackson?"

"Certainly you know that I have counseled action against the Creek these many months. It was my intention to resolve the problem once and for all when I brought the militia to Natchez earlier this year. Unfortunately, the government did not yet have the stomach for war in the south—not with the enemy already engaged in the north. But now they can hardly back down—not with so loud a public clamor."

"What has that to do with us?" Ta-na-wun-da interjected.

"I have finally been offered a commission worthy of undertaking. I am to assume charge of a force of several thousand militiamen at Fayetteville and march south, cutting a swath through the heart of the Creek Nation and destroying once and for all their ability to wage war." He pressed his right palm flat upon the desk as he fixed Ta-na and then Hawk with his uncompromising gaze. "An effective military operation requires an able chief of scouts, and I have it on good authority that Renno's son may be just the man."

Hawk was about to speak when Ta-na asked, "And which of Renno's sons might that be?"

"I have no doubt that either of you would make a formidable chief of scouts. But I was referring to you, Ta-na-wun-da. As for you, Captain Harper, it is my hope that you will put your uniform back on—temporarily, if that is your desire—and ride at my side as a militia officer."

"Take arms against the Creek?" Hawk's tone was cautious as he weighed and rejected the offer.

"I know you have suffered personal tragedy at Creek hands, so I need not recount the horrors they visited upon those poor defenders of Fort Mims. This is a time when all Tennessee—indeed, all America—must stand united against a common enemy." He faced Ta-na-wun-da. "And mark me well: Unless the Seneca, the Cherokee, and other tribes loyal to our nation demonstrate that loyalty by standing alongside us, the public clamor will soon turn from merely the Creek and Tecumseh to all Indians on American soil."

Though Ta-na-wun-da's expression did not change, Hawk sensed he was churning with anger. It was no secret that Jackson, like most Americans, saw the Indian nations as living on soil owned by the United States. With such an attitude it was inevitable Indians eventually would have to assimilate—if that were even possible—or face being driven from what remained of their homeland.

"Perhaps this is not the best moment to respond to your offer, General Jackson," Hawk said in an attempt to steer the conversation to safer ground. "We've only just—"

"Of course not," Jackson interrupted, standing from the desk. "I did not expect you to answer right away." He moved to the door and opened it for them. "But when I heard what happened—and who we were entertaining in our guardhouse—I thought it a fortuitous opportunity I could not let pass."

"Will you be heading to Fayetteville soon?" Hawk asked, following Jackson and his brother outside and across the courtyard.

"That depends on when you boys are leaving."

"Us?"

"I had it in mind to stop at Rusog's Town before going to Fayetteville. I want to see how your father is doing, and—"

"He is better," Ta-na said a bit curtly.

"Excellent. But I'd like to visit with my old friend before beginning our campaign. And it would be an opportunity to gauge the temper of Rusog and his Cherokees." He halted and turned to Hawk. "If you have no objection, I would like to accompany you to Huntington Castle."

"Of course not, General," Hawk replied, a bit disconcerted.

"Good."

It was decided they would leave at dawn, and Hawk and General Jackson shook hands. When Jackson turned to shake Ta-na's hand, the young Seneca made no move to reciprocate the gesture. With a respectful nod, Jackson headed back across the courtyard.

"What do you think of that?" Hawk asked his brother when they were alone.

"Not much," Ta-na-wun-da replied. He started toward town.

Hawk fell into pace beside him. "I take it you have no desire to be Jackson's scout."

"First they have us arrested, and then they offer us a post." Ta-na gave a low grunt of disapproval.

"How *did* that happen, anyway? Getting arrested, I mean."

"After the barman put you under, they tossed you into the street."

"And you?"

Ta-na's expression betrayed the hint of a smile. "I let them strike me a while longer. Then I chose to join you."

"And the guardhouse?"

Ta-na chuckled. "Turns out the Scotsman you were fighting is in the militia. He had us carted off."

"A militiaman, eh?" Hawk rubbed the bump at the back of his head. "It just might be worth considering General Jackson's offer. If nothing else, I could then teach that fellow a few manners."

"You're not really considering it, are you?" Ta-na asked incredulously.

Hawk clapped him on the back. "I'm only kidding. The last place I want to be right now is in a uniform— and in the middle of Creek country."

"Good."

"Come on," Hawk declared, picking up the pace. "I don't know about you, but I could use a drink."

"You're not intending to return to that tavern, are you?"

"One thing I'll say about Nashville—there's no shortage of taverns. You pick the establishment, I'll buy the ale."

"Now, there's a far more tempting offer than General Jackson's," Ta-na declared as they headed down the street.

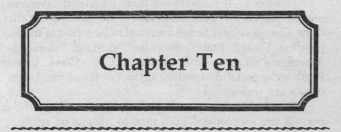

Chapter Ten

When Major-General Andrew Jackson arrived at Huntington Castle with Hawk, Ta-na-wun-da, and a military aide, it was soon apparent he had more in mind than simply visiting an old friend. He asked for and was granted a council with the Cherokee and Seneca elders and made an impassioned speech, seeking their support in the war against the Creek. The assembly was held in a small meeting lodge behind Huntington Castle so that Renno, who was still weak, could more easily attend. Joining him were Chief Rusog and most of the elders of both tribes. Also invited to attend were Hawk Harper and some of the younger warriors, including Ta-na and Ho-ta-kwa.

Jackson was well-known to the senior warriors of Rusog's Town. He had made his reputation as a fearless Indian fighter and in his youth had even battled the Cherokee. But the days of blood were past, with the Cherokee and their Seneca friends having chosen to live in peace with their American neighbors. Their land had been reduced to barely one third its original size, so they could no longer support themselves by hunting and had become farmers. Increasingly they were adopting the ways of the whites—from clothing to education to the very homes they lived in—in the hope that by doing so they would be able to protect their remaining homeland for their children and their children's children.

Jackson well understood their fears and concerns, and he played on them masterfully. He pointed out that if the Cherokee and Seneca wanted to be a part of the expanding United States, they had to stand beside the Americans when trouble arose. And the Creek to the south were certainly trouble, at least as far as the Americans were concerned.

Concluding his speech, Jackson stood in front of the council fire and looked from man to man as he spoke.

"Know that the time of reckoning is at hand. The Creek have made their position known by their heartless deeds at Fort Mims and elsewhere. Now we Americans are determined to force them off our lands. But a greater issue weighs upon the shoulders of my friends gathered here tonight. Many in our young nation do not believe that white man and red can live alongside one another and share the same land. However, when I come here to Rusog's Town, I have reason to believe this is possible— even desirable. But it will only happen if we stand together in times of crisis as well as plenty."

Jackson circled the fire until he stood in front of Chief Rusog of the Cherokee. "I must speak plainly, Chief Rusog. I come here from Nashville, where feelings are running strong against you. There are those who would have us remove not only the Creek but the Cherokee and Seneca and, indeed, all Indians whose homelands lie within the borders of the United States. This sentiment is spreading among our people, and it can only be doused by decisive action. I ask you and your people to join me as I take such action against the Creek."

Walking to where Renno and some other Senecas were seated, the general placed a fist upon his chest. "The Creek are no friends of yours. They have proven their treachery time and again, raiding not only our settlements but even some Cherokee villages that lie to the south."

He turned to Renno, who was again wearing the sachem's headdress. "You and I have known each other these many years. And you know and understand the ways of our people and our government. It is true that the men who sit in the halls of government in Washington often say one thing and do another—but you also know I have always spoken plainly with you, even when my words brought no comfort to your people. Tonight I speak as plain and as true as I have ever done. There are men in Washington who are advocating that all tribes, Seneca and Cherokee included, be forced beyond the Father of Waters, the great Mississippi. They turn to men such as me to counsel them on the feasibility of such a removal and how best to accomplish it. I have continued to argue that whites and some Indians can live in harmony, as indeed you have shown here in Rusog's Town. But the same does not hold true for the Creek. Mark my words, they *will* be removed. And if I am to prevent similar action from being taken against our friends gathered here tonight, I must show that we are neither white nor Indian but that we are brothers, united against a common foe."

Jackson turned and addressed the full council. "I ask you to stand at my side as we seek justice for those who died so brutally at Fort Mims—for those who suffer and die every day as a result of Creek treachery. Join me in Fayetteville one week from today as we begin our march south."

Having spoken, General Jackson left the lodge and returned to Renno's house. The council deliberated his request, discussing both sides of the issue, and in the end it was decided that each Cherokee and Seneca warrior would be asked to make his own decision. Those who chose to join Jackson's march would assemble in two days' time and ride to Fayetteville.

* * *

Following the council meeting, the Indians returned to their village while Renno headed into the mansion to inform Andrew Jackson of the decision. Ta-na-wun-da took leave of his brother and followed the others to Rusog's Town, where he was staying with his aunt and young cousins in the cabin of his late uncle, El-i-chi.

Hawk Harper started into the house, but as he approached the veranda he changed his mind and continued out into the fields of Huntington Castle, mulling over all that had been said. He walked alone, wishing his younger brother were at his side. Perhaps by talking things through with Ta-na he could figure out what he should do. But during the council's deliberations, Ta-na had made it clear he did not believe they should join Jackson's militia—especially since El-i-chi had been killed and Renno wounded because of that very militia. Hawk knew he had to make his own decision, and he wondered if perhaps it was meant to be that way.

"I can't believe I'm even considering it," Hawk said aloud, as if Ta-na were there. "The idea is preposterous. I owe them nothing—isn't that what you would tell me, Ta-na?"

Turning slightly to the left, he headed toward a tree that stood alone in the light of the rising moon.

"On the one hand, I'm a soldier—or at least I was. It's my responsibility, isn't it?" He shook his head uncertainly. "But what do I owe them? I've sacrificed enough to duty, haven't I? If I hadn't accepted that appointment to the Flint River Agency . . ."

The stark image of the bodies of his wife and son engulfed him. The thought of returning to the land of the Creek made his stomach roil.

"No!" he blurted, shaking a fist. "I owe them nothing. It doesn't matter what General Jackson says or wants. I don't have to do this thing. Ta-na is right."

He walked until he reached the tree. In the faint

blue light he saw the dark, splattered stain of blood where the firing squad had executed El-i-chi's murderer.

Revenge . . . retribution . . . justice . . .

The words rolled through him, one upon the other. He had already taken his revenge, first against the killers of his wife and son and more recently against the Creek warriors who had visited his lair in the Ozarks. How could he even consider seeking more?

"Is it revenge?" he asked aloud, running his hand along the bloodstained bark. "Or is it justice? Duty?"

He had had his revenge, and what had he received in return? Suddenly, a single word whispered within him: *mercy*. He had been shown mercy.

He thought of the woman named Ma-ton-ga. Of how she could have taken revenge upon him but instead nursed him to health.

He whispered her name in English: "Place-Where-the-Sun-Sleeps. . . ." He looked first to the west, then to the south, for Ma-ton-ga had not gone to the place of the setting sun but had returned home. To the south. To the land of the Creek.

Panic rushed through him. Andrew Jackson planned to march his militia through the heart of the Creek Nation, and he did not intend to show any mercy. Hawk understood the tactic from a military point of view. But Jackson's army would not encounter armed Creek warriors alone. There would be women and children—innocents like Ma-ton-ga. Like Naomi Harper and Joseph Standing Bear.

Who would speak for Ma-ton-ga? he asked himself. Who would make certain that another Naomi and Joseph were not forced to die? If he did not stand up for them, who would? It was a debt he owed to Ma-ton-ga and, through her, to all the innocent victims of war.

Hawk turned away from the killing tree and gazed at the lights of Huntington Castle. He was not so naive as to think he could halt a massacre, if that was the militia's intent. But if he was on hand, perhaps he could help see to it that retribution was tempered with compassion.

Hawk knew he could not forestall such a tragedy on his own. But General Andrew Jackson might be able to do precisely that—and Hawk intended to make sure he did. He would tell Ta-na-wun-da of his decision, then return to the mansion and inform Renno and General Jackson.

As Hawk headed toward Rusog's Town, he thought of his young son, Michael Soaring Hawk, who was probably getting ready for bed that very moment under his grandmother's loving eye. He would have to tell Michael as well. That would be the most difficult task of all.

A half hour later Hawk hurried up the stairs of Huntington Castle to the room he shared with his son. Fortunately a lamp was still burning, and he quietly pushed open the door to find Beth reading a story to Michael. The boy's face brightened upon spying his father in the doorway.

Putting down the book, Beth smiled at her stepson. "Come to say another good-night, have you?" She rose and joined Hawk at the door. "I'll just leave you boys alone," she said, gently touching his arm. Slipping into the hall, she closed the door behind her.

As Hawk crossed the room, Michael shifted to make room on the bed. Hawk sat down and leaned against the headboard, and Michael snuggled into the crook of his arm.

"Was Grandma Beth reading you a story?" he asked.

"The one about the bear," Michael told him.

Hawk did not know the story but nodded as if he did.

"They didn't kill the bear cub," the boy explained. "He was only wounded."

"That's good, isn't it?"

Michael nodded. "I didn't want them to kill the cub. But they thought he was a wolf."

"You have to be very careful in the woods. You have to know exactly what you are shooting."

"Grandpa told me that."

"And he's right."

"He said I have to be careful if I want to go hunting," Michael explained, then added almost casually, "'cause rifles can kill people. Like Mother and Joseph."

Hawk was pleased that Michael still did not know the gruesome details of how his mother and brother had died, believing they had been shot. But he was somewhat taken aback that his son spoke so matter-of-factly about their deaths. Then he realized it was through such detachment that the young boy was able to assimilate his great loss.

"Yes, rifles can kill people. They also provide food and protection."

"I would never kill anyone," Michael declared, looking up at his father. "Only rabbits and such."

"Good."

Hawk fell silent, wondering how he would tell the boy about his decision. Finally he realized he had to be as direct with his son as the boy had been with him.

"Michael," he began, placing a hand on the boy's chest. "I am sorry, but I must go away for a while."

Michael's eyes widened and suddenly looked very sad.

"Do you know the man who rode home with your Uncle Ta-na and me?"

Michael shrugged.

"His name is General Andrew Jackson, and he is a friend of Grandpa Renno's."

"He's a soldier," Michael said with renewed enthusiasm, apparently forgetting for the moment that his father had mentioned leaving.

"Yes. He's in charge of the Tennessee militia. Do you know why he came here?"

The boy shrugged again.

"He has to march his army south to Mississippi Territory. You've heard of Mississippi, haven't you?" When Michael nodded, he continued, "And when a whole army is on the move, it is very important that good guides show them the way. Guides like Ta-na-wun-da and me."

"You went all the way to the Sp . . . Sp . . . Specific Ocean."

"The Pacific Ocean," Hawk gently corrected him. "Yes, I did. And I've been all through the Mississippi Territory. So General Jackson wants me to lead him there."

Michael wrapped his arms around his father's neck and whispered into his ear, "Can I go, too? Please?"

Pulling Michael slightly away, Hawk smiled at his son. "I would love for you to come along, but General Jackson will only take men older than sixteen."

"I'm six."

"*Almost* six. And not yet sixteen."

"I won't get in the way. Promise."

"I know you wouldn't. But this is something I must do alone."

"What about Uncle Ta-na? He's going, isn't he? Is he sixteen?"

"He's much older. He must be twenty by now. But I don't think he is going. Just me."

Slinking down on the bed, Michael folded his arms and frowned. "I don't want you to go away again."

"This time it will only be for a short while."

"How long?"

"A few weeks. Not much more."

Michael's frown faltered slightly, and he stole a glance at his father. "You promise?"

"I promise. And when I return, we will go hunting together."

"Really?" the boy said eagerly, his face brightening considerably.

"Just you and me. And that new rifle of yours."

Michael threw his arms around Hawk. "Then you better get going."

"You want me to leave already?" Hawk asked with a mock pout.

"That way you'll get back quicker."

"All right, son."

Hawk rose and covered Michael with the blankets. He kissed him on the forehead, turned down the wick on the lamp, and started from the room.

"Father?" Michael called after him.

"Yes?"

"Grandma taught me a new word."

"What is it?"

"*Kononkwa*. It's Seneca."

"Yes, I know," he whispered in reply.

"Kononkwa, Father."

Hawk struggled to keep his voice from breaking as he repeated the expression in English. "I love you, too, Michael Soaring Hawk."

Late that night, Ta-na-wun-da strode through the yard of his father's home. As he peered through the darkness at the imposing edifice of Huntington Castle, he thought of Gao, his brother in the spirit, fighting the Americans to the north. And of Little Hawk, his brother by blood, about to ride south with General Andrew Jackson's militia and take the battle into the homeland of the Creek. With the Harper mansion before him and Rusog's Town behind, Ta-na sensed he stood halfway between these two worlds. Like Gao, he was only one-quarter white, and thus his loyalties flowed most strongly with his Seneca blood. But it was the blood of Renno, the white Indian, and it coursed through his veins like a thundering river.

He neared the mansion and saw a figure seated on the veranda with a candle lamp beside him. It was Renno, who had sent for him at El-i-chi's cabin.

"I have come, Father," Ta-na called, halting about ten feet from the steps.

"I wanted to speak with you, Ta-na-wun-da." Renno gestured at the chair beside him.

Ta-na started forward, then hesitated, wanting suddenly to maintain some distance from the world that Huntington Castle represented. "I will remain down here," he said softly but determinedly.

Ta-na felt his father's eyes boring through him. When Renno spoke his voice held both compassion and strength. "Then I will join you. It is good to feel the earth beneath one's feet."

Renno carried the candle lamp down the stairs, and Ta-na noticed that his feet were bare. The night was cool, the ground cold beneath Ta-na's moccasins, and he felt ashamed that he had not considered his father's comfort.

Apparently sensing his son's unease and wanting to put his mind at peace, Renno smiled and said, "You know how we cut small holes in the bottom of our children's moccasins? A sachem once told me that if we didn't, our children would think the entire earth was covered with leather." He chuckled. "That same sachem preferred eating with his hands to using the white man's silverware. He said eating with a fork and spoon is like making love through an interpreter."

There was a long silence as father and son stared at each other. Finally Ta-na said, "Why did you send for me?"

Renno's expression darkened considerably. "Your brother announced that he intends to ride with the militia into Creek country. He won't even wait for the Cherokee-Seneca force but will accompany General Jackson to Fayetteville at dawn."

"Yes," Ta-na replied. "He came to the cabin to tell me of his decision."

Renno nodded. "Yes, he said you decided against accepting the general's offer to serve as chief of scouts."

"That is so."

"Ta-na-wun-da, know that this is a difficult thing for

me to do. But I must ask you to reconsider your decision."

Ta-na tried to mask his surprise. "You would have me join the campaign against the Creek?"

"They are no friend of ours."

"True. But neither is the Tennessee militia. They killed our sachem."

"One drunken soldier killed El-i-chi. I know this to be true, for he shot me, also."

"To him, it was like shooting a dog." Ta-na saw Renno's jaw tighten and instantly regretted the words, but he continued. "I only speak the truth. To a white man —even a friend such as General Jackson—you will always be a half-breed. And even though I am only one-quarter white, to them I am a full-blood. A chief of scouts, at best."

"I understand how you feel, Ta-na, and I did not ask you here to debate whether or not Indians can ever fully belong to the United States. I ask only that you reconsider your decision—and not for me or for the country."

"Then why?"

"For your brother." He hesitated, then went on, "Actually, for your nephew Michael Soaring Hawk. It would tear open my heart to lose my son, but I do not think I could survive if my grandson were to lose his father."

"Have you asked Little Hawk not to go?"

"I cannot do that. He has made his decision, and I can only try to see that it doesn't end in tragedy."

Ta-na felt a stab of pain in his own heart. He wanted to ask Renno how he could ask a sacrifice of one son but not the other, how Little Hawk's decision mattered but not his own. But he kept silent.

"I realize this seems unfair," Renno continued. "I know I should not ask one son to go into battle to protect the other. But somehow I'm certain that if you are together, neither of you will be hurt. I have seen you ride home side by side, our family reunited."

"Little Hawk does not need his younger brother to take care of him."

"Perhaps not. But Michael needs someone to watch after his father. And I need to know that my son has a friend at his side—that my two sons stand beside each other, no matter the danger. I ask this of you because I cannot do it myself. If I had my strength back, I would serve as General Jackson's scout."

Again Ta-na felt a touch of shame and looked down at the ground. "I did not think of my brother's danger, only that I do not wish to take arms against my other brothers and sisters, even though they are Creek."

"You must listen to your own counsel, Ta-na. If you do not believe you should do this thing, then you must not."

Ta-na nodded, then looked up into his father's eyes. "You have given me much to think about. I will smoke on it tonight."

"Good." Renno gripped his younger son's forearms. "I want only what is best for our family."

"Did the manitous speak to you? Did they say I should ride with Little Hawk?"

"No. They are silent. These words come from the heart of a father who does not want to lose his son." He paused, then added, "Either of his sons."

Ta-na-wun-da returned his father's grip, then turned and walked off into the night.

At dawn Renno stood in the yard, holding the reins of his elder son's gray gelding. A few feet away, Andrew Jackson and his aide were making final adjustments to their saddles, the general insisting on doing his own work despite his left arm still being in a sling. On the veranda, Beth and Michael Soaring Hawk waited impatiently for Hawk Harper to make his appearance.

Renno felt a burst of pride when the front door opened and Hawk came out. "Captain Hawk Harper," he muttered under his breath upon seeing his son's blue uniform for the first time in more than a year. Hawk looked a bit uncomfortable, but Renno knew that would pass as soon as he was back among the troops.

In truth, Hawk had resigned his Marine commission when he went to the Ozarks. But Andrew Jackson had given him a temporary appointment to the Tennessee militia and authorized him to wear his former uniform and rank insignia for the duration of the conflict with the Creek, saying it would boost the morale of his men to ride behind an officer of the regular army.

Renno held the skittish gelding steady as Hawk kissed his stepmother good-bye, then scooped up Michael and brought him down from the veranda.

"There you go," Hawk said, hoisting Michael into the saddle. He climbed up behind the boy, and Renno handed him the reins.

Renno watched Hawk ride with his son around the yard a couple of times. When they returned, Renno waited until father and son shared a final hug before helping Michael from the saddle.

"Listen to your grandma and grandpa," Hawk called down to his son. "And keep that rifle of yours clean; we want it in good firing order when we go on our hunt."

"Don't worry about Michael. We'll take good care of him. Isn't that right?" Renno asked the boy, who grinned and nodded.

Hawk jerked the reins, turning the horse toward where General Jackson and his aide were mounting up. It took a moment for Jackson to accomplish the feat, but afterward he sat his horse as if born to the saddle.

"Good day, Mrs. Harper," the general called to Beth as he swept his hat in a flourish. Then he gave his old friend Renno a smart salute. "I wish you could be at my side, like in the old days."

"Just take care of my son," Renno replied.

Jackson grinned. "We'll have your boy back in no time . . . provided you send us some of your best warriors to help against the Creek. If not, there's no telling how long it will be before I can spare young Captain Harper." Jackson kneed his mount forward and started at a brisk trot down the lane that led from Huntington Castle.

Hawk held back a moment, staring across the fields toward Rusog's Town. Then he turned to his father. "Tell Ta-na-wun-da good-bye for me."

"I will." Renno forced a smile to mask his disappointment that Ta-na was not on hand, apparently having decided against going along. "Son, you be sure to stick close to General Jackson. That old warhorse seems to know exactly where to stand to avoid the bullets."

"Then why is he wearing a sling?" Hawk called back with a grin as he kicked the horse into a gallop.

While watching his son fall in alongside Andrew Jackson and his aide, Renno noticed beyond them a faint swirl of dust that grew larger as it approached. "Ta-na-wun-da . . ." he whispered with certainty.

Indeed, moments later his younger son reined his horse beside Hawk's gray gelding. They conversed a moment, and then Ta-na trotted toward the house and pulled to a halt about fifty feet from Renno. Riding bareback on El-i-chi's favorite pinto, he was dressed in buckskin leggings and breeches with a beaded vest. A rifle was slung over one shoulder, and El-i-chi's war shield hung at his hip.

Ta-na-wun-da raised a hand in greeting and in farewell. Renno lifted his own hand in reply. Then the young warrior spun the pony around and galloped after his brother.

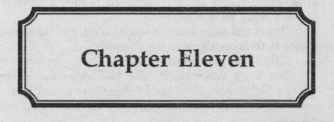

Chapter Eleven

 Renno sat on a sofa in the elegant parlor of Huntington Castle, looking out across the fields toward Rusog's Town. It was the fourth of October. Almost a week had passed since his sons, Little Hawk and Ta-na-wun-da, had accompanied Major-General Andrew Jackson to Fayetteville, with a force of more than two hundred Cherokee and Seneca warriors following two days later.

His deep concern when Hawk had announced his intention to join the Creek campaign had been replaced with the certainty that Hawk would return, as would Ta-na-wun-da. The manitous had promised Renno he would not leave this earth until he had passed the sachem's headdress to his son. Until he had brought his family together again.

He recalled the words of his brother in the land between this world and the next—when he thought he was about to die:

You must bring them together, El-i-chi had told him. *Little Hawk, Ta-na-wun-da, and Gao. And then you must pass the sachem's headdress to your son. . . . Only then*

may we ride to the longhouse of our mother and father.
Only then may we hunt at each other's side. . . .

And with Hawk and Ta-na in the south and Gao in
the north, surely that day had not yet come.

"Little Hawk, Ta-na, and Gao," he whispered, nodding with certainty as he recalled his brother's promise.
"I must bring them together."

"What was that, dear?" a voice called, and he turned
to see Beth come through the doorway.

"Oh, I was just thinking aloud."

"Anything interesting?" She brushed some of the
graying blond locks from his forehead and kissed him.

"I was just thinking about the boys . . . and
El-i-chi."

She sat beside him. "I miss him, too. And I can't
stop worrying about the boys."

"Don't be concerned about them," Renno said, taking her hand. "They will come home unharmed."

"Are you sure of it?" she asked, staring into his eyes
as if gauging the depth of his certainty.

He nodded. "The manitous have told me so."

She smiled, and he could almost hear her sigh of
relief.

"Then I will not worry about them any longer. Instead I'll worry about you."

"Me?"

"Yes, you." She gave his hand a squeeze. "You have
been spending far too much time sitting in this house. I
watch you looking out the window, and I know you want
to be out and about rather than recuperating indoors—or
at most, on the veranda."

"I'm fine," he lied. In fact, he had been thinking the
same thing but had not broached the topic, since he
knew how concerned she was about his health.

"Yes, you are fine," she agreed. "Which is why I
think you need to get away."

"Away?" he said incredulously. "But where?"

"Ever since Hawk left, all Michael can do is talk

about the hunt they will go on when he returns. He wants so much to make his father proud of him."

"Hawk couldn't be prouder of the boy."

"I know. But it is natural for a son to worry about what his father thinks of him—even a six-year-old boy. And I think he is secretly a bit afraid about being out in the wilderness. That's why I thought you might take him on an outing. Not too far away—just an overnight trip. Perhaps hunt a few rabbits or the like. It will give him a lot more confidence when Hawk returns."

Renno thought it over. "Yes, a hunting trip. It would do the child good."

"Both children."

He gave her a pout, but her loving grin soon had him smiling as well. Pulling her close, he whispered, "Yes, this little boy could use an adventure, too."

That same evening, Gao left his wife in their tepee and headed a short distance down the Thames River from the Indian encampment. Ever since the British had abandoned Detroit following their recent loss to Oliver Perry in the Battle of Lake Erie, Tecumseh's forces had been pushed deeper into Canada. They were just over a hundred miles to the east now, with only about five hundred warriors left and with few women among them. The rest had moved farther east, beyond the range of the fighting to come. For it had become increasingly clear that a major engagement was only days, if not hours, away.

A force of about six hundred British soldiers was encamped only a few miles away, but even combined with Tecumseh's forces, the redcoats were no match for the three thousand heavily armed American troops close on their trail. The previous night there had been a brief skirmish between the Indians and the Americans, and Tecumseh knew that if they did not choose a place to stand and fight, they would find themselves overrun. That was something he would not allow, so he had called a council meeting along the banks of the Thames, just outside their encampment.

Gao was joined by several other young warriors as he approached the council fire. Already on hand were Tecumseh's eleven closest advisers: his oldest friend and fellow Shawnee Wasegoboah; Potawatomi warriors Black Partridge, Sauganash, Chaubenee, and Waubansee; Sac warrior Black Hawk; Chippewa brothers Ooshawanoo and Little Pine; and chiefs Stiahta of the Wyandot, Naiwash of the Ottawa, and Carrymaunee of the Winnebago. Gao and a couple of other younger men had been invited, but they sat in the shadows beyond the range of the light, outside the circle of twelve seated on logs around the fire.

When Tecumseh rose, the group fell silent. The Shawnee leader looked from one man to the next, until he had fixed his gaze on each of the eleven. Then he stared into the fire.

He was an impressive figure. Though of average height and physique, he emanated an aura of power. It was partly due to his erect, almost graceful posture. But mostly it was evident in his eyes, which spoke to Gao more deeply than even his celebrated oratory. Tonight he wore the signs of rank given him by his people and by the British military: a large medal bearing the image of King George III, a silver necklace strung with bear claws, a pair of ornate bracelets, and a headband with two white-tipped eagle feathers.

It seemed as if many minutes passed in silence. When Tecumseh finally spoke, his words were so measured and soft that Gao had to cup his hands behind his ears to make them out.

"My friends. My brothers. Hear my words. Tomorrow we face our final battle. In this battle, I will die."

There was a collective gasp, and the assembled chiefs began whispering among themselves. Gao felt someone grab his arm, and he glanced over to see a young Chippewa warrior, his face filled with agony and distress. Gao felt curiously detached, and he wondered why. It was almost as if Tecumseh's voice had been his own.

At last Tecumseh raised his hand, and the men grew quiet again.

"My friends . . . my people . . . my love for you is too great to see you sacrificed in so unequal a contest. Tomorrow there will be no victory, only sorrow. I would try to talk you out of this battle, but you have made it clear to me that you do not wish to run and will fight the Americans here and now. So I will stand with my people."

Turning, he walked to his blanket and mat, which were spread on the ground and laid out with his personal weapons. Picking up the sword given to him by the British General Brock, he presented it to his closest friend, Chaubenee. Next he handed his pistols to Sauganash and Stiahta and his tomahawk to Black Hawk, then distributed to the others his medal and other signs of rank.

He left his fine flintlock rifle for last. Holding it forth, he said to Wasegoboah, "If you are able, stay close to me in battle tomorrow. When I fall, take this rod and strike my body four times."

He drew the ramrod from below the barrel and presented it to Wasegoboah, then handed him the rifle.

"If you are able to do this, I will rise again and will lead you to victory. But if I fall and you are unable to strike my body, you must all retreat at once, for our cause will be lost."

Everyone present heard the words and did not doubt them. For it was Tecumseh who had spoken.

The only weapon that remained to Tecumseh was the war club at his belt. He clasped his hand over it and declared, "I keep only this war club, which has slain many of my enemies. My final wish is that tomorrow I may meet the American general in battle and he will be its final victim."

Tecumseh turned and walked off into the night. Gao

sat there in the shadows, listening to the silence that hung like death over the assembly.

Renno and Michael Soaring Hawk set out from Huntington Castle at dawn, Renno walking and his grandson astride a pony. The boy gripped the sides of the small mount with his knees, trying not to wobble on the blanket that served as a saddle. Renno had offered to carry Michael's flintlock rifle, but he would not hear of it, and so Renno had attached a beaded strap and hung it around the pony's neck. Renno's own rifle was slung over his shoulder.

They headed west toward the Tennessee River. The first flocks of Canadian geese were migrating from the north, and Renno hoped to bring one home for an early Thanksgiving celebration.

It was late morning when they approached a sheltered valley whose small lake was a favorite gathering place for geese. Michael was getting quite impatient, and Renno decided to camp there, whether any geese were on hand or not. Fortunately he heard their distinctive honking as they entered the valley.

"When can I shoot?" the boy called ahead to his grandfather, who was leading the pony.

"You must be quiet on a hunt," Renno replied, looking back with the faintest of frowns. "It will serve no purpose to announce we're here."

Michael nodded and clamped shut his lips, signaling that he understood. Renno noticed he was not gripping the pony's mane so tightly anymore. In fact, only one hand was holding on. The other was caressing the rifle.

Turning away so that the boy would not see his grin, Renno steered the pony to a stand of bushes. Helping Michael down, he took the rifle from around the animal's neck and then showed Michael how to tie the reins to a sturdy branch. He handed him the gun, then loaded his own rifle with powder and ball. Kneeling, he gave Michael the powder horn.

"Let me see how you do it," he prompted.

Michael eagerly went to work, pouring a measure of gunpowder down the barrel and following it with some wadding and a lead ball from the small cartridge bag at his side. The rifle was a short one, and Michael was able to draw the ramrod and set the ball in place.

"Excellent," Renno declared, nodding approvingly. "Don't forget the charge," he added, gesturing for Michael to pour some powder in the flashpan.

Renno made sure the cover was in place over the flashpan and the hammer uncocked. Then he motioned Michael toward the lake, which sat hidden among the trees ahead. Taking the blanket off the pony's back, he followed his grandson, watching him closely and occasionally whispering advice on how to carry the rifle and make his approach.

They slipped into the trees and eased toward the lake, pausing every now and then to listen to the geese. When they were almost at the water's edge, Renno tapped Michael's shoulder and had him crouch among the underbrush. Then he put down the blanket and quietly parted the branches so that they could see their quarry. Several dozen geese were in a fairly tight group not far from shore.

"Can I shoot now, Grandpa?" Michael asked in a strained, excited whisper.

"They'll fly off when they hear the shot," Renno explained, "so we will fire together. Which one do you want?"

"That big one over there." Michael jabbed a finger toward a large goose swimming somewhat apart from the others.

"That's a good one. I'll go for that one way over there." He indicated a bird far to the left. "Do you remember what I told you when we were shooting at targets?"

"To hold my breath?"

"Yes. And aim a bit low—at the water just under the

goose. The ball will come up a bit, and you'll hit your mark." He laid a hand on Michael's shoulder. "All right, you can pull back the hammer. Then take your aim and fire whenever you're ready. I'll shoot as soon as you do."

Renno moved off a little to the left and cocked his own rifle as he watched the boy do likewise. Michael looked very serious and determined as he raised the rifle and held it as steady as possible. Renno continued to watch him out of the corner of his eye while bringing up his own barrel and taking aim. There was an audible gasp as Michael drew in his breath and held it. Then he slowly squeezed the trigger.

As soon as Michael's hammer snapped down onto the pan and the powder flashed, Renno pulled his own trigger, their weapons firing an instant apart. The double explosion thundered across the lake, and the geese took off en masse in a riot of flapping and honking.

"Look!" Michael shouted, pointing to the lone object bobbing in the churning water.

"You hit him!" Renno exclaimed, clapping the boy on the back. "I am afraid I didn't do as well."

"That's all right, Grandpa," Michael said, looking up at him with an expression of true compassion. "You can share mine."

"Good."

"And we don't have to tell Grandma."

"Of course we do! We are going to tell everyone how you got that goose with a single shot!"

Renno led the way down to the water's edge and started to remove his shirt.

"No, Grandpa. I want to get it."

"It's pretty far away," Renno said, though in truth it was floating no more than ten feet from shore.

"I can swim that far. Really. Can I?"

"Well, I suppose so. After all, it's your goose."

He helped the boy strip off his clothes and watched as he walked into the lake, never flinching as the cold water rose around him. After he had gone about five feet, the water was at his chest, and he had to start swimming.

"Don't try to grab it," Renno called as the boy paddled toward the goose. "Just swim around behind it and push it in front of you while swimming back."

Michael did as directed and soon had the goose in front of him as he headed for shore. Renno could see the stain of blood on the animal and prayed there were not two bullet holes; he did not want to explain how his own shot had gone so far astray as to hit Michael's goose.

Renno walked out into the water to meet his grandson. He saw the boy's broad grin, his look of keen determination, and for an instant saw Little Hawk. Then the image shifted, and it was as if he were seeing himself as a child, swimming in the lake of the Seneca in their homeland of western New York.

Renno shook his head to clear it and saw Michael standing in front of him in waist-deep water. "You look just like your father," he said with a smile.

"I do?" Michael asked eagerly, lifting the goose and presenting it to his grandfather.

Renno tousled the boy's blond locks. "The exact image. Now, let's get you dried off."

While retrieving the blanket, he quickly examined the bird and confirmed there was only one wound—from Renno's larger-bore rifle. Kneeling, he held open the blanket. As he wrapped it around Michael and rubbed him dry, he felt strangely light-headed and had to pause a moment before continuing. The sensation increased when he stood, and he quickly sat down to keep from passing out.

"What's wrong, Grandpa?" Michael asked, noticing the strange look on Renno's face.

"Just a little dizzy. That's all."

"Is it because you were shot?" the boy asked, moving behind his grandfather and touching the spot where the bullet had entered the top of his shoulder.

"I . . ."

Renno's vision clouded over, and he felt himself falling backward. He had a sensation of landing but did not feel the ground beneath him.

"You must bring them together," a voice intoned. "Little Hawk, Ta-na-wun-da, and Gao. Why have you not brought them together?"

"El-i-chi?" Renno called as he fought to see through the ever-darkening swirl of fog.

"My son . . . Help my son find his way home. . . ."

"But where? Where will I find him?"

"Go to the land of our ancestors. Go to the lake of the Seneca. Find my son and lead him home. When he has made the journey, your own son shall be restored to you. Only then can the headdress be passed from one sachem to the next. Only then may we hunt at each other's side. . . ."

"Yes . . . the lake of the Seneca," Renno whispered. "I will go to the lake of the Seneca."

He struggled to see the manitou of El-i-chi. But all was darkness, all was silence. Then another voice intruded on his consciousness. A small voice. The voice of a frightened child.

"Grandpa! Grandpa! Wake up!"

Renno felt himself moving, sensed hands pushing and pulling at him. The darkness passed away as mysteriously as it had come. A blond-haired boy was leaning over him, eyes wide with worry as he begged his grandfather to come back.

"I . . . I'm all right," Renno muttered, lifting his head from the ground.

Michael wiped the back of his hand across his cheeks, and Renno saw the tears spilling from his eyes.

"It's all right," he said, sitting up. He pressed his hands to the ground, waiting as the world slowly settled into place.

"What's wrong?" the boy asked. "Are you sick?"

"It . . . it was just the wound. You were right. I'll just rest a moment; then I'll be fine." He looked up at his grandson and grinned. "I'm all right now. Really I am."

Michael did not seem convinced, but he nodded and summoned up a smile.

"Was I talking?" Renno asked. "Did I say anything foolish?"

The boy seemed confused and merely shrugged. Renno sensed that he might have heard something but was too frightened to say. Placing a hand on Michael's shoulder, he told him, "It was just like a dream. That can happen when someone is feeling poorly. Do you understand?"

Michael's nod was tentative, uncertain.

"You know, it would worry your grandmother if she thought I was still feeling poorly. She might not let us go hunting again. Do you think we can keep this our secret? Just you and me?"

This time Michael's nod held more conviction.

"Good."

With some effort, Renno pulled himself to his feet and stood there a moment regaining his balance.

"Now, young fellow, what do you say we look around for a place to make camp?"

"Grandpa?" Michael asked, tugging at Renno's shirt.

"Yes?"

"Can we go home?"

"Now? This afternoon?"

The boy lowered his head as if in shame and mumbled, "Yes, sir."

"Why, that's a splendid idea," Renno declared. "We have caught our prey, and a good hunter takes his prize home as quickly as possible to keep it from spoiling." He cupped his hand under Michael's chin and lifted his head. "That is what a good hunter does."

"Really?" Michael asked, his face brightening somewhat.

"It certainly is. And do you know something else a good hunter does?"

"What?"

"He puts his clothes on first."

Renno bent down and tickled his grandson's bare belly, setting the boy howling with delight.

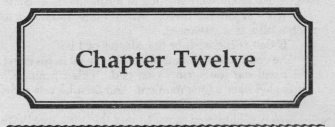

Chapter Twelve

 Gao stood just inside the open entrance of his tepee, the first faint light of dawn visible at his back. Though it was the season when the trees lose their leaves, he was wearing his summer war outfit: grayish-brown linen shirt over a buckskin breechclout, buffalo-hide moccasins, and red cloth headband. His black hair hung loose to his shoulders, a pair of eagle feathers dangling behind his left ear. Tucked beneath a beaded wampum belt were a tomahawk and a long-bladed knife. A medicine pouch was slung over one shoulder, a shot pouch over the other. Hanging at his side was a powder horn, carved with images of birds and bears. Suspended from his right hand was a war club, fashioned from a length of cow's tail, with a large rock sewn into one end and a loop cut into the other for his wrist.

Mist-on-the-Water came near and handed him his flintlock rifle, which she had cleaned and oiled.

"I wish you did not have to go," she said in the Seneca language of her husband.

By way of an answer, Gao told her, "Do not strike

the tepee today." He paused until she nodded. "You must follow the river upstream to where the other women make their camp." He referred to the larger encampment of women, children, and civilians—British and Indian—farther to the east, beyond where General Henry Proctor's British forces were digging in for the battle to come.

"You will join me there," Mist-on-the-Water said, as much a plea as a statement.

"If that is the wish of the Master of Life."

She embraced him and buried her head in his chest.

"I will see you again," Gao said. "This I promise."

He held her a long moment. And then he was gone.

Gao was hunkered down among the birch trees with a group of other warriors, waiting for the Americans to launch their attack. Shortly after dawn, Tecumseh had led his men to meet their British allies on a carriage road that ran alongside the north bank of the Thames River. The British force was positioned along the road, while the Indians guarded a parallel strip of woods about fifty yards to the north. To make their attack the Americans would have to come on the road or through the woods, for between the two was a swampy thicket, with more extensive swampland beyond the woods.

Morning dragged into early afternoon, and still there was no sign of General William Henry Harrison's army. Gao and his companions occasionally changed positions, keeping an eye on the approaches to the east and west and on the British force, which was deployed in two lines, their single six-pound cannon in the middle of the road. With three thousand well-armed Americans expected—at least one thousand of them on horseback—the Indians wondered whether the British would stand and fight or abandon their positions at the report of gunfire.

The first sound Gao heard was not a musket blast but a bullet that came whizzing through the trees. He ducked instinctively. Hearing a grunt, he looked up and saw Tecumseh not ten feet away, clutching the left side of his chest as he fell to the ground.

Gao was one of a dozen warriors who raced to his side. In shock they looked down at their fallen leader, but to their great amazement he pulled his hand from his chest, and there was no blood.

They had all heard the bullet. Tecumseh had even felt its sting. Yet now the pain was gone, with no sign that he had ever been struck.

"Matchemeneto!" a Shawnee cried, naming the spirit known as the Evil One.

"It is a bad sign," Tecumseh said somberly as he rose from the ground.

His friend Chaubenee agreed it was a bad omen and advised him to leave immediately. The others concurred, promising they would remain behind to fight.

Tecumseh would not hear of it and directed the men back to their positions, saying, "I stand with my people and will not run from Matchemeneto."

Gao moved off toward the east, crouching behind the trunk of a fallen pine. It was then that bugles blared, sounding the charge, followed by the muffled report of rifles from the direction of the carriage road.

Less than a minute later, a sudden and eerie silence fell over the battlefield. Gao strained to hear what was going on, but the hush was broken only by the occasional distant and unintelligible shout. A few more minutes passed, and then Indian runners started arriving from the direction of the road, reporting on what had transpired.

The news spread among Tecumseh's forces in a flurry of hand signs and whispers. The British troops, attacked by a force of mounted dragoons twice their size, had fired a single volley and then beat a hasty retreat down the road, abandoning their cannon and many of their weapons.

None of the Indians were surprised. They had hoped, however, that the British would at least slow the Americans' advance. Now, with General Proctor's forces in chaotic retreat, the dragoons could turn their full attention to the Indians in the narrow strip of woodland.

They were coming—between five hundred and a thousand mounted soldiers, with another two thousand infantrymen and additional cavalry ready to follow.

Gao double-checked the charge in his rifle and thumbed back the hammer. A warrior standing a few feet away waved frantically at him, and he lifted his head and listened. To the west, brush and branches were snapping, the sounds growing rapidly louder.

Horses! Gao thought, easing his rifle barrel over the top of the fallen tree trunk. He stared down the sights, waiting for the riders to appear.

A cluster of twenty mounted soldiers emerged not more than fifty yards away, brandishing swords and pistols as they spurred their mounts through the brush. Gao held back until he heard one of the Indians—Wasegoboah, he thought—let loose a piercing war cry. Gao had already chosen his target, and he pulled the trigger, a dozen other Indian rifles and muskets firing in unison.

Three soldiers and one horse went down under the hail of bullets. The others pulled back, but only for a moment. When they reappeared, they numbered more than a hundred.

Gao had already reloaded; he took what proved to be an ineffective shot and hurriedly poured another charge down the barrel. All around him, his comrades where shouting and firing their weapons, forcing the Americans to take cover. Every now and then a horseman would emerge from the thicker forest, urging his comrades on. It was difficult to get a good shot through the brush at the swerving targets, and many of the bullets downed horse rather than rider.

Gao found himself under sustained fire from two different positions. When both groups of soldiers simultaneously paused to reload, he fell back and ran toward where some of Tecumseh's men were attacking the

Americans' flank. He caught sight of Wasegoboah and
several others hunkered down among some bushes to his
left. The Shawnee warrior waved him over, and Gao
shifted direction and sprinted to him.

Wasegoboah pointed to the right across a small
clearing, and Gao saw a group of horsemen hidden in the
trees on the opposite side, preparing to make a charge.
The Indians readied their weapons, Wasegoboah proudly
wielding Tecumseh's ornately engraved flintlock rifle.

Gao recalled their leader's words when he had honored Wasegoboah with the weapon: *If you are able, stay
close to me in battle tomorrow.* Suddenly he felt a shiver
of fear and looked around to see if Tecumseh was
near . . . to see if he was still with them.

There he stood, apart from the others behind a birch
less than ten yards away. He had removed his shirt and
held his war club cradled in his hands. It was covered
with blood.

Their eyes met, and Tecumseh gave a slow, solemn
nod. Then he raised his war club and pointed at the
horsemen, now advancing across the clearing.

Gao spun around and took aim at the lead rider. He
wore the uniform of an officer of great rank—a colonel,
Gao suspected. He knew many of his comrades would be
aiming at this great prize and hoped at least one of their
bullets would find its mark.

At Wasegoboah's signal, they opened fire. The colonel's uniform was torn open by half a dozen bullets. His
white horse fared no better, with streams of blood bursting all over his body. The horse stumbled and fell, landing on top of its severely wounded rider.

Another horseman went down as well, and after that
the others pulled back into the forest. As the Indians
reloaded, they realized the colonel had somehow survived and was struggling to free himself from beneath the
horse.

Wasegoboah could not resist so worthy a prize. Taking advantage of the lull in the shooting, he leaped from

his cover, Tecumseh's rifle in one hand and a tomahawk in the other. As he raced toward the wounded officer, another soldier rode into the clearing and took aim at the Shawnee. Wasegoboah raised the rifle and fired, blasting the man from his saddle.

Gao saw another horseman come forward to protect the wounded officer. Taking careful aim, Gao squeezed the trigger. The bullet smacked into the man's shoulder. He lost his gun but managed to stay in the saddle as he retreated into the woods.

The colonel was still pinned under the mortally wounded horse and was frantically groping at one of the saddlebags, perhaps searching for a pistol or other weapon. Racing up to him, Wasegoboah kicked his hand away from the bag. With a whoop of victory, the Shawnee warrior raised his tomahawk over his head. But as he swung it down, a rifle fired from the trees on the far side of the clearing. Wasegoboah's body stiffened; the tomahawk slipped from his grip, just missing the officer. Then Wasegoboah went limp and flopped backward onto the ground, the side of his head blown away by the blast.

Gao and his comrades cried out in sorrow and rage. Rising from his hiding place, he stared in disbelief at the body of Tecumseh's beloved friend. A bullet whistled past, but Gao did not hear it. His eyes were locked on Tecumseh's rifle, lying a few feet from Wasegoboah's body. His thoughts were on Tecumseh's words: *When I fall, take this rod and strike my body four times.*

If they did not recover the ramrod, all would be lost. Tecumseh would die.

Gao dropped his empty rifle and stepped from the bushes into the small clearing. Someone shouted for him to get back. A hand tugged at his shirt, but he jerked free and broke into a sprint. Rifles and pistols opened fire, small plumes of dust kicking up all around him.

He was halfway to Tecumseh's flintlock when the first bullet struck him in the left shoulder. He staggered slightly but kept going. A second bullet smacked into his thigh, knocking him to the ground. He continued on, crawling until his fingers tightened around the stock of the rifle. He drew it close, cradling it lovingly in his arms.

He managed to stand; then, dragging his right leg, he limped back to his comrades. Behind him, four soldiers came riding out of the brush. The Indians opened fire, but other riders appeared now—dozens of them—some racing to their colonel's side, others pinning down the Indians with withering fire.

Gao waited for the bullets to find him and prayed he would have the strength to make it back to the trees. But it was not a bullet that struck him. Instead he heard the whinny of a horse at his back, and as he whirled around, he was struck in the face by the barrel of a rifle, wielded like a club by the rider.

The world went dark as Tecumseh's flintlock slipped from his grasp, and he fell headlong to the ground.

Renno and Michael Soaring Hawk were approaching Huntington Castle when Renno heard a cry of despair and knew it was his nephew Gao. The voice of the manitou had followed him on the journey home from their aborted hunting trip, calling to him with increased urgency:

You must bring them together—Little Hawk, Ta-na-wun-da, and Gao. Go to the land of our ancestors. Go to the lake of the Seneca. Find my son and lead him home. Help him make the journey home. . . .

And now it was not just the manitou of El-i-chi that cried out to Renno. It was Gao himself, his voice filled with terrible dread.

Renno knew he could not turn his back on his brother, nor could he close his ears to his nephew's cry. Something was horribly wrong, and the sachem of the Seneca had to see it put right.

Beth came out into the yard to meet her husband and grandson. "You are home so soon," she said when

Renno led the pony to where she was standing. "Didn't you want to spend the night?" she asked Michael, taking the goose he held out.

"It's a big one, isn't it?" Michael said proudly.

"Yes, I should say so."

"He got it with a single shot," Renno put in.

"And so you decided to come home?"

Michael gave his grandfather a nervous glance, then said without conviction, "I, um, wanted to show it to you."

Renno helped him off the pony's back. "We'll speak of it later," he told his wife, his eyes telling her she should let the matter drop.

"Well, let's get this goose into the kitchen," she said. "Tomorrow we will have a real feast."

"Can I carry it?" the boy asked, reaching up for it.

"Of course. You're the hunter, aren't you?" She handed it back, and he ran with it to the veranda. She turned to her husband and lowered her voice so that Michael would not hear. "What really happened?"

"There is something I have to do."

She looked at him curiously. "You returned because you forgot to do something?"

He shook his head. "We came back because I spoke to my brother. I am afraid it frightened the boy."

"Your brother?"

"El-i-chi came to me. He asked for a favor."

"And Michael saw this?" she said incredulously.

"No. But he heard me speaking back. He must have thought I was ill."

"Are you?"

"I'm fine," he said a bit testily. "But the manitou of my brother has spoken. And now there's something I must do."

Michael called from the veranda, "Are you coming, Grandma?"

"In a moment, dear," she replied. "You take that goose to the pantry; I'll be right there."

Michael jerked open the door and disappeared inside.

Beth turned to her husband, her expression one of dread. "Just what have the manitous asked you to do?"

"I must go north. I must find El-i-chi's firstborn and bring him home."

"Gao? But he is with Tecumseh."

"Then that is where I will go."

"You can't!" she implored, gripping his arm. "You are hardly back on your feet. You can't really be considering such a foolhardy act."

"We will talk of it later. Now I must see to this mare."

Beth's voice rose higher in desperation. "I won't let you! Not by yourself. Not all the way to—"

"It is something I must do," he said firmly. "I leave at dawn." He turned and led the pony toward the barn.

When Gao regained consciousness, he was not in the clearing where Wasegoboah had been shot; he was lying among some bushes in the middle of the woods. He was bare-chested, his shirt having been cut into makeshift bandages and tied around his shoulder and thigh. It took a moment to remember where he was, but then he heard the gunfire and knew they were still battling the Americans along the Thames River.

"Rest easy," a voice whispered as he tried to sit up.

Gao tried to focus on the man hovering over him. For a moment he thought he was dreaming, but then he breathed the man's name: "Tecumseh . . ."

"If I had a hundred more like you, we would take this day," the Shawnee said, keeping his voice low.

Gao saw that Tecumseh had traded his war club for a rifle. Uncertain if it was the one Wasegoboah had dropped, he pointed at it and looked up questioningly.

Tecumseh shook his head. "The Americans have it. They do not realize the prize they hold."

"We must get out of here!" Gao said, rising to a sitting position. "Before—"

"Shh!" another voice called, and Gao saw several other warriors in the vicinity. "They come again!"

Tecumseh handed Gao a loaded pistol and laid a comforting hand on his good left shoulder. Leaning close, he whispered, "Stay here. I go ahead." Then he turned and slipped away through the woods.

Gao winced as he grabbed onto the bush and rose to his feet. He clutched the pistol in his fist and cocked the hammer, then took a cautious step in the direction his leader had gone. The gunshots sounded much closer now; a skirmish of some sort was taking place nearby.

The young Seneca warrior moved as quietly through the forest as his wounded right leg would allow. Seeing puffs of black-powder smoke, he made his way from tree to tree until he joined up with other Indians, who were firing at a group of soldiers pinned down in a stand of birches about fifty feet away. Between the two groups lay the bodies of a gray-haired soldier and an Indian. With a start, Gao recognized the Indian as the Wyandot chief Stiahta.

It was obvious both men were dead, yet a young soldier—a private from the looks of him—emerged from behind a tree and went crawling toward the gray-haired man. The Indians watched a moment, transfixed by his courageous but foolhardy action. Then one by one they took their shots. Incredibly, the bullets failed to find their mark. Soon the private had the dead soldier's shot pouch and rifle in hand and was scrambling back to the trees.

Gao raised his own weapon to fire but realized it was too long a shot for a pistol. He found himself almost cheering the young soldier on as he dashed into the safety of the trees, bullets whizzing all around him.

The Indians began moving to the right, following the Potawatomi warrior Chaubenee, who still carried Tecumseh's sword. As Gao hobbled after them he caught a glimpse of their Shawnee leader slipping in and out among the birches, exhorting them to keep up the battle.

Then Gao saw where Tecumseh and Chaubenee were headed. A group of soldiers was moving through the woods and had spread out somewhat, leaving them exposed to attack. Tecumseh closed in on the lead man, whom Gao recognized as the same private who had retrieved his dead comrade's rifle. The private was partially hidden behind a tree, and Tecumseh moved to where he could get a decent shot. As he brought up his rifle, another soldier emerged from behind a tree and yelled, "Look out, King!"

Tecumseh whirled to his right and took aim at the man who had shouted. Simultaneously, the young private leveled the rifle he had retrieved and fired. The gun had been loaded with a double shot, and the pair of balls tore into the left side of Tecumseh's chest, just below the nipple. He was knocked off his feet, his heart still before he hit the ground.

Gao did not have to wait for Chaubenee's command before he and his comrades broke from the trees and charged the soldiers' position. Their war cry shook the branches as they fired, reloaded, and fired again, driving the soldiers back by the fury of their assault.

For a few minutes the guns fell silent. Gao, Chaubenee, and the others stood over Tecumseh's body. He was dead. Exactly as he had predicted. And no rod of iron would bring him back to life.

Chaubenee gave the death wail. It was taken up by one warrior after another until the forest rang with its cry. He did not have to give the order to retreat; they all knew the battle was over. They slipped away into the woods, some to safety, others into the hands of the waiting Americans.

Gao was one of the unfortunate ones. The wounds to his shoulder and thigh slowed him considerably as he tried to evade the soldiers and make his way to where Mist-on-the-Water was waiting for him. He had not gotten far when he stumbled into a party of Americans. Facing a dozen rifles, he dropped his weapons and waited for the muzzle blasts to put an end to the nightmare that had descended upon him.

There was to be no such release. Instead, an officer shouted, "He was with Tecumseh! Take him!" A moment later, several of the soldiers grabbed him and tied his hands behind his back.

Gao's body went limp as they dragged him toward the American lines. He did not struggle. He did not even cry out. For it no longer mattered.

Tecumseh was gone. And with him, all their dreams had died.

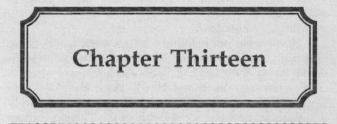

Chapter Thirteen

Captain Hawk Harper had not seen his brother in two days. As chief scout, Ta-na-wun-da had ridden ahead, across the Coosa River and into the heart of Creek country, leaving the militia to follow. Now Jackson's Army, as it was being called, was encamped at Fort Strother, thirteen miles west of the Creek villages of Tallasahatchee. And one of Ta-na's runners had just reported that two hundred Creek warriors were gathered there, spoiling for a fight.

Hawk did not doubt that General Jackson would give it to them. But with two thousand men under his command, plus nearly three hundred Cherokee and Seneca warriors who had joined the campaign, it essentially would be a rout.

The coming battle was not the only thing on Hawk's mind as he sat in the plank shack that served as headquarters and listened to Jackson and the other officers discuss plans of attack. He was also wondering if his brother had received the report he had forwarded with a runner.

Tecumseh is dead, he thought, shaking his head in amazement. The Shawnee warrior-prophet had been shot four weeks ago in a one-sided battle on the Thames River in Canada. Many of his followers had been killed or captured during the engagement, and those who had survived were struggling deep into the Canadian wilderness.

Killed or captured . . .

Hawk could not help but fear the worst had befallen his cousin Gao. How would Ta-na-wun-da react? he wondered. Ta-na and Gao had been as close as brothers—closer even than Ta-na and Hawk. How, also, were the Creek warriors at Tallasahatchee taking the news? Surely if the militia knew about the Battle of the Thames, Indian runners from Canada were already spreading the word among the Creeks and other tribes loyal to Tecumseh.

The very same thought must have been on the minds of the others, for Captain Scott Ridgley smacked a fist onto the top of the map table and exclaimed, "Good Lord, an opportunity has presented itself, and I think we should press it to our full advantage. The Creeks thought Tecumseh a god. With him dead, it will break their will and send them scurrying off like lost pups. I say attack at once."

"We can't be sure they're even aware of what happened in Canada," a lieutenant commented.

"Don't you know anything about Indian ways?" Ridgley taunted. "There is no way *we* could hear about such an event without *their* getting word a day or two before. They know, all right. And when we reach Tallasahatchee, they'll scatter to the wind."

Hawk rose from his chair. "I agree with Captain Ridgley that they know. But it does not necessarily follow that this will work to our advantage. Ta-na-wun-da indicates they are eager for a fight and warns us to be cautious about—"

"Ta-na-wun-da?" Ridgley cut him off with a sneer. "That's just one Indian talking for another."

Hawk's jaw clenched, but he remained calm. "Ta-na-wun-da is not just an Indian. He is a Seneca, and he does not lie."

"I didn't call your brother a liar," Ridgley replied. "But Indians think alike, and we'd do well to keep our own counsel on these matters."

"Your argument is ridiculous on the face of it," Hawk shot back. "If they really think alike—which they don't—then we must accept that Ta-na knows what the Creeks will do and pay heed to his advice."

"I said Indians think alike. That doesn't mean Ta-na-wun-da is telling us what *he* really thinks." Ridgley sat down and folded his arms across his chest, as if indicating the matter was closed.

"Then you *are* calling him a liar," Hawk snapped.

"Not a liar. But an Indian. One who would prefer we spent our weeks wandering around down here and never engaged the enemy."

"Enough!" a deep voice boomed.

All eyes swung to Major-General Andrew Jackson, who rose from his seat off to the side and approached the table. Drawing his pistol, he placed it atop the map.

"Caution does not translate to cowardice or treason," he said emphatically, narrowing one eye as he fixed his gaze on Captain Ridgley. The general next turned his attention to Hawk Harper. "And while I respect the advice of our chief of scouts, it is for us military leaders to turn that advice into strategy. I agree that the Creek are spoiling for action. And if we do not bring it to them, we can be sure they will bring it to us—and on terms not necessarily in our favor. We do not need a hornet's nest of some two hundred Creek warriors dogging our trail wherever we go. We must destroy the nest before the hornets take to the field—and we must do it at once."

He crossed the room and opened the door to stare out across the fort compound for a moment. Then he turned back to the officers.

"Captain Harper, given that we are firm in our resolve to engage the enemy, how would you set about accomplishing our purpose?"

Hawk sighed inwardly. He had hoped the question would not be posed to him, but it had, and there was only one answer, which every man in the room knew. Rising, he approached the table, picked up General Jackson's pistol, and pointed the barrel at Tallasahatchee.

"We number two thousand to their two hundred. The land around Tallasahatchee is ideal for an encircling action. We can close the noose and demand either surrender or death."

He glanced at Jackson, who nodded in approval.

"I would add one cautionary note," Hawk continued, looking directly at Captain Ridgley. "The concerns of our chief of scouts should be taken under advisement. A careful reading of his report shows that his worry is that in engaging the enemy in battle, we do not leave ourselves vulnerable to unexpected attack. We know of two hundred Creek warriors massed thirteen miles to our east. Undoubtedly others are in the vicinity. While we march on Tallasahatchee, we could be leaving this fort open to the very sort of attack we came here to prevent." He put the pistol back down on the table.

"And what would you have us do?" Jackson asked.

"We possess an overwhelming advantage. If it were my command, I would lead one half against Tallasahatchee and keep the rest here, to protect the fort and stand in reserve, should we need reinforcements."

"And you, Captain Ridgley?"

The captain frowned but nodded and said gruffly, "It is a well-reasoned plan."

"Good," Jackson declared. "And the honor of engaging the enemy shall fall to my good friend, General Coffee." He nodded toward an officer who sat alone in the corner. "His force of nine hundred should be sufficient to teach the Creek a lesson they will not soon forget. If any of the younger officers wish to participate in the action, please let General Coffee know of your intentions. I will leave it to him to make the final assignments."

He started toward the open doorway, then paused and looked back.

"I want us to be in position before daylight. Speed is of the essence if we are to remove the hornet's sting."

Turning, he strode briskly into the cool evening air.

Hawk Harper rode at the front of one of three columns of combined infantry and cavalry. His own company was at Fort Strother, but he had been temporarily assigned to one of the mounted units marching on Tallasahatchee. It had taken much of the night to cover the thirteen miles between the fort and the cluster of Creek villages. But the imminence of dawn and the availability of a broad, well-marked road enabled them to traverse the final few miles rapidly.

Several times they had received messages from the scouts, brought by Seneca and Cherokee runners. No direct word had come from Ta-na-wun-da, however, with one report placing him in the vicinity of Tallasahatchee and another claiming he had departed the region to scout other Creek strongholds to the south. Hawk suspected the latter to be the case; Ta-na's services would be better utilized making sure the militia was not surprised by any rearguard action.

As they neared the villages, the militia slowed their pace and began to fan out, one column circling to the south and another to the north, to surround the enemy and cut off any possibility of escape. Hawk's column intended to launch a direct assault from the west, which would either force a surrender or drive the Creeks into the waiting arms of the encircling forces.

The militia did not launch the attack, however. The Creeks had their own scouts and apparently knew of the army's approach. Rather than use the darkness to slip away before the militia arrived, they met their enemy

head-on, at a place where Hawk's column would have to
cross a broad, open field.

The battle began in silence, with a single arrow that
pierced the neck of a lieutenant's horse, dropping the
animal and spilling the rider. A titter of laughter spread
through the ranks as the near troops saw the horse go
down and assumed it had stumbled in the dark. The
snickering ceased a moment later when a hundred muskets and rifles opened fire from a line of birches to the
right. As the soldiers scrambled for their own weapons,
another volley rang out, this one from a stand of trees to
the left, catching the troops in a cross fire.

Hawk saw two militiamen go down. He also saw a
Creek warrior who had been hiding in the tall grasses—
and who had loosed the first arrow—scurrying back to
the safety of the trees. Raising his pistol, he fired at the
man, but already the distance was too great, and he soon
disappeared among the birches.

Sporadic gunfire broke out from the militia, some
firing to the left, others to the right. Turning his mount,
Hawk rode down the ranks, directing the foot soldiers
into the cover of the tall grass and signaling the horsemen under his command to prepare for a charge.

It took a few moments for the officers to coordinate
their efforts—enough time for a second volley from both
groups of Creeks. Fortunately the distance was a bit far
for accurate shooting, and the militia sustained only one
additional casualty. Then, as the Indians switched from
volleying to random fire, Hawk Harper led his men in a
wide, sweeping charge that brought them around the far
end of the right-hand stand of trees.

The riders thundered along the rear side of the
copse, taking sporadic fire and returning it with pistol
and carbine. As they circled the far end and rode back
along the front, Hawk tried to count how many Indians
were hidden among the birches and underbrush. He esti-
mated as many as thirty-five. If an equal number were in

the trees across the way, that left two thirds of the Creek force elsewhere—perhaps in the villages themselves.

Hawk led his men beyond the range of the Indian guns to rest and reload. The infantry, meanwhile, moved ever closer through the grass, protected to some extent by a gentle rise of land between the road and the trees. Hawk could hear some distant fighting to the north and south of Tallasahatchee and surmised that the rest of the Creek force had engaged the flanks of the militia. It was a bold but risky move. By dividing into small groups, they could attack all three columns converging on their villages. But each Creek band would find itself facing more than three hundred militiamen and be quickly overrun.

Hawk waited until the foot soldiers fired their first organized volley and were met by a smattering of return fire from the trees. Then he raised his pistol and began the second charge. The infantry got off a second volley before the horsemen came sweeping between them and the trees, peppering the birches with gunfire.

Slowing his horse and letting the others gallop past him, Hawk heard a screeching whinny and spun around to see a horse go down, spilling its rider and tumbling over him in a flailing of hooves and head. He doubted anyone could survive such a fall, but a moment later the soldier scrambled to his feet and started hobbling away from the nearby trees.

Then several shots rang out, and the man went down. Hawk was already riding toward him when the militiaman rose, staggering across the field only to be shot again.

A warrior emerged from the trees and sprinted toward the fallen soldier, tomahawk raised high. Hawk slowed his horse, jabbed his empty pistol beneath his belt, and drew his rifle from its scabbard. Cocking the hammer, he took aim as best he could and fired. The tomahawk flew from the warrior's hand, and he went down on one knee, clutching his shoulder. But then he was up again and running toward the soldier.

Hawk kicked his horse forward. Leaning low in the saddle to present as small a target as possible, he bore down on the man. The thunderous hooves alerted the warrior, who spun around, a long scalping knife glinting in his hand. Hawk dropped the reins and guided the animal with his knees as he grabbed his rifle by the barrel and swung it like a club. The stock caught the Indian on his wounded shoulder, knocking him from his feet and sending the rifle spinning from Hawk's hands.

The Creek was up in an instant and bounded toward Hawk, whose gray gelding reared and almost threw him. When the animal landed back on its front hooves, the warrior was there to meet it, his knife laying open a gash along the horse's neck. With a triumphant shout, he jerked back the knife and leaped at the rider. Hawk managed to free his boot from the stirrup and caught the man in the jaw, sending him reeling backward. But it stunned him only momentarily, and again he came at horse and rider.

All around them, bullets kicked up dirt and whined through the air, with at least one smacking into the thick leather saddle. The gelding brayed in fear and pain as it stamped and turned in a circle, exposing Hawk's back to the warrior. Hawk fought the reins, trying to keep the man in sight as the animal pranced and spun back around.

Keening, the Creek warrior lunged at Hawk with the long-bladed knife, but the cry became a gasp of fear, for he found himself staring down the barrel of Hawk's second pistol, which he had jerked from a saddlebag. Hammer thudded against flashpan, and the gun recoiled with a burst of flame and smoke. The lead ball caught the man on the bridge of the nose, driving bone through brain as it took away the back of his head.

The warrior's body had not even flopped to the ground when Hawk rode past at a gallop, his gelding's neck wound spraying blood.

The wounded soldier was still alive, gamely trying to

crawl toward the militia lines. Hawk slipped the second pistol beneath his belt as he reined in his mount. Leaping from the saddle, he grabbed the burly man around the chest while keeping a tight grip on the reins. He helped the man to his feet and saw that his face and chest were covered with blood, his matted hair gleaming red in the thin morning light.

"Steady, now!" Hawk called to both man and horse as he wrestled the fellow into the saddle. Stuffing the reins in the bewildered man's hands, he slapped the animal's rump and set him running toward the infantry lines.

Dropping to the ground, Hawk crawled over to the dead Indian. The gunfire was now sporadic, with significantly less coming from the trees. Either the concerted volleying from the militia was taking its toll, or the Creeks were cutting their losses and making a run for it.

It took a moment for Hawk to find and retrieve his rifle. Taking shelter in a small depression in the ground, he loaded the rifle and the brace of pistols at his belt. He peered over the top of the depression and watched the nearby trees until he saw the flare from a muzzle. Sighting on it, he fired his rifle. An Indian came staggering through the underbrush and fell to the ground.

Hawk could see now that many of the Creek were running through the fields beyond the copse, toward what appeared to be a village in the distance. The mounted militia was in pursuit, their pistols taking a devastating toll on the fleeing Indians.

Hawk kept firing until one of the horsemen came galloping over with a riderless mount in tow. Shoving the pistols under his belt, he grabbed his rifle and raced toward the man, who slowed enough for him to leap onto the spare horse. Then they galloped toward the Tallasahatchee villages.

The remainder of the engagement brought Hawk little pride or pleasure. Though it was clear the battle was won and that the Creeks were now putting up only token resistance, General Coffee ordered the soldiers to press their assault on the villages. The separate units of horsemen and infantry finished encircling the area and then moved in. No warriors were spared, and even some women and children fell under the punishing fire of the Tennessee militia.

Hawk and a few other officers eventually succeeded in ending the carnage, but not before almost two hundred Creek warriors lay dead in the villages and surrounding fields. Few were taken prisoner, for most were determined to fight to the death. When the militiamen began searching lodge to lodge, rounding up whoever was left, they found only women, children, the aged, and the infirm. Eighty-four souls were herded together and marched toward Fort Strother. Then Tallasahatchee was put to the torch.

A few wagons, brought along from the fort, were used to transport the five dead and forty wounded among the militia. As Hawk Harper rode away from the burning villages, he headed over to them to check on the man he had rescued. Approaching the caravan, he saw a horse tied to the back of the lead wagon; it was his gray gelding, stepping proudly and looking none the worse for wear, despite the neck wound it had sustained.

Dismounting, he walked alongside the gelding, checking the wound. The gash had been closed with some heavy thread, the kind used for repairing field tents.

"Thought a brave feller like that oughta get some attention, too."

Hawk turned to the soldier seated on the tail of the wagon, his left arm in a sling. It was not the man Hawk was seeking, however, for he was older and fairly slight.

"Did the best I could," he continued, gesturing at the horse's neck. "The surgeons were all busy, and I figured I'd better do somethin' to stop that bleeding. All I had was my sewing kit."

"You did a fine job," Hawk told him, shaking his good hand. "I'm most grateful."

"Don't like to see anything suffer—even a horse."

The wagon bounced over a rut, and the soldier had to hold on to keep from spilling out.

Hawk tied his borrowed mount to the wagon and asked, "Do you happen to know what became of the man who was riding my horse?"

"The one you got out of that field?"

Hawk nodded.

"Sure." He jerked a thumb over his shoulder. "He's in the corner up front. All shot up but alive."

"Thanks."

Hawk walked to the front of the wagon, peering over the side as he matched his stride to the vehicle's. He immediately recognized the burly private, who had sustained wounds to the leg and back. The man was lying on his side, propped up with blankets, and was conscious though quite pale and weak.

The soldier seemed strangely familiar, and with a start Hawk remembered where they had first met. The man's hair was red not from blood, but naturally so. And his powerful physique was that of a farmer, which probably explained how he had survived his wounds.

The private stared up at Hawk, and his lips quirked into an embarrassed smile. "Y-you're the one who put me on that . . . that horse, ain't you?" he stammered weakly.

"Lie easy, soldier," Hawk told him as he kept pace with the wagon.

"I-I'm sorry. Real sorry."

"I'd have done the same for any man."

"I mean about Nashville. I was drunk. I had no cause t'lay into you like I done."

"Giles, right?"

"Yes, sir. Private Giles McPherson."

"Well, forget about all that, Giles."

"If there's anythin' I can—"

"Just rest easy and get better." Grinning, Hawk rubbed his chin as if it were sore. "And remind me never to get in an argument with you again."

"No, sir, 'tis me who should be avoidin' fights. Emily's always tellin' me t'watch my temper."

"Emily?"

"My wife."

Hawk nodded, his thoughts returning to the years of his youth. "It's a beautiful name. My mother's name was Emily."

"If she's anythin' like my Emily, she was a saint."

"Yes, that she was."

With some effort, the farmer offered his hand. "You're a brave man, Captain. Thank you for what you done."

Hawk shook his hand, then gestured at the bandages around his chest and leg. "Think you'll be all right?"

"What, this?" Giles shook his head. " 'Tweren't nothin', really. I've been laid up worse by the kick of a brood mare. A few days, I'll be fit t'take on another hundred o' them Creeks."

"Let's hope it doesn't come to that. Maybe after today, they'll lay down their arms."

"I wouldn't wager on that, Captain. I surely wouldn't. My money has us seein' more action within the week."

Giles McPherson's prediction proved accurate. Four days later, Ta-na-wun-da arrived at Fort Strother from his scouting foray through the regions to the south, bringing troubling news of an encampment of Creeks being threatened by a larger force of their fellow Indians. In the wake of the battle at Tallasahatchee, the smaller band had advocated that tribal representatives meet with General Jackson to sue for peace. Considered traitors, they were now holed up at Talladega, besieged by a force numbering into the many hundreds.

It took only a few minutes for the general to make

his decision. Two thirds of the militia would leave that day for Talladega. Though it was already late afternoon, Jackson wanted the troops ready to pull out at midnight. They would march through the night and all the next day, traversing the thirty miles to Talladega. It was the seventh of November, and Andrew Jackson intended to have his men in position and ready to launch their attack at dawn of the ninth.

Chapter Fourteen

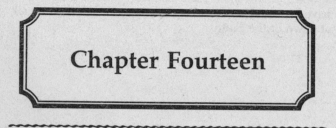Hawk Harper was delighted when the sun at last broke over the low hills to the east. It had been darker than expected during the night, and he estimated they had made only about eight miles thus far. With daylight breaking, they could increase their pace and hopefully reach their destination—a point about six miles north of Talladega—before dark. They would then rest prior to traversing the final miles before the next dawn.

Hawk was astride his trusty gray gelding, nibbling a hard, unsalted biscuit, when his younger brother came riding up from the rear.

"Enjoying breakfast?" Ta-na-wun-da asked as he slowed his pinto to a walk.

"So, there you are," Hawk said cheerfully. "I figured with another battle coming, you'd already headed off in the other direction."

Ta-na gave a mock frown. "*I* ride alone through the heart of Creek country. When *you* ride, you have a thousand soldiers at your side."

"But the Creek are in front of us. What were you

doing back there?" He gestured in the direction from which Ta-na had come.

"I returned to the fort to get this." He patted the leather courier bag hanging at his side. "One of our Seneca runners brought dispatches from Fayetteville."

"Anything of interest?"

It was Ta-na's turn to grin. "I am only a scout. What would I know about the contents of dispatches?"

"Little brother, I'd wager that you, that runner, and half the Cherokee and Seneca riding along with us already know everything in that bag."

"Well, there's nothing of interest except the newspaper." He opened the bag and removed a folded copy of the *Gazette*, which he handed his brother. "I don't think General Jackson would mind you getting a first look."

Hawk studied the front page. As he had expected, the main topic of news was the defeat of the British at the Battle of the Thames. He scanned the articles for any word about Tecumseh, and his brother leaned closer and pointed to the bottom of the page. Looking there, Hawk saw what purported to be a description of the last moments of the warrior-prophet. It concluded with something of a tribute to the man who had fought so tenaciously for his people and their cause:

> Thus fell Tecumseh, the most celebrated warrior that ever raised the tomahawk against us, and with him has fallen the last hope of our Indian enemies. This mighty leader was the determined foe of civilization and had for years been laboring to unite all the Indian tribes in resisting the progress of the settlements westward. Had such a man opposed the European colonists on their first arrival, this continent, in all probability, would still be a wilderness.
>
> To those who prefer a savage, uncultivated wasteland, inhabited by wolves and panthers and by men more savage still, to the busy city,

to the peaceful hamlet and cottage, to science
and the comforts of civilization, it may be a
source of regret that Tecumseh came too late.
But if the cultivation of the earth, and the cultivation of the human intellect and the human
virtues are agreeable in the sight of the Cre-
ator, it may be a just cause of felicitation that
this champion of barbarism chose to ally himself with Great Britain. For in so doing, he has
drawn destruction upon his own head, by sav-
agely daring what was beyond his strength.

And so Tecumseh has fallen, mourned by
his friends and respected by his enemies as a
great and magnanimous chief. He received the
stamp of greatness from the hand of nature;
born with no title to command but his innate
virtues, tribe after tribe yielded submission to
him at once. Had his lot been cast in a different
state of society, he would have shone as one of
the most distinguished of men. For despite the
lowly state into which he was born, Tecumseh
possessed the soul of a hero.

"Will you be riding ahead?" Hawk asked as he returned the newspaper to his brother, who stuffed it back
into the courier bag.

"This time the numbers we face are many. I will
remain until the battle is won."

"Is their force larger than at Tallasahatchee?"

Ta-na-wun-da nodded. "Creeks are converging from
all directions. By the time we reach Talladega, their numbers could approach our own."

"Then this may be it . . . the final battle."

"Do you really believe that, Captain Hawk Harper?"
Ta-na's formality unnerved his brother. "When you chose
to ride south with General Jackson, did you think there
would be one great victory, and then the Creek would
abandon their homes and disappear into the west? Did

you not believe the general when he said he would burn a path all the way to Mobile?"

"To be honest, I don't know what I thought or why I even came along. Something just . . ." He shook his head in consternation.

"Something has spoken to you," Ta-na declared. "Yes, perhaps I have heard it too."

"What do you think it is?"

Ta-na stared straight ahead as he considered the question. A smile played at the corners of his mouth. "Fate? Destiny? The voices of the manitous?" He chuckled. "No, it is probably nothing so grand." He drew in a breath, held it a moment, and let it out slowly. "It is probably as simple as that smell all around us," he said, looking at his brother.

Hawk eyed him uncertainly.

"Leather," Ta-na-wun-da declared. "Leather, smoking rifles, and soldiers on the march." He slapped his reins against the pinto's neck and kicked the horse into a trot, calling behind him as he rode off, "I will see you in Talladega, brother!"

Far to the north, the cousin of Ta-na-wun-da and Hawk Harper lay in a cold, vermin-ridden cell at Fort Niagara, one hundred fifty miles east of where Tecumseh had breathed his last. In the weeks since the Battle of the Thames, Gao's thigh wound had healed nicely, and he could stand and move around on his own. However, in recent days his shoulder had taken a turn for the worse. The American army surgeon had done an adequate job removing the bullet, but the conditions in which he was being kept had led inevitably to infection, and he suffered from a fever that would not abate. Gao was less concerned for himself than he was for his wife, Mist-on-the-Water.

He had made it a point to speak no English in front of the soldiers, which led some of them to speak more freely around him than they might otherwise have done.

From what little he had gleaned, he knew the Indian movement had all but crumbled and most of Tecumseh's followers had disbanded and were returning to their respective homes. He prayed Mist-on-the-Water was doing so as well—perhaps heading south to Rusog's Town on the chance her husband would eventually find his way there.

But Gao no longer expected that to happen. When first captured, he had thought he would be executed right there on the field of battle. Then he saw prisoners being released, and his hopes had soared. But the officer who had been among his captors had seen him with Tecumseh, and Gao, with eleven others known to have been close to the great chief, had been singled out for special treatment, including lengthy interrogations and a long journey. They were taken first to Detroit, then by boat along Lake Erie to Fort Niagara, just north of Buffalo on the Niagara River. Despite questioning en route, Gao and his fellow prisoners had told their captors nothing, and they had begun to hope for eventual release. That hope faded upon arriving at Fort Niagara.

The fort was a shambles, having sustained heavy damage the previous year during a bombardment by the English at Fort George on the opposite side of the Niagara River. But recently Fort George had fallen to American hands, and the region had become relatively quiet. Half the troops had been transferred to the fort across the river, leaving Niagara undermanned, with many of its soldiers sick or wounded. They blamed their current state of affairs on the fallen Shawnee leader and his followers, convinced that without Indian support the British could not have pressed their campaigns so boldly.

It was the misfortune of Gao and his companions that their arrival at Fort Niagara coincided with that of Colonel Charles Stringfellow. Reputed to be a brutally effective interrogator, he had been sent from Albany to obtain information from any British or Indian prisoners who had fallen into American hands.

When Stringfellow made his first visit to the guard-house, Gao and the other prisoners gathered at the barred windows of their cells to catch a glimpse of him making his way across the parade ground. He was tall and appeared somewhat gangly and out of place in uniform, but he walked with a self-assured, almost arrogant stride. The colonel got closer, and Gao saw the black patch over his left eye and the prominent scar that ran down the side of his face. A British sword must have made the scar, Gao thought ruefully. He knew a wound like that could destroy not only a man's eye but his soul.

Yes, Colonel Charles Stringfellow looked like a man who took great pleasure in his work.

A few minutes later a pair of guards entered Gao's cell and roughly shackled his hands behind his back. He gritted his teeth against the pain that shot through his wounded shoulder, determined not to let his agony show as they marched him down the hall to the interrogation room. Five of the other Indians were already there, lined up against one wall, and Gao stoically took his place at the end of the line.

Stringfellow was seated in a chair in the middle of a room otherwise devoid of furniture. Six armed guards stood at various points around the room. Also on hand was Major Caleb Wilson, who had some knowledge of several Indian languages and had interrogated Gao and the others without success upon their arrival at Fort Niagara. Wilson was serving as temporary commandant of the fort but was outranked by the visiting colonel.

Stringfellow's single dark eye was cold, almost disinterested, as he looked from one prisoner to the next. With a slight flick of the hand, he signaled Major Wilson to come forward. Wilson conferred briefly with the colonel, then tried to get a response from the Indians, using what at times was a chaotic and poorly pronounced blend of Shawnee, Creek, and Potawatomi. Stringfellow, meanwhile, turned partially to the right and folded one leg over the other, staring off into the distance as if thoroughly bored by the proceedings.

Though the major's command of Indian languages was rudimentary at best, Gao had no trouble understanding him, since he first asked each question in English for the colonel's benefit. Gao knew his companions also understood the gist of what was being said, even if they had trouble following the actual words, but to a man they made no response. For his part, Gao was far more interested in what the colonel was thinking than in what Major Wilson was asking.

Stringfellow gave the first signs of impatience when the questioning shifted to the topic of Tecumseh's death. Without altering his position, he fixed his gaze on each prisoner in turn, lightly drumming the arm of his chair with his fingertips.

"Did Tecumseh make any predictions about his death?" the major asked.

Gao struggled to keep from laughing, for when Wilson translated the words into Shawnee, they came out something like, "Did Tecumseh know he was dead?"

Major Wilson asked several more questions about their fallen leader, concluding with, "What did Tecumseh tell his followers to do if he were to die?"

Stringfellow changed with a suddenness that surprised everyone, Gao included. The colonel bounded out of the chair, took three quick steps toward the prisoner standing farthest to the right, and brutally backhanded him, whacking his head against the brick wall.

"These *creatures* are playing with you," he snarled, turning to the stunned officer.

"Perhaps if we were to—"

"We have given your methods a try, Major. Now we will use mine."

He removed his blue jacket and handed it to Wilson. When he turned toward the prisoners again, his eye gleamed dangerously. He approached the warrior he had struck. The man was almost a foot shorter but stared at Stringfellow with no sign of fear.

"I don't have to talk Shawnee, now do I, boy?" He gently patted the prisoner's cheek where he had struck it. "You understand me, don't you?"

The warrior's hands were shackled behind him, yet he seemed on the verge of leaping at the colonel. Stringfellow smiled, almost challenging the fellow to make a move. Then he stepped to the left, in front of the second man in line.

"We speak the same language, don't we?"

Without awaiting a response, he rammed his fist into the man's stomach, doubling him over. The warrior gasped, struggling for air. When at last he started to straighten, the colonel viciously kneed him on the bridge of the nose, slamming him against the wall.

The man slid down the bricks, blood pouring from his nose. But the moment his knees touched the floor, he forced himself back up. He stood tottering a moment. Then he let out a keening wail and charged, driving Stringfellow backward into the chair, which tumbled over, sending the colonel sprawling to the floor, the Indian landing on top of him.

Unable to use his hands, the prisoner tried to bite his tormentor, but several guards pounced on him and hauled him to his feet, then pummeled him.

"Leave him be!" Stringfellow shouted, pushing away the major, who tried to help him. Getting up off the floor, he repeated his order and motioned for the guards to drag the man back to the wall.

Two held him in place; the other guards trained their rifles on the rest of the prisoners. As Stringfellow approached he drew a pistol from his belt and cocked it. He wore a chilling grin as he pressed the barrel firmly against the warrior's forehead.

"Yes, we understand each other," he declared. "Now, I will ask you a simple question, and you will answer—or else I will pull this trigger." Without shifting his gaze, he called over his shoulder, "Translate that into Shawnee, Major, just in case he doesn't speak the king's English—even though he does the king's bidding."

Major Wilson came forward, his voice somewhat feeble as he did his best to pass along the colonel's warning. Gao noted that he concluded with a personal plea that the prisoner comply because the colonel "means what he says, and there is no one here to stop him."

"Now ask him this," Stringfellow added. "Where can we find the Shawnee Prophet?" He spoke of Tenskwatawa, whose prophecies had actually been the work of his brother, Tecumseh. He had not been at the Battle of the Thames and was still on the loose, capable perhaps of uniting Tecumseh's followers. Gao finally understood why they had been kept prisoners.

The major asked the question in Shawnee, then repeated it in several other languages. The prisoner did not react, his eyes never wavering as he stared at the colonel.

With a sigh, Stringfellow pulled the pistol back from the man's forehead and shook his head in dismay. "You and your friends are beginning to bore me," he muttered.

Abruptly swinging the pistol to the right, at the man standing at the end of the line, he pulled the trigger. There was a flash of sparks and smoke, and then the charge went off with a thunderous boom, sending the lead slug into the very cheek he had patted so gently a few minutes before. The blast blew off the back of the man's skull, splattering the wall with blood and brains. His limp body flopped to the floor.

Colonel Stringfellow methodically reloaded his pistol as the cloying black smoke cleared. He walked up to the prisoner with the bloody nose and again pointed the barrel at his face.

"This time we won't need you to translate, Major Wilson," he called behind him. "This fellow knows precisely what I am talking about." He angled his head slightly. "Now, don't you?" he asked as he pulled back the hammer and it locked in place with a rasping *clink*.

Gao's ears were still ringing from the sound of the gunshot. He glanced at the guards, who seemed more than eager to bring their own guns into play. Then he looked at the colonel and the warrior who faced him. Just beyond them, a pool of blood oozed from under the body of the dead Shawnee and spread slowly across the floor.

"What is it to be?" the colonel demanded. "Will you answer, or must I waste another bullet?"

"He does not speak English," Gao blurted, taking a half step forward.

All eyes—and rifles—turned to him. The colonel's pistol was still trained on the other prisoner, but his attention was riveted upon the man who had spoken in such perfect English.

Gao took another cautious step. "He is Wyandot and does not understand you or the major."

Slowly, the pistol barrel lowered, and Stringfellow faced the speaker. "And who might you be?" he asked, his tone almost pleasant as he uncocked the hammer and replaced the gun beneath his belt.

"I am Gao of the Seneca."

"Seneca?" Stringfellow's eyebrows raised. "I did not realize your people ran with Tecumseh."

"We each choose our own battles. My choice was to stand beside Tecumseh."

"You appear to be an educated man. Surely you did not learn such perfect English among the Seneca."

When Gao did not reply, the colonel walked over to Major Wilson and conferred in hushed tones. He nodded several times, then reapproached the young Seneca warrior.

"I am told you did not respond to the major's earlier interrogations. And today you speak only to protect one of your friends. Are you going to make me shoot each one of them to get the answers to a few simple questions?"

Gao stood as erect as possible, hoping the officer would not consider the fevered sweat on his forehead a sign of fear. "We are each prepared to die," he intoned in as even a voice as he could muster. "Indeed, we are already dead."

The colonel chuckled. Drawing his pistol again, he pointed the barrel at the body lying a few feet away. "That poor savage is certainly dead." He waved the gun at the others. "But the rest of you are very much alive. It is your choice whether or not you join him."

"We do not hold the rifles," Gao said plainly.

"Ah, but your tongues are on the triggers. Speak, and no more need die."

"We know about words," Gao declared, setting his jaw stubbornly. "We know how the Great Father in Washington"—he said the term with more than a measure of disdain—"uses words to kill his red children. Words are like bullets—and we will not shoot them into our own hearts." He stepped back against the wall. "Fire your weapons," he challenged. "I have looked into your eye, into your soul, and I speak truthfully when I say that we are already dead."

Stringfellow slowly brought up his weapon, thumbing back the hammer as he aimed it at Gao's face. They both stood motionless, each staring down the barrel, each gauging his adversary's determination and strength.

A faint smile played at the corners of the colonel's mouth. Releasing his breath, he drew the gun back, tipping it up as he uncocked it.

"Yes, you are dead," he said in an undertone, the tension releasing from his body. "I guess I will have to bring you back to life." He turned to the guards. "Take them back to their cells. All of them"—he waggled the pistol at Gao—"except that one."

All but two of the guards hurried forward and ushered the other prisoners from the room.

"Seat him in the chair," the colonel ordered, and the remaining guards grabbed Gao by the arms and dragged him to the overturned chair in the middle of the room. Setting it upright, they dumped him onto it.

"It seems we no longer need your services, Major

Wilson," Stringfellow said, his tone smug and patronizing. "When this Seneca warrior again finds his voice, he will do so in English."

The major hesitated, looking back and forth between Gao and the colonel.

"I said that will be all, Major."

The officer appeared on the verge of speaking. Then, frowning, he spun on his heels and stalked out of the interrogation room, slamming the door behind him.

"That's better." Stringfellow slowly circled the chair. "Much better."

Removing his pistol, he handed it to one of the guards.

"Major Wilson means well, but his methods are so very tedious. Don't you agree?"

Stepping beside Gao, he gripped the young prisoner's shoulder directly on the gunshot wound.

"He tells me you have already suffered at the hands of our troops over on the Thames. Is that correct?"

The colonel's fingers clamped down like a vise, shooting pain across Gao's shoulder and down his chest. He tried not to wince.

"Yes, you are dead. But you do not have to suffer. All I want to know is where we can find the so-called Shawnee Prophet. From what I've been told, Tecumseh himself wasn't very fond of his brother. Surely he would not object to your giving him up."

Gao fought the pain and forced himself to look up at the colonel. "You will get no more words from me."

"Good." Stringfellow relaxed his grip. "I was hoping you wouldn't make it too easy." He waved the guards over. "Spread his legs . . . wide."

Each man grabbed a leg and yanked it up and outward, jerking Gao off the chair. He came crashing down on his back, smacking his head on the floor, hands pinned beneath him. Blinking against the pain, he saw the colonel standing over him, a boot raised over his spread-eagled legs. He shut his eyes and prepared himself for a blow to his genitals. Instead, the heel of the boot crashed down on the precise spot on his right thigh where he had taken the bullet.

Gao gasped, biting his lip to keep from screaming. The colonel raised his foot again and stomped even harder. Then he landed a crushing kick on Gao's bad shoulder.

"Remain silent for all I care," Stringfellow said, placing another well-aimed kick to his shoulder. "You will be talking soon enough. Indeed, we won't be able to shut you up."

His booted foot struck again, catching Gao in the cheek and laying open a bloody gash down the side of his face. The young Seneca mercifully fainted.

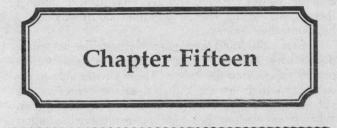

Chapter Fifteen

Just before dawn on Tuesday, November 9, 1813, the Tennessee militia approached the Creek encampment at Talladega. Having learned a lesson from the surprise attack at Tallasahatchee, they sent an advance force of allied Indians to encircle the area and secure the perimeter before they arrived. It proved to be a simple task, for the Creeks were not on their guard and had retired to their lodges, apparently having subdued any opposition from within their own ranks. The militia was easily able to move into position without being seen.

As the first light of day broke over the Creek village, a bugler sounded the attack. The bulk of General Jackson's forces had been well deployed and was protected by the cover of the surrounding woods, and it was left to the mounted troops to bring the battle to the enemy. Hawk Harper was among them as they charged from four different points, firing their weapons and then pulling back to reload and launch another attack. The infantry, meanwhile, tightened the circle, marching through the trees and then across the surrounding fields until they were within eighty yards of the town.

At the first blare of the bugle, hundreds of Creek warriors poured from dwellings, some still yanking on their clothes, others firing haphazardly into the air. It was a simple matter for the mounted troops to ride through their midst, picking off man after man and driving others back into their lodges.

After a third and then a fourth charge the horsemen pulled back, and the infantry opened fire, sending repeated volleys into the lodges. Those Creeks able to escape from their homes gathered at the center of the village, where they tried to organize a counterattack. When it was obvious they could not overcome the larger, better-armed militia, they concentrated their attention on a single point at the western end of town.

At first the militia did not grasp what the Creeks were doing, the Indians being astute enough to deploy a portion of their forces around the village so as not to reveal their growing concentration to the west. But with the infantry in that area coming under heavier attack, the strategy revealed itself, and General Jackson gave the order to reinforce the western line.

Hawk and the other mounted militiamen were sent around the perimeter to add their numbers to the infantry, ensuring that the line would hold and the enemy could not escape in that direction. The Creeks, however, had thrown up some crude defensive works, making it increasingly dangerous for the horsemen to launch an effective charge. After a few abortive attempts, they were ordered to dismount and join the infantrymen on the line. Hawk argued they should remain mounted and continue to protect the entire perimeter, but he was overruled and reluctantly took his place with the others near the western edge of town.

Soon after he began firing from the shelter of a small hillock, he suspected there was more to the Creek plan than first perceived. By his estimate, no more than three hundred warriors were concentrated at the western defensive works, with perhaps another hundred spread around the rest of the village. Yet Ta-na-wun-da had reported upwards of one thousand fighters on hand at Talladega. Either some of that force had already departed the village, or they were being held back as reinforcements or for some other purpose entirely.

Cautiously peering over the hillock, he looked left and right. The militia was moving through the trees and across the fields, converging on this same location—leaving the eastern side of the perimeter poorly defended.

Scrambling through the trees to his tethered gelding, Hawk leaped into the saddle and went galloping back, calling for the other horsemen to join him. Some responded, but others were either unaware of his call or were pinned down by gunfire. When word finally reached the bugler, he sounded the call, and soon a number of horsemen had mounted up. At Hawk's command, they swept around to the south, heading toward the eastern perimeter.

Even as the small body of mounted troops was on the move, the hundreds of Creeks amassed at the eastern edge of the village were making their break. They burst from cover, a few on horseback, most on foot, and went racing across the open field, firing muskets and arrows at the sparse ranks of the militia. Simultaneously, the smaller force to the west rushed the enemy lines, deflecting attention from the bold flight for freedom taking place in the east. It was a desperate plan, designed to draw the soldiers away from the village. The women, children, and elders who were forced to remain behind could only pray that the soldiers would not take reprisals against them once the fighting ended.

Hawk and his men set a breakneck pace around the perimeter of the militia lines in an attempt to cut off the fleeing warriors, whose leaders were mounted. The infantry on that side of the village, vastly outnumbered by the hundreds of Creeks who fell upon them, struggled to pull back to more defensible positions. Fortunately the Indians were more concerned with making their escape than with inflicting casualties on the enemy. Still, the toll of the dead and wounded steadily rose.

The mounted militiamen were embroiled in a furious charge against the Creeks on horseback, who were leading the escape toward a string of low mountains in the distance. A running gun battle erupted, with the Indians suffering heavy losses as one after another was shot off his horse. Some of the animals were struck as well, spilling their riders, who were then overrun by the soldiers.

The pursuit went on for miles until all the Creek horsemen had either been killed or had made their escape. The militiamen then shifted their attention to the warriors on foot. They turned their mounts and came galloping back, scattering the fleeing Indians and turning most of them toward the village. But by now the infantry had regrouped, cutting them off from the rear. The Creeks found themselves trapped between the infantry and a growing force of horsemen.

For more than an hour, the warriors refused to surrender, fighting on valiantly despite overwhelming odds. They did not lay down their arms until almost two hundred of them lay dead or dying in the open fields.

Hawk and his men rounded up the survivors and marched them back toward Talladega. Sporadic gunfire could still be heard, but the battle was over, with only small pockets of resistance still being flushed out. As Hawk neared the now-silent perimeter line, he saw a rider approaching from the village and recognized the pinto as Ta-na-wun-da's. Relief flooded through him, and he rode out to greet his brother.

The Seneca scout pulled his horse to a halt and gazed across the field at the spectacle of several hundred defeated warriors being marched back to the village they had tried to escape. Behind him, wisps of smoke rose above the village as the militia methodically searched and set fire to each building.

"Is it finished?" Hawk asked, reining in beside his brother.

Ta-na glanced over his shoulder and frowned. "I fear it has just begun."

"What do you mean?"

"There is much anger among your soldiers," Ta-na replied, emphasizing the word *your*.

Hawk observed the village. "They're not executing prisoners, are they?"

"Each man is taking his own revenge. General Jackson seems unwilling to interfere." Ta-na's eyes narrowed to dark points. "These are the people who murdered Naomi and Joseph. What will your revenge be, Little Hawk?"

"My name is Harper. Captain Hawk Harper," he snapped, frowning angrily. "As for revenge, it has no place on the field of honor." He kicked his horse into a gallop and headed for the village.

As Hawk rode among the burning lodges, he understood what Ta-na-wun-da had meant. Some of the troops were operating in an orderly fashion, rounding up the occupants of a building before setting it afire. Others were behaving like madmen, hauling women and children from their homes, shooting any warrior they came upon, sometimes putting buildings to the torch without confirming they were empty. Screams could be heard from within as the structures went up in flames. All around the village, soldiers were shouting, "Fort Mims! Fort Mims!" as if the words alone justified any action.

It took a moment for Hawk to fully comprehend what he was seeing. Then he leaped from his horse, sword in hand, and entered the fray. One man was dragging a youth barely in his teens along the ground toward one of the burning buildings, apparently to add him to the pyre. Dashing forward, Hawk swung his sword broadside against the fellow's back, knocking him to his

knees. When he tried to get back up, he was met by
Hawk's boot, which sent him sprawling unconscious in
the dirt. The boy scrambled to his feet and ran off.

Hawk then turned his attention to a soldier pinning
a fairly young Creek woman to the ground as his partner
tried to grab her flailing legs. Yanking the first man to his
feet, Hawk threw him backward onto the ground. The
other soldier started to come to his friend's aid but was
quickly dispatched by a blow to the back of the head
from Ta-na-wun-da's rifle butt.

Hawk smiled at his brother, then helped the woman
to her feet. He led her through the smoky, blazing village
until he found some soldiers who were working to round
up and protect the prisoners. Turning her over to them,
Hawk waded back into the madness, Ta-na-wun-da at his
side.

Fortunately Hawk and Ta-na weren't the only ones
outraged into action to end the massacre. Order was
slowly restored, but not before some three hundred
Creeks—a number of them women and children—lay
dead in the village and surrounding countryside.

As the militia began moving the prisoners out of
Talladega to a nearby encampment, Hawk and Ta-na
walked through the smoldering ruins. A number of militiamen were rummaging for souvenirs or anything of
value, but the brothers ignored them, concentrating instead on finding survivors or any soldiers taking advantage of them. Several times they discovered women
being held in lodges; each time the women had been
raped or were about to suffer that fate. The mere sight of
Hawk in his captain's uniform was enough to get them
freed without further incident.

There were only two lodges left to check, each
charred and smoldering but still intact. As Hawk and
Ta-na approached the first, they heard a woman's muffled
cry. Breaking into a run, they burst through the open
doorway and found three militiamen holding a woman
spread-eagled on the ground, while a fourth mounted

her. Her buckskin skirt was pulled up over her head, and the man was grunting as he plunged into her.

Hawk was on him in an instant, hurling him off the woman and across the hard-packed ground. When one of the others tried to intercede, Ta-na-wun-da leaped forward and felled him with a single blow to the jaw. He turned to the other two, who backed toward the doorway, raising their hands in submission.

The first man yanked up his pants and scrambled to his feet. Enraged, apparently caring not that Hawk was a captain, he lowered his head and charged into Hawk, sending him careening across the lodge. The two men landed hard, but Hawk managed to roll free, and he jumped to his feet.

The soldier stood up a bit more slowly, drawing something from his boot. Hawk saw the glint of metal in the man's hand as he lunged again. Stepping deftly to the side, Hawk clapped his fists on the back of the man's neck, knocking him to his knees.

Ta-na was about to step in and finish him off, but Hawk waved him away. Ta-na then turned to confront the pair of soldiers in the doorway, but they quickly ran out into the village.

The rapist was struggling to stand. Hawk approached cautiously, waiting to see what he would do. Groaning, the soldier lifted himself partway off the ground, then collapsed again, his body twitching a few times before becoming still. A stream of blood flowed out from beneath his belly across the ground, pooling on the hard-packed earth.

"Damn fool," Hawk muttered as he knelt and rolled the soldier onto his back. The man's own knife protruded from his gut.

Hawk jerked the knife free and tossed it across the lodge. Turning, he saw his brother comforting the sobbing woman, cradling her head in his lap. As Hawk stepped toward her, she reached up to him, her eyes beseeching, her lips mouthing his name.

Hawk just stood there, gazing at her in disbelief. He tried to speak—to ask if it was really her and what she was doing there. The only sound he could utter was, *"Ma-ton-ga . . ."*

General Andrew Jackson looked up from his maps as Hawk Harper entered the tent that served as field headquarters for the militia. He motioned for the young captain to approach, then went back to his maps, still not speaking. After long, wordless minutes, he stood and paced to the rear of the tent. When he turned and looked back at Hawk, it was more in sadness than anger.

"Is there anything I can do to convince you to stay?" he asked, easing his left arm from the sling to flex and rub his stiff fingers.

"I'm determined to return home," Hawk told him.

Jackson came a few steps closer. "We finally have them on the run. Why leave now? You have served admirably; you should be there to see this thing through."

"You don't need me."

"Maybe not, Captain Harper, but I *want* you. And I should think that you, of all people, would want to see that these Creek bastards no longer have the strength or means to terrorize innocent people."

"I have seen enough."

Jackson drew in a breath and slowly exhaled, his eyes narrowing in thought. "Yes, we have all seen enough," he replied with a nod. "I know how you feel about Talladega, and I assure you, it is not my desire to have our soldiers dishonor themselves on the field of battle. Which is all the more reason for you to remain. We need men like you to help rein in these boys—to forestall any needless killing."

"Each day I fear that Tecumseh may have been right about us," Hawk commented. "Nothing will stop us from killing until every last Indian is forced west of the Mississippi. Maybe we'll keep on killing until we've driven them across the Rockies and into the Pacific Ocean."

"You sound like an Indian now."

"Whether I admit it or not, one quarter of my blood is Seneca. And I am tired of watching my people—white and red alike—destroy one another."

The general sat back at his table. "Let me speak plainly with you, Captain Harper," he said, folding his hands in front of him. "You can view what happened at Talladega as a massacre, but it was not. Fort Mims, attacked without cause, was a massacre, with every last man, woman, and child murdered by those heathens. At Talladega, the enemy was given the opportunity to surrender. If they had done so sooner, no innocents would have lost their lives. Because they put up such resistance, causing so many casualties among our men, there were some excesses in the aftermath." His voice lowered almost to a hush as he added, "There always will be excess in war. Many of our fellows have lost family and friends to Indian raids; we cannot blame them for wanting a bit of revenge when they get the chance."

"I don't blame them," Hawk replied. "I understand them only too well."

Jackson leaned forward and eyed the younger man closely. "Then why are you leaving? Our cause is just, and for the most part the Creeks can expect honorable treatment at our hands. If there was some excess, at least it has put them on notice that we are firm in our resolve and shall not turn back until our cause is won."

"Until they are driven across the Mississippi," Hawk said simply.

"Until they surrender the rightful land of these United States of America."

"Sorry, General, but I will no longer be a party to this excuse for Indian removal—and massacre."

There was a long silence, then General Jackson rose and approached. "I regret that you feel as you do. But you have served me well, and you are not bound to the Tennessee militia. When you return to Huntington Castle, give my regards to your father and stepmother."

The two men shook hands. Hawk started to leave, then turned around and said, "There is another thing, General."

"Yes?"

"My brother has requested to accompany me."

"I have already given my permission."

"Yes. And I'm afraid I must impose on our friendship for one other favor."

Jackson's eyebrows rose, but he remained silent.

"It regards a woman prisoner."

Jackson nodded. "I was told you have taken an interest in one of our Creek captives."

"It is more than an interest. It is a debt I must repay. When I was in the Ozarks, this woman saved my life. I would like to bring her back to Rusog's Town with me."

Jackson studied Hawk a moment, then said, "Don't you think it curious that you should find her here among so many?"

"Perhaps that's why I came to Talladega."

"Are you a believer in destiny?"

Hawk grinned. "Destiny doesn't care whether I believe or not."

"Well, I don't wish to stand in the way of destiny. If she is willing, you may take her with you."

"Thank you, General." Hawk saluted, then strode from the tent.

Ma-ton-ga gripped the mane of the bay mare given her by the white man named Hawk. It was an unshod Creek pony, one of the horses taken during battle. She wondered, now that she was his prisoner, if he would take her as well. It did not matter. She had been used before, and still she was alive—while so many others had passed beyond. Thunder Arrow, Running Fox, Talks-with-Clouds. The people of Tallasahatchee and Talladega. Even the Panther Passing Across. And untold numbers yet to die.

She rode between the gray gelding and the pinto, the white man on her left, the Seneca on her right. The younger one had said his name was Ta-na-wun-da, which in the Seneca language meant Swift Waters. The older one had more than one name. At the cave he had told her his white name: Hawk Harper. But the Seneca said he was called Os-sweh-ga-da-ah Ne-wa-ah, the Little Hawk—and that they were brothers.

How could this be? she asked herself. One's hair was as golden as corn, his brother's as black as a new-moon sky.

The lowering sun painted the west with bands of orange and gold. There was a glow to the south as well, and she turned to gaze a final time upon the smoldering lodges her people had called home . . . until that morning, when the white soldiers arrived.

Her face was expressionless. She would not show them her pain or the tears in her heart. She would ride north with them, across the Coosa River and into Cherokee country beyond. She would go wherever they took her, for twice now she had crossed paths with this little hawk with golden feathers. And each time, someone had been saved while others had died.

It was the will of the Master of Life. She would fight it no longer.

Ma-tun-ga gripped the sides of the pony with her legs and stared straight ahead. She felt his eyes upon her. She heard his voice but understood only a few of his words: *north, father, hunting, home.* And her name. She had heard it spoken in English before, but never with such gentleness. Especially from a *shemanese*—a white man—even if he were a shemanese Indian.

Place-Where-the-Sun-Sleeps . . .

She looked to her left, beyond the man with hair as golden as the sun. She saw herself walking there, bathed in its glow, warm in its embrace. Sleeping in that land where the sun lies down at night.

The white Indian watched her, his eyes as blue as

the sky, his smile as warm as the sun. She gazed into those eyes and saw herself walking there, embraced by the warmth and the light.

Ma-ton-ga turned away, holding tighter to the pony's mane. She stared straight ahead, her face carved from stone.

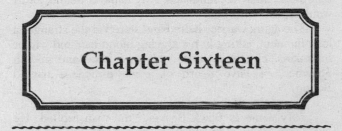

Chapter Sixteen

Renno Harper rode toward the small band of Indians. They were as bedraggled as the others he had passed on his journey north. Each group possessed only one or two ponies, with the men, women, and children forced to carry most of their possessions on their backs. There was a bite to the November air, and most of the travelers wore several layers of clothing—a curious mixture of Creek, Shawnee, and other designs. Renno knew at once that this group of about two dozen had been part of Tecumseh's Pan-Indian movement and were now trying to reach their former homes in the south before the winter snows arrived.

Renno reined in his horse and waited for them to approach. He was impressed with how straight they held themselves despite their burdens and defeat. But as they drew closer, he recognized the same look in their eyes that he had found in each party he had encountered. Behind the strength, beyond the stoic pride, the spirit had gone out of them. Their leader had been taken from them; they would fight no more.

Dismounting, Renno dropped the reins and walked toward the headman, who carried a pair of rifles instead of a pack and was leading one of the ponies. He was about Renno's age and wore the paint of a Shawnee.

The white Indian raised his hand in friendship and said in the Shawnee language, "My name is Renno, and I would speak with you."

The aging warrior halted and stared at the stranger a long moment, taking in his graying blond hair and winter buckskins. Finally he raised his own hand and said in Shawnee, "I have heard of a white Seneca named Renno."

"I am that Renno."

"My name is Black Beaver," the man replied. He put down his burden, and they gripped their right forearms in greeting.

Slowly the others came to a halt and lowered their packs to the ground. Renno shared with Black Beaver news from the south, including the war between the Tennessee militia and the Creek Nation. Word of the massacre at Fort Mims had reached Tecumseh's followers, but they did not yet know about General Andrew Jackson's incursion into Creek lands. Black Beaver took the news without emotion, as if expecting only the worst now that Tecumseh had died.

The Shawnee then spoke, telling of their own situation and how, following the disastrous Battle of the Thames, Tecumseh's followers had left in small groups for their respective homes. Renno had heard the same story from several other parties he had encountered, but he did not interrupt, merely nodding in understanding.

When Black Beaver finished, Renno said, "I have come north seeking my nephew. He is of the Seneca, and his name is Gao." He avoided directly asking if the man knew Gao because questioning any but the closest of friends was considered poor manners.

Black Beaver was silent a moment, then gave a slow nod. "I fought beside this Gao of the Seneca."

Renno's heart leaped. This was the first person who had direct knowledge of his nephew. Renno wanted to pummel him with questions, but he forced himself to remain silent and wait for the man to continue.

"Yes, he was a brave warrior," Black Beaver went on. "At the very end, he stood at the Panther's side."

"I make this journey to learn where my nephew now stands or to bring home his body from where it lies," Renno said solemnly.

Black Beaver nodded. "I wish I could make your journey a shorter and happier one, but Gao is not among us. Nor will you find him among the warriors making the long march home. With my own eyes I saw him take two bullets from the rifles of the white soldiers."

The words struck Renno like a fist. He wanted to cry out that Black Beaver was wrong—that the manitous had made a promise, and they never lied. Instead he lowered his gaze and said in a voice that cracked with emotion, "I will seek his body on the field of battle."

"You will not find him there," Black Beaver told him, raising a cautioning hand. "He fell, but the Panther touched his wounds, and he stood to fight again. He was still fighting when the Panther dropped and the battle was lost."

"He is alive?" Renno pressed, momentarily forgetting proper etiquette.

"That I cannot tell you," Black Beaver replied, shaking his head. "And what I *can* tell you will bring little comfort, for I heard that your nephew was among those captured by the Americans."

"Then he may still be alive." Renno allowed himself the faintest of smiles.

"At the end of the battle, many of our men were captured. All but a small number were released to return to their homes. Gao was among those few taken by boat to their fort on the eastern bank of the Niagara."

"Fort Niagara," Renno said, his gaze shifting to the northeast.

"The Seneca warrior is strong and may have recovered from his wounds. Perhaps the Americans will release him, now that the war is done."

Renno knew that even though Tecumseh's followers had given up the fight, the battle still raged between the British and the Americans. It was entirely possible that Gao would languish in prison for the duration of the war. But he was alive—of that Renno was certain. And with the help of the manitous, he would set his nephew free.

"Thank you for your help," he told the Shawnee. "I must continue my journey now, to the American fort."

"My friend, there is one thing more," Black Beaver added as Renno started to turn away. "Your nephew had a Potawatomi wife."

"Mist-on-the-Water!" Renno exclaimed, having totally forgotten her in the excitement of learning about his nephew's fate.

"She is not among us," Black Beaver said, guessing the question in the other man's mind. "But the wife of my son is her friend and may know of her fate."

Turning, he called a name and gestured to a group of women standing nearby. One of them picked up her pack and came forward.

"This is Singing Bird," he said, motioning for the woman to put down her load and come closer. She complied and stood a few feet away, eyes lowered.

"Singing Bird," he said, turning to his daughter-in-law, "this traveler is the uncle of the Seneca named Gao. He seeks news of his nephew's wife."

She looked up at Renno with a mixture of curiosity and fear.

"You may tell us of your friend," Black Beaver instructed her.

"When the Americans released our warriors," she began in a soft, hesitant voice, addressing her father-in-law rather than Renno, "Mist-on-the-Water learned that Gao had been taken to the fort on the Niagara. I told her to wait for him at the lodge of his father, but she chose a different path."

"Tell us of this path," Black Beaver gently prodded.

She looked nervously between the two men, then announced, "She has gone to the Niagara to find her husband. I am afraid she travels alone."

Somehow the news did not surprise Renno, and he nodded and declared, "I, too, will go to the Niagara."

"You are two days' ride from Detroit but only one from Lake Erie," Black Beaver pointed out. "If you follow the southern bank of that lake, you will reach the Niagara sooner than if you travel through Detroit and across the Canadas."

"Your words have wisdom; I will heed your advice." Renno offered his hand, and the two men again gripped forearms. Smiling at the young woman named Singing Bird, he said to Black Beaver, "Please thank your son's wife for me."

Renno mounted up, angling northeast toward Lake Erie and Fort Niagara beyond. When he turned to give a final wave of farewell, Black Beaver and his people were taking up their burdens to continue their slow, steady march.

Hawk Harper climbed down from the saddle and took the veranda steps two at a time. Just as he reached for the front door it flew open, and his stepmother rushed into his arms.

"You're home!" she exclaimed, hugging and kissing him. "And Ta-na!" she added when her younger stepson came up the steps, and she embraced him, as well.

"Where's Michael?" Hawk asked, looking through the doorway into the dark interior of Huntington Castle.

"He's visiting his cousins in the village."

"And Father?" Ta-na put in.

"He . . . he isn't here," she replied hesitantly.

Hawk realized she was staring at the Creek woman, who remained seated on the back of the pony.

"Beth, this is Ma-ton-ga," he announced. "We found her in Talladega, and I was hoping she could stay with us for a while."

"But of course," Beth declared. She walked to the top of the steps and said to the Creek woman, "Welcome to Huntington Castle."

Coming up beside Beth, Hawk said a few words in Creek to Ma-ton-ga, who cocked her head slightly as she eyed the white woman. Grabbing hold of the pony's mane, she slid to the ground and stood with her hands folded across her chest.

"She doesn't speak much, I'm afraid," Hawk told his stepmother.

"That's quite all right," Beth said, directing the comment to the woman. "Lots of folks talk a lot but have nothing much worth saying."

"So, where is Father?" Hawk asked, looking around.

Beth opened her mouth to speak, and her lower lip started trembling. Pulling a handkerchief from her sleeve, she dabbed at her eyes. "I . . . I'm sorry," she stammered.

"What is it?" Ta-na asked, wrapping an arm around her shoulder and pulling her close. "Has something happened?"

"He rode off a week after you left."

"Rode off? Where?" Hawk pressed.

"He didn't quite say."

"But that's impossible. Renno would never leave without letting you know where he was going. He must have said *something*."

"He . . . he said where he was going, but he didn't know where it was," she mumbled, the tears coming freely now.

"Sit down," Ta-na urged, leading her back across the veranda.

She let herself be helped into one of the chairs, but when she tried to speak, the words got all jumbled, and she started to sob.

"It's all right, Beth," Hawk said soothingly, kneeling and taking her hands. "Just take it slow and start from the beginning."

Nodding, she took a deep breath and held it a moment. She exhaled, calmed somewhat, and managed to say, "I told him not to go alone. It was too soon. He was still recuperating."

"What did he say when he left?" Hawk asked.

She stared into his eyes a moment, then looked up at Ta-na-wun-da. "Your cousin," she whispered, her eyes welling again with tears. "He went to find your cousin."

"Gao?" Ta-na said in disbelief, and Beth lowered her eyes and nodded. "But he's probably in Canada somewhere. Is Renno going all the way there?"

She shrugged. "He said he had to bring Gao home. That's all he told me." She began to sob again. "I begged him not to go," she muttered, shaking her head. "I'm so worried about him."

"Don't worry, Beth," Hawk said taking her hand. "We'll bring him home." He looked up at his brother, who nodded. "We'll bring both of them home."

Later that day, Hawk Harper stood beside his son while Michael aimed his rifle at an old, rotting log that Hawk had thrown out into the water. It was the very same lake where Michael and his grandfather had shot the goose. During their ride, Hawk had explained that he would be leaving at dawn to find Renno and that their hunting trip would have to wait until he returned. Michael had taken the news well and was not even particularly disturbed to discover that the geese were no longer in residence. He seemed content to just be firing the gun, taking particular delight when one of his shots smacked into the hollow wood.

Michael held his breath and squeezed the trigger. The gun fired with a bit more force than usual, almost knocking him off his feet. He looked up in surprise at his father, who was trying not to chuckle.

"I think you poured a bit too much powder down the barrel," Hawk explained. "Try a mite less this time."

As the boy measured out the charge, he nodded to his right and said, "That's where I shot at the goose."

"From those bushes?"

Michael nodded. "Grandpa wasn't so lucky."

"Yes. He missed his shot, didn't he?" Hawk already knew the truth from Beth but did a good job of maintaining the ruse.

"I'm not supposed to say."

"Grandpa told you it was a secret?"

"Well . . . I told him I wouldn't tell." Michael slid out the ramrod, turned it around, and pushed the ball down the grooved barrel. "He was pretty sad."

"A hunter can't expect to make every shot."

" 'Specially when he's sick."

"Yes. That gunshot wound probably still hurt a lot. It would throw off even the best hunter."

Michael replaced the ramrod and looked up at his father, shielding his eyes from the sun. "That wasn't it. He just sort of got sick. Over there." He pointed toward a spot near the edge of the lake.

"What do you mean?" Hawk knelt and touched his son's forearm. "How did he get sick?"

"I swam back with the goose. Then he started looking real funny, and he fell down. I was kinda scared."

"Was he in pain?"

"I don't think so," Michael said with a shrug.

"Did he say anything?"

"He was talking a lot."

"What did he tell you?"

"He wasn't talking to me." Michael fidgeted. "It was . . . sort of like a. . . ." Frowning, he looked down.

"It's all right, Michael," Hawk reassured the boy. "Renno wouldn't mind you talking about it with your own father. What was it like?"

"A dream," he replied, almost beneath his breath.

Hawk lifted the boy's chin until their eyes met. "What kind of dream?"

Again Michael shrugged. "I was a little scared. It sounded like he was talking to someone, but nobody was there."

"What exactly did he say, Michael?"

"He was calling Uncle El-i-chi. And talking about that lake he's always telling us about, where he and Uncle El-i-chi used to swim when they were boys."

"The lake of the Seneca?"

"Yes, that's it." Michael's face brightened. "He said he would go to the lake of the Seneca."

"Grandpa said that? Are you certain?"

Michael nodded.

"Did he say anything else?"

"That was all. Then he woke up and felt better."

Hawk Harper thought a moment, then stood and gripped his son's shoulder. "Take one more shot, son. Then we have to ride home."

Michael took careful aim and fired, the bullet thumping into the log and setting it rolling in place in the water. He negotiated for one final shot, and then they headed over to where Hawk's horse was tethered.

"Father?" Michael asked as Hawk cinched the saddle and untied the reins.

"Yes?"

"Uncle El-i-chi isn't coming home again, is he?"

Hawk stopped what he was doing and turned to his son. "No, Michael. Your uncle will not be coming back."

"But if he's in heaven, how come we can hear him?"

"Maybe Grandpa didn't hear him. Maybe it was only a dream, like you said."

"No, they were talking to each other," Michael stated emphatically. "I heard."

"What you heard was Grandpa Renno. Sometimes when someone is dreaming, they—"

"No. I heard *them* talking."

"You heard *them*?" Hawk said incredulously. "*Both* of them?"

Michael hesitated, then nodded weakly. "I . . . I didn't tell Grandpa. I thought he might get mad."

Hawk reached down and lifted the boy into his arms. Cupping his chin, he said, "No one would ever get mad about something like that. You weren't sneaking around, were you?"

Michael shook his head.

"Then you did nothing wrong. But you need to tell me what Uncle El-i-chi was saying."

"He was real quiet. Like he was whispering."

"And what was he whispering?"

"Something about you and Uncle Ta-na coming home. And something about Cousin Gao."

"Gao?" Hawk asked, his eyes widening.

"I think he was telling Grandpa to go find Cousin Gao at that lake."

"The lake of the Seneca?"

"Yes. He wanted Grandpa to bring him home." Michael paused. "That's all I heard."

Nodding, Hawk gave his son a quick hug and lifted him into the saddle.

"Father?" Michael asked, looking back at him. "Will Grandpa Renno be mad at me?"

"No, Michael, he won't," he assured him. "In fact, he is going to be very, very happy. For right now, though, Beth has promised us a big supper, so let's get back to Huntington Castle."

Climbing up behind his son, he kicked the horse into a trot, and they headed up the hill toward home.

Chapter Seventeen

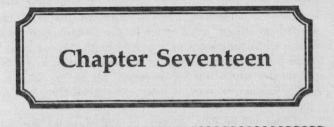

Hawk Harper stalked out of his late uncle El-i-chi's cabin in Rusog's Town, shaking his head in frustration. Ta-na-wun-da was standing nearby, speaking with El-i-chi's widow, and when he saw his brother's expression, he whispered something to her and went over to see what the problem was.

"My Creek cannot be *that* bad," Hawk declared, throwing up his hands in defeat.

"She understands you," Ta-na said. "Let us go now."

"Ta-na, your Creek is much better. Can you tell her? Try to explain why she cannot come."

Ta-na eyed his brother, clearly far from pleased at the prospect, but he let out a sigh and nodded. "I will speak with her. But she already understands." He started into the cabin.

"Tell her we have to travel quickly—a woman would slow us down."

"I know what to say," Ta-na called over his shoulder.

"And a Creek might not be too welcome where we

are headed," he added, but Ta-na-wun-da had already disappeared inside, shutting the door behind him.

Hawk stared at the closed door, thinking how stubborn Ma-ton-ga could be. She rarely spoke and pretended not to understand what they were saying—when it suited her. But if she was in need of something, she had no problem making her wishes known. Just now she wanted not to be left behind in the Cherokee-Seneca village while they went in search of Renno. Hawk really could not blame her, since he and Ta-na were the only people she knew. But he also could not be expected to take a woman on such a long and potentially perilous journey.

"She will be fine," a voice behind him said, and he turned to see Ah-wa-o standing there. The death of her husband had aged her, and the added worry about Gao's fate was not easing her burden. Yet she forced a smile as she laid a gentle hand on his arm.

"I know she will. But I feel responsible. I didn't even ask if she wanted to come here with us."

"And what would have happened had you not brought her?" Ah-wa-o asked.

Her nephew shrugged.

"Didn't you say there is only death in the Creek lands right now? When this war is over, she can return if she chooses. For now, you are her protector, which is why she does not want you to leave without her."

"You are certain you don't mind her staying with you? Beth offered to let her stay there, but—"

"Ma-ton-ga will be more at home among the people of Rusog's Town than in that big house." She gestured in the direction of Huntington Castle. "And I am happy to help you, just as you and your father are helping my son."

Hawk leaned close and touched his cheek to hers. "We are going to find Gao," he assured her.

She pulled away slightly, revealing tears in her eyes.

"Search for your father. When you find Renno, you will find my son. Of this I am certain."

The cabin door opened, and Ta-na-wun-da emerged. He nodded at Hawk, indicating he had succeeded in his task. Hawk caught a glimpse of Ma-ton-ga watching him through the window. She looked scared and hurt—much the way Michael had looked a short while ago when the brothers rode away from Huntington Castle. He tried not to dwell on it. As he followed Ta-na-wun-da to where their horses were standing, he told himself that he had no other choice.

Hawk hoisted himself into the saddle and gave Ah-wa-o and Ma-ton-ga a farewell wave. Then he and Ta-na wheeled their horses and rode hard northward.

Gao lay on the floor of the cell, his hands shackled in front of him, his eyes swollen almost shut, his shoulder oozing a fetid-smelling pus. He had not seen Charles Stringfellow in several days and wondered if the colonel had grown tired of his sport. But Stringfellow was not one to acknowledge defeat so easily. Most likely he was waiting for Gao to recover his strength a bit. That way Gao would not pass out during the next interrogation, as he had done during the previous one.

In the interim, Stringfellow was keeping himself busy with the other prisoners. Gao could hear the grunts and moans whenever one of them was dragged to the interrogation room down the hall, and his heart swelled with pride to know that none of them had given the colonel the satisfaction of hearing them scream or beg for mercy.

With each day that passed, Gao knew death grew ever closer. Surely by now the colonel was convinced the Indians would never talk, and soon he would end the matter by having the lot of them shot. The only hope Gao still allowed himself was that he would first have the opportunity to put Charles Stringfellow in his grave.

Gao heard a key turn in the padlock of the cell door,

and he rolled onto his right side, his back to the doorway, and pretended to sleep. The massive iron-reinforced door swung open, and two people entered the room. Gao recognized the shuffling gait of one as belonging to a particularly sadistic corporal. When the footfalls stopped near his head, he knew he was about to be struck. In fact, it was this same guard's black boot that had closed up Gao's eyes.

The young Seneca relaxed his body and awaited the blow. Instead, the heel of the boot touched his raised left cheek and began to press downward, softly at first and then with increasing strength.

"Leave him be, Lemuels," the other man said.

Gao was fairly certain the voice was that of a private named Marris, who treated the prisoners with a bit more respect than the other guards.

"Don't worry. I ain't gonna hurt him." Lemuels gave a final, vicious twist of the boot, then withdrew his foot. "Don't need to. He's hurtin' bad enough."

"Come on," Marris said. "Tell him, and let's get out of here."

The sadistic guard stepped around Gao's prone body and knelt in front of his face. Grabbing his hair, Lemuels lifted his head slightly and hissed, "I been told there's someone sniffin' around the fort, lookin' for you. A squaw girl, and a real good looker, from what I hear. Says she followed you all the way here from the Thames."

Gao's heart raced, and he opened his eyes as wide as the swelling would allow.

"I knew you was awake," Lemuels said with a cruel grin. "Is this squaw your sister or somethin'?"

"It's his wife," his partner put in.

"I know that," Lemuels snapped. "But that don't mean she ain't his sister. You know how these Injuns are." Again he grinned at Gao, revealing tobacco-stained teeth. "Ain't that so, red man?" He let go of Gao's hair.

"Come on," Marris said uncomfortably.

"You wanna see her?" Lemuels asked the prisoner. "What's her name? Mist-somethin'?"

"Mist-on-the-Water," Marris put in.

"That's it. They tell me she's a real pretty one, though I ain't yet had the pleasure of her acquaintance."

Gao struggled to sit up. Staring directly at Corporal Lemuels, he said in a low but firm voice, "Where is my wife?"

"Oh, so you're interested, are you?" Lemuels turned and poked Marris in the arm. "Wants to see his wife. So do I. Don't you, too, Marris?"

"Come on," Marris urged, turning toward the door. "You told him about his wife. Now, let's get out of here."

Lemuels chuckled. "That's right," he said to Gao. "She's lookin', but she ain't gonna find you. Not unless you give the colonel what he wants. Meanwhile, I plan to take a bit of what *I* want. A bit of what that squaw's got t'give."

"You bastard!" Gao screamed, launching himself at the corporal. He slammed full force into Lemuels, knocking him back against the wall. Clenching his shackled hands together, he brought them down on the guard's temple, knocking him to his knees, stunned.

Private Marris was on Gao in an instant, yanking him away from Lemuels. But Gao managed to grasp Marris by his jacket lapels and throw him across the cell.

Seeing that Lemuels was struggling to his feet, Gao lashed out with his callused bare foot, catching him on the jaw and knocking him back down again. Marris grabbed hold of his arm, but he jerked free and leaped over Lemuels and through the open doorway. Turning to the left, he came to a shuddering halt. A pair of guards stood a few feet away, their pistols leveled at him. He spun around and saw a third guard come dashing out of the interrogation room, his rifle at the ready.

"Son of a bitch!" Lemuels roared as he came bursting through the doorway. He reached Gao in three short strides and threw a right cross to the jaw before Gao could even raise a hand to defend himself. A second blow knocked him to the floor, and then two of the guards grabbed his ankles and dragged him back into the cell. The last thing he saw was Lemuels standing over him, grinning viciously as he slammed his heel down on Gao's face.

Hawk Harper and Ta-na-wun-da set a quick, steady pace north beyond the Cherokee lands and across Tennessee. They traveled light, catching what sleep they could beneath the stars. Both wore buckskins and a heavy wool outer jacket, and Ta-na was even using a lightweight saddle, having decided it would be prudent to look and act like a white as much as possible.

Toward the end of the third full day of travel, they reached a region of central Kentucky known as the Barrens. It had once been a place of great forests, but over the centuries the Indians had burned off the trees to provide grazing land for the vast herds of buffalo that had roamed east of the Mississippi River. Now the region was almost devoid of trees and well fit its name.

They rode down a dusty hillside and saw a pair of riders about fifty yards away across a dry streambed. Apparently a small pool was hidden among the rocks, for the horses had their heads down as if drinking. Turning in their direction, Hawk and Ta-na rode toward them, raising their hands in greeting.

Hawk eyed the two strangers as he neared them. Though nothing specific about their looks signaled caution, he kept his hand near the pistol at his belt. The more heavyset of the pair was probably in his late forties and had a scruffy salt-and-pepper beard. His clothing was trail worn and in need of needle and thread, but his flat-crowned hat might have just come from a hatmaker's. His brown-haired companion was about Hawk's age and wore a rather sporty wool suit that seemed more appropriate for a store clerk than someone in the wilds of the Barrens.

"Mind if our horses take a drink?" Hawk asked, indicating the pool of rainwater.

"Suit yourself." The older one motioned for them to proceed.

"My name's Hawk Harper," he introduced himself as his gelding dipped its head toward the water. Beside him, Ta-na-wun-da also brought his horse over to drink.

"Who's your friend?" the man asked, eyeing Ta-na warily.

"Ta-na-wun-da," Hawk replied.

"Where's he from?"

"Rusog's Town."

"That's down Tennessee way, ain't it?" the younger man put in. His companion shot him an annoyed glance.

"It's in the Cherokee lands," Hawk explained.

"Where you headed?" the first man asked.

"Just passing through, Mr. . . .?"

"Name's Conners. This here is Purdy Smith."

"Pleased to make your acquaintance," Hawk said, nodding to each.

Conners gave a low grunt in reply as he continued to eye Ta-na suspiciously.

"You fellows from around these parts?" Hawk asked by way of conversation.

"No," the one named Purdy said. "A group of us come over from—"

"Shut up!" the bigger man hissed, then turned to Hawk. "Don't matter where we're from. We're just passing through, like you."

"I only asked because we're headed northeast, and if you've come from up there, you might know what the weather's been like."

"Downright warm. Almost December, and still there ain't been no snow to speak of."

"It's probably waiting for us to get there," Hawk said with a mock frown.

Conners glanced over at the small packs tied to the

backs of their saddles. "You boys 'pear to be traveling light. You sure you're ready for winter?"

"We'll manage."

"I suppose you can buy what you need—if you got enough gold, that is." His left eye narrowed slightly.

"You travel with less than we do," Ta-na-wun-da pointed out, gesturing at their empty saddlebags.

"So, you can speak, can you?" Conners said, his tone condescending. "Well, the boy and me do all right by ourselves. Don't we, Purdy?" He turned to his young partner and grinned.

"Sure do."

Hawk's horse finished drinking, and he pulled the reins, moving the animal back a few steps. "We'll be moving on now," he said. "Good day to you both."

"How about you, Indian?" Purdy asked. "Ain't you gonna wish us a good day?"

Ta-na stared at the man a long moment, then turned his horse and started away. He could hear the white man chuckling behind him.

As the brothers rode off, they glanced back several times to confirm that the two strangers were still at the pool.

"Friendly folks," Ta-na commented when they were out of earshot.

"Think they're highwaymen?"

"If so, they weren't doing their job, just letting us ride off like that."

"Maybe not," Hawk agreed. "Or maybe they saw my hand resting near the butt of this pistol."

"Nervous?" Ta-na teased.

"No. Prudent."

"Me, too. I even managed to cock mine."

"I guess we're just too fierce for them," Hawk joked. "Either that or our bags look like poor pickings."

"You mean yours isn't full of gold, like mine?"

"Hell, little brother, if that were true, I'd rob you myself."

* * *

An hour later, they made camp in one of the few copses they had seen in the entire Barrens. The grove consisted of little more than a few dozen stunted beeches scattered among thickets and some boulders, but at least the trees provided a ready source of firewood and the rocks and underbrush served as a windbreak from the night breeze. After tending to their horses, they built a fire and had some dried meat and biscuits. They then laid out their bedrolls, planning to sleep a few hours and hit the trail again as soon as the moon rose.

Their preparations were interrupted by the sound of horses at least half a dozen, riding hard from the south. Ta-na-wun-da quickly smothered the fire, and they grabbed their rifles and checked their charges as they took positions behind some boulders and underbrush. The sun had dipped below the horizon, but there was enough light to make out the riders. Hawk counted six horses but seven men, two of them doubled up on a chestnut mare. They called to one another as they approached and spread out around the trees.

"I see their horses!" one exclaimed, and Hawk recognized the voice of Purdy Smith.

"Hello!" shouted another—the heavyset man with the salt-and-pepper beard.

Hawk knew there was no point in pretending not to be there. He glanced over at Ta-na, who nodded.

"What do you want, Conners?" Hawk called out.

"These are the rest of my friends. Turns out they was lagging a bit because one of their horses had to be put down. That's when Purdy and me remembered that fine pinto and gray you boys are riding." He shifted on the saddle, his gaze taking in the grove, gauging where the two of them might be hiding. "It's like this," he went on, walking his horse a few steps closer. "We was wondering if you fellows'd care to make a trade."

"What kind of trade?" Hawk asked, raising the rifle barrel slightly in anticipation of the answer.

"Your horses for your lives."

In reply, Hawk and Ta-na cocked their weapons, which clinked loudly.

"Now, boys, it don't gotta be that way. We've no quarrel with you, but we need them horses."

"The only thing you'll get is a chestful of lead if you don't turn that horse around and ride off," Hawk warned.

"That may be, but while you pull that trigger, the whole lot of us'll be rushing them trees. I don't think that Injun friend of yours can handle six at once."

As if on command, the other six men cocked their own weapons. Conners alone still had not drawn his gun.

"Take a few seconds to make up your minds. Then send them horses on out, and we'll be on our way. If not, we're coming in after them—and you."

The riders continued to spread out. When they had completely surrounded the copse, they halted and sat their mounts, the silence broken only by the occasional whinny or stamping of a horse.

Hawk and Ta-na used hand signs to coordinate their plans. Hawk had a rifle and his brace of pistols. Unfortunately only the rifle was loaded, and he began loading the pistols as quietly as possible. Ta-na, meanwhile, had his rifle and a tomahawk. Another pistol was in his saddlebag, and he signed that he would retrieve it and take up a position on the far side of the trees.

"You boys come to your senses?" Conners asked.

Hawk did not reply. Tucking his pistols beneath his belt, he shouldered his rifle again and poked the barrel through the underbrush, training it on the bearded man.

With a shout, Conners dropped low on the back of his horse and spurred it forward. Several shots rang out at once, Hawk's among them. It went high and missed as Conners wheeled his horse to the side and headed for a point off to Hawk's left.

Jumping up, Hawk slipped back through the trees, seeking a new position. He caught sight of a rider entering the copse and ran toward him, pistol raised. The man

saw him coming and swung his rifle around, but Hawk
got off his shot first, the blast knocking the man from his
saddle. Before his horse could run off, Hawk caught hold
of the reins, calmed down the animal, and leaped into the
saddle.

Being on the outlaw's horse enabled Hawk to ride
right up to another of the ambushers, who had dismounted and was just entering the trees on foot. By the
time the man realized the rider was not a friend, Hawk
had fired his second pistol, the slug catching the man in
the neck. He staggered a few feet, blood spurting from
the wound, then fell to the ground.

Dropping from the saddle, Hawk was hurriedly
pouring powder down the barrel of his pistol when a
keening Indian war cry split the air. For a moment he
thought it was his brother, but the sound came from opposite where Ta-na had gone. Spinning in its direction,
he discovered Conners on his horse only twenty feet
away, raising his pistol to fire.

Hawk heard a distinct *whoosh*, and something thudded into the outlaw's back. Conners was thrown forward
against the animal's neck, his pistol dropping from nerveless fingers. He tried to turn around to see what had
struck him but tumbled off the saddle. He landed
facedown in the dirt, the fletched shaft of an arrow protruding from his back.

Conners's horse bolted away, and Hawk saw another
horse and rider in the distance, just beyond the trees. He
caught only a glimpse as the person rode off around the
copse—enough to determine that it was not Ta-na-
wun-da but another Indian in traditional garb, wielding a
bow and shield.

Hawk snatched up the loaded pistol Conners had
dropped and ran back through the trees to where their
horses were tied. Shots were still ringing out, so at least
some of the remaining four outlaws were alive. One, in
fact, had sneaked through the grove on foot and was in
the process of untying the pinto and the gray.

Hawk was approaching the man when an arrow whistled through the trees and caught the outlaw in the chest. He staggered backward a few feet, and a second arrow struck him in the side, knocking him off his feet.

Hawk looked around for another ambusher to take on, then realized the guns had fallen silent. He cautiously proceeded through the trees to the opposite side of the copse, where the shadowed figure of a man, tomahawk in hand, was standing over a body. He called his brother's name, and Ta-na-wun-da turned toward him and raised an arm to indicate he was all right.

Hawk sprinted over to his brother. Ta-na reported that he had killed two of the outlaws. Hawk had done likewise, with the remaining three being dispatched by the Indian who had come upon the scene.

Calling out a greeting first in English, then in Seneca, Hawk and Ta-na stepped from the trees into the gathering darkness of the Barrens. Twenty yards away, the Indian sat bareback on a bay pony, bow in one hand, war shield in the other. Using knees to control the animal, the Indian approached at a walk and stopped only a few feet away. It was too dark to clearly discern features, and it took the brothers a moment to recognize the person who had come to their assistance.

"What are you doing here?" Hawk blurted, running up to the pony. "Why aren't you back at the village?"

Lowering the tip of the bow until it pointed at Hawk, the Indian said in halting English, "Ma-ton-ga follow Hawk and Swift Waters. Ma-ton-ga not be left behind."

Ta-na-wun-da stepped beside his brother and said in Creek to the young woman, "You followed us all this way?"

She nodded.

"And those?" he asked, pointing at the bow and shield. "They belong to my uncle, the sachem El-i-chi. You took them?"

"I did not steal them," she replied in her language,

looking back and forth between the brothers. "When Ah-wa-o knew I would not remain there, she give them to me for my journey."

"She knows you are here?" Hawk put in, also in Creek.

"Ah-wa-o is a good woman," Ma-ton-ga told him. The hint of a smile played upon her lips as she added, "Even if she is Seneca."

"And you shoot a bow well—for a Creek."

"I can track without being seen," she added. "You will let me come with you." It was more a statement than a request.

Hawk saw the determination in her eyes. He knew if he tried to send her away she would simply continue to follow—as she had shown herself quite capable of doing. It was obvious she would not slow them down, and there was no denying she had already proven herself useful.

Turning to his brother, Hawk said in English, "What do you think?"

"I think we had better do something about those bodies and then get some sleep. We have a long trail ahead of us."

"Come," Hawk told the woman, gesturing for her to follow.

Ma-ton-ga slid off the pony and led it in among the trees.

Chapter Eighteen

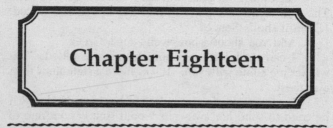

Mist-on-the-Water stood at the back gate of Fort Niagara, waiting in the cold drizzle for someone to take notice of her. She had come there several times during the past week, each time turned away without any word of her husband. She was certain he was still alive and in their custody, for she could read it in the eyes of the various soldiers who sent her away. And each time she would come back hoping to plead her case to someone new—to someone who would take pity and help her out. She was certain such a man could be found if she was tenacious enough.

Mist-on-the-Water well understood the white world. She herself was half white, her father being a French trapper who had married the sister of the Potawatomi chief, Main Poche. But her mother had succumbed to the white man's disease—whiskey—and eventually her father sold them to an abusive army sergeant at Fort Sackville on the Wabash River. She had spent four years at that fort, until she fell in love with Gao and he had taken her away.

Yes, she understood the ways of the whites. And she

wondered how high a price they would expect her to pay for her husband's release. That she would pay it she did not for an instant doubt.

The first glimmer of hope came that rainy morning when the small door in the larger double gate was opened and she saw the uniform of the man who opened it. He was an officer—a captain, no less. Until then she had spoken with no one higher than a sergeant, and she knew they would not be able to deliver on any promise made. A captain, however, was a different matter entirely.

"My name is Mist-on-the-Water, and I have come for my husband," she said in French-accented English.

"You have, have you?" the officer asked. He held the door open only a crack and peered out at her from under a slouch hat pulled low to protect his face from the rain. "And who might your husband be?"

"His name is Gao, and he is of the Seneca. He was made your prisoner after the Battle of the Thames."

The captain looked her up and down, but she was unable to read his expression. He had a pleasant enough face, despite the trim brown beard and much longer mustache. She hoped that whatever price he demanded, he would at least treat her fairly.

"Yes, I know of a prisoner named Gao," he told her.

She felt her heart race.

"And I know of you." He pulled the door open wider and stepped out. "You have been here before."

"Many times."

"Why do you keep coming back?"

"To take my husband home to his people."

"His people have no home. They have been scattered to the winds."

"His father's people live in the Cherokee lands to the south. That is where I will take him."

"He is a prisoner of war. What makes you think we would release him?"

"He will fight against you no more."

The captain grinned. "From what I hear, he's fighting us even now."

"Then he is all right?" she said eagerly.

"He's alive, if that's what you mean. But he was shot up pretty bad when we found him."

She boldly reached forward and placed a hand on the captain's jacket sleeve. "He is of no further use to you. Let him return to his family."

The officer looked down at her hand. She let it linger a moment longer, then withdrew it.

"So, you want me to simply open the door of his cell and let him go. And why should I do that?"

"Because a woman asks you to show mercy." She lowered her eyes.

"Do you understand the risk I would be taking?"

"But you are an officer. Can you not grant pardon to a prisoner of war?"

"Well, yes, I suppose I could. But I would have to get approval. It would take some maneuvering."

"Then you will do this for me?" she asked, her eyes widening with hope as she stared up at him.

"That all depends on what this prisoner's wife is willing to do for me."

"And what would you have me do?" she asked, resigned to the answer.

The soldier's high-pitched moaning sounded to Mist-on-the-Water like a frightened animal caught in one of her father's traps. He had only just entered her, and already his body was beginning to stiffen and jerk as he released himself within her. While leading her over to the supply shed, he had told her he had not been with a woman in seven moons—and he clearly had not lied. In fact, he had been in such a hurry to correct the situation that he had done little more than open his pants and lift up her buckskin skirt. She was especially grateful he had not tried to kiss her, for she cringed whenever his beard touched her face.

Mist-on-the-Water stared up at the ceiling of the shed, counting the rough-hewn planks as she waited for him to finish. With one final lunge, he let out a groan and collapsed on top of her. She lay there without moving, feeling his chest heave and smelling the tobacco on his skin, wondering if he had a wife somewhere and if she would be willing to make such a sacrifice for him, praying that he would honor the promise he had made.

At last the captain lifted himself off her and stood. Mist-on-the-Water quickly pulled down her skirt and got up, picking her robe up off the floor and wrapping it around her. She noticed his nervous gestures as he closed his pants, and she sensed that with his manhood having softened, his resolve had lost its firmness as well.

"I'll see what I can do for your husband," he muttered, tucking his shirt into his waistband and putting on his jacket. He focused beyond her, unwilling to look her in the eyes.

"You said you would release my husband," she said, taking hold of his arm.

"It isn't that simple." He pulled his arm free. "I have to write up an order of release and get it approved by the commandant. And then—"

"But you said—"

"I know what I said," he snapped. "I meant it, too. But I can't just march over there and walk out with your husband."

He pushed past her to the shed door and reached for the doorknob. Then he turned and stared at her for a long moment, as if weighing a decision.

"Can you return this afternoon?" he finally asked. "I can make arrangements by then."

She hesitated, trying to read his expression. He was not entirely sincere, she was certain, yet she sensed he was not simply trying to get rid of her.

"I will return," she told him.

"Come back an hour before sunset." He pulled open

the door. "Now, get going. And don't tell anyone about. . . ." He gestured toward where they had lain.

She followed him back to the gate. It was not until she heard it close behind her that she allowed herself to cry.

The sun had dipped almost to the horizon, and Mist-on-the-Water began to think the captain would not appear at the gate. When at last he did, she felt a flood of relief—as well as the desperate fear that he intended to have her a second time and send her away empty-handed again.

That will not happen, she told herself. This time she was prepared. She would leave with her husband, or the captain would never have another woman.

It came as no surprise when he led her into the fort and back along the wall to the same shed they had used that morning. When he closed the door behind her and started to take off his jacket, she backed away from him and stood shaking her head.

"I told you, it's quite a favor you're asking," he said, approaching her. "You've got to show me some favors in return."

"I have come for my husband."

"And you will leave with him," the captain declared.

"Today?" she pressed.

"This very night." He had his jacket in his hands, and he reached into a pocket for a folded and sealed piece of paper. "It's an order of release, signed by the commandant," he explained, holding it out to her.

She took a cautious step forward and reached for the document, but he snatched it away.

"You'll get it just as soon as we finish our own little business." He stuffed the paper back into the pocket and dropped the jacket on the floor.

With a sigh of resignation, Mist-on-the-Water removed her robe and spread it on the dusty floor. Lying on top of it, she once again fixed her gaze on the planks overhead and hiked up her buckskin skirt.

This time the captain took somewhat more time in concluding his efforts. Mist-on-the-Water put up with his crude attentions in silence, focusing her attention on her future with Gao. She prayed only that this man's seed would not take root within her and that her husband would forgive her for what she was doing.

The officer finally finished, and Mist-on-the-Water straightened her clothing, brushed off her robe, and wrapped it back around her. She waited as patiently as possible while he dressed himself, then said, "You will bring me my husband now."

He chuckled. "I can't do that."

"But you promised." Her hands clenched into fists, anger flaring in her eyes.

"Hold on," he said, raising an appeasing hand. "You'll get what's coming to you. But I can't march over there and bring him back." He reached into his pocket and produced the document. "It took me quite a bit of work to get this, and I don't want it known who gave it to you. All you gotta do is take it to the guardhouse and present it to the soldiers on duty. They'll know what to do."

He held the document forth. She reached for it, hesitated, then snatched it from his hand.

"Just don't break those seals," he said, indicating the double wax seal on the back. "If you do, it won't be official anymore, and they may not release him."

"I must take this to the guardhouse?" she asked uncertainly.

"Don't worry. You won't raise an eyebrow. Indian squaws come and go around here; some of our fellows even take them for wives." He opened the door. "I'll show you where it is."

She followed him across the compound. A number of soldiers were milling about, and other than an occasional glance, they paid little attention to her. Those who were close enough saluted the captain, then went back about their business.

The guardhouse was a freestanding wood structure at the rear of the parade ground, not far from the gate where she had entered. As they neared the building, the captain halted and said, "He's in there with the others. Just show them that paper, and they'll take care of you."

She was about to speak, but he turned and walked away. She stood there a moment, staring at the guardhouse, looking around at the soldiers in the parade ground. Realizing she had better act before suspicions were aroused, she headed over to the door and knocked.

A moment later the door creaked open, and a burly black-haired private stuck his head out. "What the hell d'you want?" he demanded.

In reply, she held forth the document. Taking it, he broke the seals and unfolded it. He squinted, trying to read in the fading light of dusk.

"Just a minute," he mumbled.

He closed the door, and she heard him walking down the hall. A minute later he returned and gestured for her to enter.

"This way," he said, shutting the door behind her.

She looked down the corridor and saw what appeared to be cell doors lining either side. He led her only as far as the first door on the right. It was open, and he ushered her inside. She found herself in an office, with a corporal on duty behind the desk. In front of him was the paper given her by the captain.

"She the one?" the corporal asked.

The other soldier nodded.

"So, you came for your husband," the corporal said to her. "Well, let's take you to him." Rising, he picked up a set of keys and came around the desk.

He led the way to the first cell on the left. Unlocking the padlock, he opened the door and gestured for her to enter. She stepped to the doorway and peered inside. The cell was empty.

She started to turn around, but the soldiers pushed her into the room and followed her. The corporal was still holding the padlock with the keys dangling from it, and he closed the cell door and hung the lock from one of the bars on the small viewing window. Then he turned to her, a smug leer on his face.

"Where is my husband?" she demanded.

"You didn't really think we'd let him go, did you?"

"But I brought you a release."

His laugh was short and crude. "I sure as hell know what you brung us. Ain't that right, Parker?"

"That it is, Lemuels."

"And I sure as hell know what we're gonna give you—and it ain't your husband."

Taking two quick strides to her, Lemuels jerked the robe off her shoulders. The private circled behind and grabbed hold of her arms. She did not resist. Indeed, she had been expecting such an action. And she knew from the look in the corporal's eyes that even if she submitted to them as she had the captain, they had no intention of letting her husband go. If Gao was to be released, she would have to do it herself.

The young Potawatomi woman remained as calm as possible, giving them no reason to strike her. When the private pulled down on her arms, she allowed herself to be forced to the floor. She even helped by spreading her legs and, as the private relaxed his grip, reaching down to raise her skirt. As she did so, she slipped her other hand beneath her, to the small of her back, and then under the waist of her skirt. Her fingers closed around a knife handle, and she slowly drew the weapon out of its sheath.

"That's more like it," Lemuels said when he saw how compliant—even eager—she had become. He had already uncinched his pants, and he pulled them down and dropped to his knees in front of her.

"Leave some for me," the private told him, undoing his belt.

Lemuels did not see her hand move from behind

her back as he brought himself down on top of her. He thrust forward and let out a gasping groan as the blade slid into his chest just below the rib cage. She angled it upward, and as the knife tore through his heart, his eyes widened in surprise. His body jerked several times; then his eyes closed, and he lay still.

"Damn, that was fast," the private muttered, holding his pants around his waist to keep them from falling as he waited for Lemuels to get up. "Come on, Corporal. It's my turn."

Mist-on-the-Water pushed Lemuels off her. She was still gripping the knife, and the blade slid from his chest as he rolled over onto his back. They were both covered with the blood oozing from the corporal's chest.

It took a moment for the scene to register on the private. With a curse, he whirled around and leaped at the door. But he stumbled and fell when his pants dropped around his knees. Pulling himself up, he groped for the door handle, fumbling as he tried to yank it open.

Swiftly and silently, Mist-on-the-Water jumped to her feet and pounced on the private, stabbing him in the neck and back. He clawed at the door, sliding down it to the floor, where he sat in a spreading pool of blood, trying to scream, to cry out. All that came out was a gurgling death rattle as he fell onto his side and lay still.

Mist-on-the-Water wiped the knife blade and tucked it in the sheath at her waist, then retrieved her robe and wrapped it around her bloody clothing. Dragging the private out of the way, she removed the keys from the padlock, opened the door, and started down the corridor. One by one, she unlocked the cell doors and swung them open, calling in to the stunned prisoners to gather down at the end of the hall and wait for her.

In the last cell on the right, she saw a young warrior —the only one shackled around the wrists. She did not recognize him at first, so bruised and swollen were his features. But then he called her name, and she raced over and threw her arms around him. They stood there, gazing joyously into each other's eyes. Remembering the shackles, she quickly fumbled through the keys until she found one that worked. The irons clattered to the floor, and at last he could take her in his arms.

"What happened?" he asked. "How did you get here?"

"Later," she told him. "Right now we must get away from this place."

As they headed down the hall, Gao glanced into the first cell and saw the bodies of the two guards. He looked back at Mist-on-the-Water, and she saw the respect in his eyes for what she had done.

At the end of the hall, they entered the office and found the other prisoners distributing the few weapons on hand—three rifles and four pistols, along with a supply of powder and shot. One of them saw the couple standing in the doorway, and he came forward to present Gao with a rifle. Another man offered Mist-on-the-Water one of the pistols, but she shook her head and clasped her hand around the knife at her waist.

Quickly they made plans. With no exits other than the front door, and the only windows small barred ones, they all would have to make their break out the front, where there was a good chance of being seen by the soldiers. Despite Gao's misgivings, it was agreed that Mist-on-the-Water would go out first and see if the way was clear. Then they would slip out and make a run for the rear gate and the woods beyond.

As they filed from the office, Mist-on-the-Water walked over to the desk and retrieved the paper given her by the captain, in case Gao someday needed to prove he had been released from custody. Then she joined the others in the corridor.

Opening the front door, Mist-on-the-Water headed outside and looked across the parade ground. A few soldiers stood on the far side, smoking and talking among themselves. They were far enough away and might not cause any trouble. One soldier, however, was standing guard in front of a neighboring building, which appeared to be a headquarters of some sort.

The door behind her open a crack, she described the setting to the men inside. Then she walked boldly across the way to where the guard was standing.

"I am looking for a captain," she said to the soldier, who seemed more surprised at her command of English than at seeing an Indian woman in the fort compound. While speaking, she shifted position so that his back was to the guardhouse.

The soldier asked her the captain's name, and she said she did not know it, but she could describe him. She did so while gazing over his shoulder, and she saw the guardhouse door ease open and her husband emerge, rifle in hand. Behind him, the ten other prisoners slipped out into the parade ground. Turning to their right, they started back alongside the building, seeking the darker shadows of the perimeter wall beyond.

Mist-on-the-Water had no trouble keeping the guard engaged in conversation. But just when she thought the others would succeed in getting away, a soldier shouted an alarm and a rifle fired in warning. A moment later, other guns joined the action.

The guard turned to see what the commotion was about and caught a glimpse of the fleeing Indians. He started to raise his rifle, but Mist-on-the-Water moved up behind him and drove her blade into the small of his back. As he fell, she snatched up his rifle, then raced after her husband.

When the first shot rang out, Gao came to a shuddering halt. Waving the others past him, he looked back to check if his wife was all right and saw the guard raise his rifle. Then the man fell, and as Mist-on-the-Water grabbed the gun and ran toward Gao, a soldier came out of the headquarters to see what was going on. The man had a pistol in hand, and Gao did not wait to see if he would use it. Shouldering his rifle, he drew a bead on the soldier and pulled the trigger, catching him in the chest.

Together again, Gao and his wife sprinted through the compound, seeking the shadows as they darted from building to building. All around them, voices were shouting and guns firing. Gao managed to reload, and he shot a soldier off one of the lookout posts on the wall. Then he switched rifles with Mist-on-the-Water and kept running.

Suddenly his wife pulled up short. When Gao turned to where she was looking and saw one of his fellow prisoners lying facedown beside the fort wall, he dashed over and rolled him onto his back, only to discover a slug had struck just below the left eye, killing him instantly. Knowing there was no way to take the body with him, he grabbed his wife by the hand and continued their run.

As they moved along the wall, Gao heard someone call his name and saw an Indian waving at him from the rear gate just ahead. The surviving prisoners were making their break across the open field that separated the fort from the woods, the guards apparently overcome.

Racing through the gate and into the field, Gao pushed his wife ahead to shield her from gunfire. Behind him, soldiers were lining up along the wall, shooting into the gathering darkness at the fleeing prisoners. At least two Indians had been struck and were lying in the grass off to Gao's left. Another was trying to get to the two fallen men, so Gao continued toward the trees, intent on seeing his wife to safety.

They reached the sheltering forest, and Gao stopped quickly to reload his rifle. He looked to see if he could help the Indian rescue their fallen comrades but instead saw him driven back by the relentless gunfire, retreating beyond the range of the soldiers' rifles. He and Gao watched helplessly as the wounded prisoners crawled toward the woods, shielded only by the hazy light of dusk as bullets pounded into the dirt all around them. They made it only a few more feet before first one and then the other were struck, again and again, their bodies jerking under the impact of the slugs.

The guns fell silent; the surviving prisoners were out of the Americans' range. The soldiers pushed open the double gate and began filing out, torches in hand, lining up as they awaited the order to begin their pursuit into the woods. Gao saw Colonel Charles Stringfellow among them, his face eerily illuminated in the light of the torches. Gao also recognized two others—Indians who apparently had been caught during the escape. They were dragged in front of the colonel and forced to their knees.

Gao and his comrades stared in revulsion as Colonel Stringfellow drew his pistol. Glancing over his shoulder, Gao saw his wife standing at the edge of the trees, her hands reaching toward him, her eyes beseeching. As he turned back around, the pistol fired, and one of the prisoners buckled and fell to the ground.

With a cry of rage and sorrow, Gao sprinted toward the fort, ducking low and weaving to the left and right in a desperate effort to get within rifle range without being struck.

Even in the darkness, Mist-on-the-Water had been able to read the anguish on her husband's face. When he sounded his war cry and raced off across the field, she went after him, shouting his name, begging him to come back. She made it only about twenty yards before one of the other men intercepted her and pulled her to the ground.

She sat there sobbing, watching her husband run toward the soldiers at the fort wall. The officer who had just executed one of the captured Indians had already drawn another pistol and was holding it on the second prisoner. But his attention was diverted by the savage cry from across the field, and he turned to see what it was.

Gao must have appeared a ghostly apparition racing toward them in the murky twilight, and it took a moment for anyone to react. Then the officer swung his pistol toward Gao and fired. The shot missed, and Gao dove to his side and rolled through the grass.

The officer looked suddenly panicked, and he flung down his arm, signaling the soldiers to fire. A handful of shots rang out, and Mist-on-the-Water saw the bullets thud into the ground around her husband. He rose to his knees, brought up his rifle, and fired. A dozen more gunshots rang out, and Gao was thrown onto his back by the force of the slugs tearing into his body. Thirty yards away, Colonel Charles Stringfellow's legs collapsed, and he crumpled to the ground, a bullet hole in his forehead.

Screaming her husband's name, Mist-on-the-Water broke from the Indian's grasp and jumped up, running toward her husband with arms outstretched. But several pairs of hands grabbed her from both sides and lifted her off the ground, carrying her back to the safety of the trees, away from that field of death.

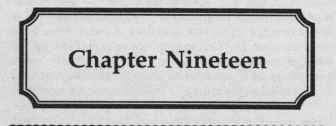

Chapter Nineteen

The horse's ears snapped upright, its head lifting from the tuft of grass it had been nibbling. Renno heard the noise as well, and he uncoiled himself from his cross-legged position by the small campfire and stood, trying to discern where the sound had come from. When it came again, he knew immediately that it was gunfire—not a single weapon but many rifles and muskets—coming from the vicinity of Fort Niagara.

The fort was only a few miles away. Renno had planned to spend the night there alongside the trail and present himself at first light. Instead he quickly smothered the fire, gathered up his deerskin robe and supplies, saddled his horse, and set off toward the fort, moving as quickly as possible in the growing dusk.

The gunfire was diminishing as the first flickering torchlights came into view. The Niagara River flowed north along the left side of the fort, with forested flatlands bordering it on the right. It was there, between the fort and the woods, that the activity was centered. As Renno drew closer he heard soldiers shouting and saw people standing near the trees. And then came a sound that sent shivers through him: the war cry of a Seneca warrior.

Renno kicked his horse into a gallop and raced toward the field. A figure, running toward the fort, was fired upon and dove to the ground. When he rose to his knees and returned fire, he was met by a volley of rifles and thrown onto his back.

Renno pulled his horse up short and stood staring in confusion at the scene a hundred yards ahead. Just beyond the edge of the forest, a woman shrieked, and several Indians dragged her from the field back into the woods. Her scream echoed louder and cut through Renno deeper than any rifle shot, for she had screamed the name of his nephew, Gao.

Renno gripped the reins as his horse stamped nervously in place. He was about to ride over to the warrior who had been shot, but a half-dozen soldiers went running across the field, grabbed the body by the arms, and dragged it back to the fort. The troops standing around the rear gate were in complete disarray, and it seemed one or more of them had been shot as well. An officer was shouting chaotic commands, and Renno surmised that he was ordering a company to take off in pursuit of the Indians.

Renno did not let himself think about the fallen warrior. It might not be Gao, he told himself. Perhaps Gao had been one of the men who had carried the woman away.

The woman . . . Mist-on-the-Water. . . .

He had to find out if it was her—and if he did not hurry, the soldiers might get to the fleeing Indians first. Reining his horse to the right, he rode toward the trees, praying that in the confusion no one from the fort would see the shadowed rider.

Though there was still a bit of hazy light, the woods were dark and dangerous for a horse and rider. Renno tied up his mount, gathered his weapons, and checked the charges, then took off at a run, weaving among the trees as he attempted to cut off the Indians. Fortunately the forest was fairly sparse, and he was able to make his way without too much difficulty. After a few minutes he heard hushed voices and branches snapping. Pulling up, he shouted a greeting in Seneca, then again in Shawnee.

The voices fell silent as he approached. He knew they would assume he was from the fort, so he repeated his greeting: "I am Renno of the Seneca, and I come in peace. I seek my nephew Gao and his wife, Mist-on-the-Water."

A moment later the dark figure of a man appeared in front of him—a warrior training a rifle on him. Renno's own rifle was slung over his shoulder, and he raised his hands to indicate he was a friend. The man came closer until he could see Renno more clearly, then looked him up and down, taking in his buckskin hunter's outfit and long, graying blond hair.

"I am Renno of the Seneca," he said again, first in English and then Shawnee, all the while keeping his empty hands raised. "I was going to the fort to find my nephew Gao when I heard the gunfire."

The man stared at him a moment longer, then struck his fist against his chest and said in English, "Laughing Crow."

He waved the barrel of the rifle, indicating that Renno should follow. Together they sprinted back through the trees to a small clearing where the others were gathered. Renno counted six Indians, including a young woman. One man had been shot in the leg; others were bandaging his wound. The woman was sitting by herself, sobbing and muttering unintelligibly.

Renno looked quickly from one man to the next but did not see his nephew. Walking over to the woman, he said, "Mist-on-the-Water?" She did not look up.

Laughing Crow approached and said in broken but understandable English, "Gao was brave Seneca. Fought with heart of panther."

Renno felt his entire body go numb. He did not cry, but the tears of Mist-on-the-Water flooded through him as if they were his own.

"His wife kill soldiers," the man continued, gesturing at the sobbing woman. "Help us get away. We were twelve. Now we are five."

The words almost did not register. But then he heard other voices—shouted voices—and he looked in the direction of the fort. The Indians turned that way as well, and one whispered in Shawnee, "They are coming!"

The bandaging had been completed, and the warriors helped up their wounded comrade, with one lifting Mist-on-the-Water to her feet. The Indian named Laughing Crow had assumed the role of leader, and he directed the others to follow him toward the east.

"Wait," Renno said to him. He brandished his rifle. "First go south and then east. I will lead them away; then I will come find you."

Laughing Crow eyed him a long moment, then nodded.

"Send one of your men to the edge of the woods just south of the fort," Renno added. "My horse is tied there; you can use it for that man." He indicated the man with the leg wound.

Laughing Crow nodded, then turned to the others and told them to follow.

Renno walked over to Mist-on-the-Water and touched her shoulder. "I will take you to your husband's home," he whispered. She did not seem to hear him, and when he knelt to look in her eyes, it was as if she were not there.

One man took her by the wrist and pulled her along after him. She did not resist but simply went where she was led.

Renno watched them disappear into the shadows. Off to his right he could hear voices growing louder and boots trampling the underbrush. He doubted the soldiers would search for long in the growing darkness, and he would make sure that whatever searching they did was in the wrong direction.

Clutching his rifle to his chest, he sprinted northward. The fort was bordered on the west by the river and on the north by Lake Ontario, so he could not go far before he would have to turn east. However, he might be able to convince them that the escaped prisoners were following the shoreline of the lake, thus confusing any renewed search the next day.

Renno ran about fifty yards, then turned and raised his rifle, firing well over the heads of the approaching troops. As he continued his run, he could hear excited shouts and guessed the soldiers were shifting toward the shot. After going another twenty yards, he drew his pistol and fired, reloading on the run. Soon his rifle and pistol were joined by others, and Renno wondered if the soldiers might even be shooting at one another in the darkness. Once, he actually saw the shadowy figure of a man, but if the man noticed Renno, he must have assumed it was another soldier, for he did not shoot.

As Renno expected, the pursuit did not last very long. He made it to the bank of the lake with the soldiers hard on his trail, but shortly after he turned east, he heard the shouted command to pull back. Apparently clearer heads had realized that the soldiers were more likely to kill each other in the dark than capture any escaped prisoners.

Turning to the south, Renno struck a path that would intersect with that of the Indians. As he neared the area where he guessed they might be, he began making the call of a nightjar, and after about ten minutes, he heard the distinctive but slightly altered sound of an owl. Heading toward the signal, he soon came upon the others, among them the wounded man, seated upon Renno's horse.

The group continued for another hour across an area of open meadows, putting several miles between themselves and the fort. Renno walked alongside Mist-on-the-

Water, who had stopped crying but now appeared to be in shock. Reaching another stretch of forest, they decided to rest for a while at its edge.

Renno conferred briefly with Laughing Crow, then sat alone with his nephew's wife. Though she did not appear to be listening, he told her who he was and where he had come from. It was when he mentioned his children that she raised her eyes and looked at him for the first time.

"My younger son is about the same age as your husband," Renno told her, sensing that he might be getting through. "His name is Ta-na-wun-da, and he was raised at Gao's side."

Her brow furrowed slightly, as if she were carefully weighing his words.

"They were truly like brothers, Gao and Ta-na-wun-da."

At last she spoke, her voice the faintest of whispers: "I know Ta-na-wun-da."

"Yes," he said eagerly, smiling at her. "He met you at Vincennes."

"Has Ta-na died, too?" she said, her voice hollow.

The words clutched at Renno's heart, for truly he could not say if his son—if either of his sons—was still alive. "I will take you to see him," he finally replied.

Her body went rigid, her eyes widening as she shook her head.

"What is it?" he asked as gently as possible. "What is wrong?"

"I cannot go with you," she said. "I will not leave my husband. I must go back for him. I must lead him home."

Lead him home . . .

In the words of his nephew's wife he heard the voice of the manitou:

Go to the land of our ancestors. Go to the lake of the Seneca. Find my son and lead him home. When he has made the journey, your own son shall be restored to you.

Only then can the headdress be passed from one sachem to the next. Only then may we hunt at each other's side. . . .

"Yes," Renno murmured, nodding in understanding as he touched Mist-on-the-Water's arm. "Yes, that is why I have come. I must take him to the land of our ancestors. I must lead him home."

She stared up at him, her head cocked slightly. "You have heard him? He speaks to you, also?"

It was Renno who now looked with curiosity. "Who is it that speaks to you?" he asked.

"My husband. He calls for me to bring him home."

"Come," Renno said, standing and offering his hands. "We are going to get your husband. We are going back."

A light of awareness seemed to come into her eyes. She grasped his forearms and rose.

Renno walked over to where Laughing Crow and the others were sitting. "I am returning to the fort," he announced. "I must retrieve the body of my nephew."

Those who spoke English looked at him as if he had lost his mind.

"Soldiers kill you," Laughing Crow said, and others nodded their accord.

"If such is the will of the Master of Life," Renno replied. "But the manitous sent me here to find my nephew and lead him home. This I shall do."

One of the Indians started to comment about the insanity of such a scheme, but Laughing Crow raised a hand to silence him. Standing, he said to Renno, "I see now where Gao get such bravery."

Mist-on-the-Water came up beside Renno. She spoke with the sureness and strength she had exhibited back at the fort when she freed them from the guardhouse. "I will join my uncle on this journey."

Recognizing the powerful spirit that again flowed through her, Laughing Crow nodded. "Yes, this you must do," he declared. "I come, too."

"No," Renno said with more abruptness than intended. "It is for Mist-on-the-Water and me to bring home our dead. You must bring home the living." His gesture took in the entire group. "Lead them beyond the lake and north into Canada. By the time winter ends, the Americans will forget you, and you can go wherever you wish."

Again Laughing Crow nodded. "Your words are wise."

Renno offered them the use of his horse, but the wounded man insisted he had only been grazed and demonstrated that he could walk without assistance. Renno agreed to keep the animal, since he would need it to transport his nephew's body.

"Walk in peace," Laughing Crow said, gripping Renno's forearm.

"Walk in peace," Renno repeated. He helped Mist-on-the-Water into the saddle and mounted up behind her. With a final wave of farewell, they rode back across the fields toward the forest and Fort Niagara beyond.

At dawn the double gates at the rear of Fort Niagara opened onto the field, and a detachment of mounted troops filed out, preparing to resume their search for the escaped prisoners. On the opposite side of the field, a blond-haired man emerged from the forest. He was dressed in the buckskins of a hunter and led a horse on which sat a young Indian woman.

Renno strode briskly toward the soldiers, questioning whether he should have let Mist-on-the-Water accompany him right up to the fort. He had wanted her to wait in the woods, but she insisted upon remaining with him, even if it meant joining her husband in death. He almost wondered if that might be her true wish, but he shook off the thought and concentrated on the task at hand.

He raised his hand in friendship. By way of response, one of the soldiers was dispatched across the field to find out who the strangers were and what they wanted.

"My name is Renno Harper," he said, halting about ten feet from the mounted officer.

"Lieutenant Armstrong," the man replied, sitting his horse. "What business have you at Fort Niagara?"

"I have come for one of the Indians you've been holding prisoner. His name is Gao, and he is of the Seneca."

The man looked quite stunned. He glanced back at the fort, then asked, "What concern are our Indian prisoners to you?"

"I would speak with your commandant."

The lieutenant glanced at Mist-on-the-Water but apparently did not recognize her. Turning back to Renno, he said, "Our commandant is a very busy man. If you have—"

"I am aware that your prisoners escaped last night. I have information that may prove of interest to the commandant."

Armstrong ran a hand along his bushy mustache as he weighed the stranger's words. Finally he nodded and said, "Wait here." Jerking back on the reins, he wheeled his horse around and trotted back to the others, reining in his horse alongside a pair of officers.

These two were a captain and a major, and they appeared to be disagreeing about the appropriate action. The major ended the conversation with a dismissive wave of the hand, then kicked his horse forward and approached the strangers.

"There is the man I told you about," Mist-on-the-Water told her father-in-law in a low voice.

"The one coming?" Renno asked.

"No. The officer who stays behind. He was the one in the shed."

Renno nodded.

The rider halted a few feet away and raised his hand, saying, "I am Major Caleb Wilson."

Renno raised his own hand and replied, "Renno Harper."

"I am told you have word of our escapees."

"I came here in search of my nephew, who was among your prisoners. His name is Gao, and he is a Seneca."

Hearing the name, the major gave a sad, almost resigned frown and nodded. Renno closely watched his reactions, trying to gauge the sincerity of what he would say.

"I knew your nephew. Though our interests were at odds, I can truly say he was a brave warrior—perhaps the most courageous I have seen. He died last night, trying to save two of his comrades who were being unjustly executed—two *more* unjust executions, I might add."

"I heard what happened from this woman." He gestured at Mist-on-the-Water. "She is the wife of my nephew and was there when he died."

Wilson eyed her with increased interest, then turned back to Renno. "If she's the woman who was seen entering our guardhouse, she is as brave as her husband. And you are equally so, to bring her here so brashly. Brave—and foolhardy, it would seem."

"May I speak plainly, Major Wilson?" Renno asked. "Please."

"I am an American, but I live among my father's people in the land of Cherokee south of Tennessee. I have long served our nation, and I took no pleasure in knowing my nephew was standing alongside the very British we fought so hard to remove from our soil. My own son is Captain Hawk Harper, a graduate of West Point."

Wilson leaned forward in the saddle. "I have heard of Captain Harper. He serves on the staff of our president, does he not?"

"He was offered such a commission but felt compelled to turn it down following the deaths of his wife and son at the hands of the Creek."

"I'm sorry to hear that."

"So, you can see that we have served our nation and made sacrifices for her. That is why, even though my nephew chose a path I did not approve of, I came here hoping to get him released into my custody. Instead I must ask that you permit me to take his body home."

Wilson looked again at Mist-on-the-Water as he said to Renno, "You mentioned to my lieutenant that you had news of the escapees. I take it this woman was among them."

"I was," Mist-on-the-Water replied boldly.

"If my soldiers knew that, they'd demand your life for the ones that were lost—especially the two guards you murdered during the escape." Dismounting, he walked up to Renno. "Why have you brought her here? What game are you playing?"

"My niece would rather die on the ground where her husband breathed his last than leave this field without him. I brought her so that she could ask for your pardon and make witness to the injustice that was done."

"Injustice?" The major eyed him suspiciously.

"When I came upon her and the other Indians, they spoke of a Colonel Charles Stringfellow. They described interrogations so brutal and executions so callous that I confess I was ashamed to be an American."

The major's shoulders slumped somewhat, and he nodded. "You may gain some satisfaction in knowing that your nephew, before dying, succeeded in taking the colonel with him."

"Unfortunately he failed in his attempt to save the two Indians who were recaptured."

"You are wrong," Wilson told him. "True, the colonel executed one of them, but he was killed before he could shoot the other."

"One is still alive?" Renno said in surprise.

"He's back in the guardhouse. There will be no more executions without due process."

Renno did not doubt that the major was speaking

the truth, and he allowed himself a smile. "Then I would ask that I be permitted to leave here with both my nephew's body and the remaining prisoner."

The major gave a rueful grin. "Instead I would ask why I should not put this woman under arrest."

"Because she was doing no more than defending herself, as were the prisoners."

"Self-defense?" he said incredulously. "I am afraid that I must be the one to speak plainly now. This niece of yours offered herself to those guards and then killed them when they were, shall we say, in a position least able to defend themselves. I do not condone the guards' breach of conduct, but I think her actions can hardly be considered self-defense."

"Not the way you describe it. But my niece tells a different story entirely. One of your officers took advantage of her, promising that if she granted him favors, he would obtain an order of release for her husband. Desperate, she agreed, and afterward he sent her to the guardhouse with a sealed order that you supposedly signed. When the guards read it, they didn't release Gao but instead dragged her into a cell and tried to rape her. She took the only action left open to her."

"There was no order of release, nor would there have been," Wilson insisted.

"No," Renno agreed. "But there was an order of sorts."

He turned to Mist-on-the Water, who reached into the pouch at her waist and removed a folded piece of paper with a broken double seal. Renno took it from her and handed it to the major.

"She retrieved it during the escape, thinking they might one day need to show that Gao had been officially released. It was not until we read it this morning that we understood the actions of those guards—and of that officer over there." He pointed with the paper toward the soldiers lined up outside the fort. "From Mist-on-the-

Water's description, I would guess that man to be Captain Bushnell."

He handed the paper to Major Wilson, who shook it open and quickly read the contents:

> Let it be known to any and all who read this—especially you, Corporal Lemuels—that the squaw who stands in front of you is a drunken Indian whore. I know because she just sold herself to me—and I didn't even need to dip into my purse to meet her price. I just told her what she wanted to hear, and I suggest you do the same. I am sending her over to you because of the debt I owe Corporal Lemuels from Tuesday last. I trust this will be considered payment in full.
>
> The whore wants us to release her husband. I suggest you give her what every squaw really wants and then give her the boot.
> —Captain Henry Bushnell

Renno could see the rage in the major's eyes as he refolded the paper. He turned and glared at the captain, who was standing beside his horse. Then he looked back at Renno.

"May I have this?" he asked, quickly adding, "You have my word that this incident will not go unpunished."

Renno nodded, and the major remounted his horse.

"I think it would be prudent for you and your niece to remain here. I shall return shortly."

He galloped back to the fort and dismounted in front of Captain Bushnell. They were soon in a heated argument and almost came to blows. Finally the major shouted an order, and several soldiers drew their weapons on the captain. He stood looking all around, as if waiting for someone to come to his defense. Finally he drew his pistol and handed it, butt first, to the major. As the captain was taken under guard into the fort, Major

Wilson grasped the reins of Bushnell's horse and led the rest of the soldiers back through the gate.

Renno and Mist-on-the-Water waited for almost ten minutes. Then several soldiers appeared at the open gate. Behind them was a young Indian, his wrists in irons. One of the soldiers—Renno thought it was Lieutenant Armstrong—undid the shackles and motioned for him to leave. He walked forward, hesitant at first, as if expecting a bullet in the back. But when he recognized Mist-on-the-Water sitting on the horse in the middle of the field, he broke into a run.

He raced up to them, and Renno grabbed him by the arm and said, "Look!" The man and Mist-on-the-Water turned to the gate as Major Wilson came riding out. Trailing him was Captain Bushnell's horse, a body draped over the saddle.

The major halted his mount in front of Renno. "I wish it had ended better," he said, extending the reins of the horse bearing Gao's body. He gestured to Mist-on-the-Water. "This horse and saddle rightfully belong to your niece. And I see no reason to hold this man any longer." He indicated the freed Indian. "Tell the others we will not pursue them. We ask only that they put down their weapons and fight our nation no longer. Tecumseh is dead; it is time we put an end to this unfortunate matter."

"Thank you, Major," Renno said, nodding in respect.

Wilson spurred his mount and returned to the fort, passing through the gate without looking back.

Renno spoke briefly with the Indian, advising him the route to follow to catch up to his companions. The young man thanked them for all they had done, then took off into the woods at a warrior's pace.

Mist-on-the-Water dismounted and approached her husband's body. He had been wrapped in a blanket before being tied in place over the saddle, and she ran her hand along his shrouded head and back. Renno came up beside her and laid his hand upon hers. She looked up at him with tears in her eyes but also with resolve.

"Are you ready?" he asked, and she nodded. "Then come." He motioned toward the forest. "Our journey is still ahead of us. We must bring your husband to the land of his ancestors. We must lead him home."

Chapter Twenty

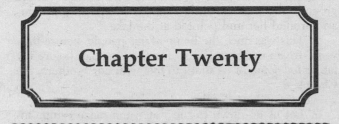 Renno sat his horse on a low bluff overlooking the headwaters of the lake of the Seneca. He gazed out across the water, thinking of the years that had passed since he had last stood on this spot—the days of his youth when he and El-i-chi ran along the banks of the long, crystal-blue lake.

Turning, he looked back at Mist-on-the-Water. She was on the horse given them by Major Wilson, which was pulling a travois they had constructed soon after leaving Fort Niagara. The body on the travois had already been prepared for burial in traditional Seneca fashion, painted with images of battle and the hunt, perfumed with herbs, and wrapped in a casing of birch bark that would serve as a coffin. She had walked alongside that travois for much of the hundred-mile journey from the Niagara, only occasionally agreeing to ride the horse. She had wanted to be at her husband's side these last days before they lowered him into the ground.

It was well into December, and the short days had grown increasingly cold. During the previous night, the cool Canadian winds had picked up moisture crossing Lake Ontario, dusting the leaves and ground with snow. Soon heavier storms would strike; Renno knew they had to finish their business quickly and head south.

He dismounted and walked back to the other horse. Reaching up, he lifted his niece-by-marriage to the ground. She was shivering slightly, and he wrapped his arm around her and pointed at the lake.

"This was once the home of our people, before they were driven north and west into the Canadas, before my father led some of us south to live with our brothers, the Cherokee."

She nodded silently.

"Let us go down to the water and make camp. Tonight I shall consult the manitous." He indicated a small hill to the right at the edge of the lake. "At dawn we shall lay your husband to rest on that hilltop, so he may walk with his ancestors."

"I am ready," Mist-on-the-Water said solemnly. She took the reins of her horse and followed Renno toward the lake.

The moon hung high above the water as Renno sat alone on a deerskin robe atop the very ground where his nephew soon would rest. Below him in the distance, near the edge of the lake, he could make out the flickering campfire he had built before leaving Mist-on-the-Water and coming alone to the top of this hill.

Renno had worked hard, digging and preparing the ground to receive his nephew's body. Fortunately the unseasonably mild winter had made interment possible, since normally the ground would have been frozen by this time. Exhausted now, he did not build a warming fire but simply sat on the robe and looked out across the dark, glowing waters. As he gazed upon the glimmering silver reflection of the moon, he called for the manitous to come. He knew they would not forsake him here, on this ground sacred to his people.

The figure that came walking up the hill was shrouded in cool moonlight. His hair was long and as golden as the sun. His eyes were as deep as the waters, as blue as the sky. His face was as familiar as a reflection in a mirror, as mysterious as Renno's own soul.

The figure approached and stood with arms folded across his chest. He wore only moccasins and a breech-clout of white leather. He spoke no words, yet his voice rang deep and true within Renno's heart.

"You have brought the son of the son of my grandson to the home of his people. You have heard our voices, and you have come."

"Renno . . ." the sachem of the Seneca whispered to his great-grandfather—the first Renno—and the manitou lowered his head and smiled. "Where is my brother?" Renno asked, looking around to see if others were present.

"El-i-chi is with me. As are Ghonkaba and Ja-gonh. And soon my great-great-grandson will make the journey and take his place at our side."

"And me?" Renno asked, raising a hand toward the figure, which seemed to hover in front of him, as solid as a man yet as translucent as a pool of water.

"First you must see the power of the sachem in your son, and you must present him with the headdress and the robe. You have completed your mission. You have brought them together, Os-sweh-ga-da-ah Ne-wa-ah, Ta-na-wun-da, and Gao."

"But my sons are far to the south, in the land of the Creek."

"They are together at last," repeated the manitou.

As the words were spoken Renno felt a rush of fear, thinking his sons might have joined Gao in death.

"Your sons still walk on the red earth of the living," the voice continued, as if reading his mind. "On the red earth of our people. Though we have been driven from this land—scattered to the north, west, and south—this place by the lake shall always be our home. It is here that each of us one day shall return. To walk beside these waters. Upon the red earth of our ancestors."

Renno started to speak, but the manitou raised a hand and exclaimed, "Hush! The sachem approaches!"

Renno thought he heard distant hooves, and he looked around, but no one else was there. He turned back and found the image of the manitou fading in front of him. He reached toward the vision, but it rose like white smoke into the light of the moon. As it passed from sight, the faintest of echoes whispered in Renno's mind:

Hush! The sachem approaches. . . .

For long minutes, Renno sat motionless. Watching. Awaiting.

All was silence. All was night.

Another half hour passed before Renno stretched his arms and rose. He was troubled by the words of the manitou, yet he knew he was following the correct path. El-i-chi had told him to lead Gao to the lake of the Seneca, to bring their three sons together. He sensed he was to bury Gao there, on that sacred spot. Perhaps afterward the young warrior would accompany Renno in spirit form to Rusog's Town, where Renno would pass the sachem's mantle to his eldest son. And then he would make his own final journey home.

Renno looked down toward the lake and saw that the light of the campfire still blazed brightly. Picking up the robe he had been sitting on, he wrapped it around his shoulders and started down the hill. When he neared the bottom, a dark shadow loomed in front of him, and he halted, trying to make it out. For a moment he thought it was Mist-on-the-Water, but it drew closer, larger, and took the form of a man. Thinking the manitou had returned, he started to call out his great-grandfather's name, but then the moonlight illuminated a face, and he gasped.

"Ta-na-wun-da!"

And then directly behind his son, another figure emerged from the darkness.

"Little Hawk!"

"Father!" they exclaimed in unison, rushing forward and gathering him in their arms.

Renno and his sons stayed up late into the night. They spoke of the passing of Tecumseh and Gao and shared all that had happened in the months since they had been together at Huntington Castle. Renno described his journey to Fort Niagara and how he and Mist-on-the-Water had recovered Gao's body. And Hawk explained how Ma-ton-ga had come to be with them and how the things Michael Soaring Hawk had heard his grandfather say in vision had convinced them to search for Renno there, at the lake of the Seneca. Sitting quietly nearby, Mist-on-the-Water and Ma-ton-ga listened intently before falling asleep only a couple of hours before dawn.

When the sun rose, the group began its solemn duties. They used the travois as a funeral bier, and Mist-on-the-Water decorated it, as well as her hair and dress, with strips of red and yellow cloth torn from pieces of clothing in the saddlebags. Meanwhile, Ma-ton-ga fashioned a small drum from a hollow log and a covering of deerskin.

Leaving the horses at the camp, Ta-na-wun-da and Hawk lifted the bier with its bark-encased body onto their shoulders, and the group climbed the hill to the burial spot Renno had prepared. The bier was placed on the ground, and the body lowered into the hole. Then, as the brothers and the women bowed their heads, Renno raised his arms toward the sky—toward Taronhiawagon, the Holder of the Heavens. As Ma-ton-ga beat the drum, Renno chanted the ancient condoling rites of his people. Each phrase began with an explosive burst, then gradually sank to the close and ended with a quick, rising inflection. Occasionally Ta-na-wun-da gave a brief, low wail of *"Haih! Haih!"* in assent.

> *"Konyennedaghkwen, onenh weghniserade*
>   *yonkwatkennison.*
> *Rawenniyo raweghniseronnyh.*
> *Ne onwa konwende yonkwatkennison nene*
>   *jiniyuneghrakwah jinisayadawen.*
> *Onenh onghwenjakonh niyonsakahhawe*
>   *jinonweh nadekakaghneronnyonghkwe.*
> *Akwah kady okaghserakonh*
>   *thadetyatroghkwanekenh."*

> *"My offspring, now this day we are met*
>   *together.*
> *The Master of Life has appointed this day.*
> *We are met together on account of the solemn*
>   *event that has befallen us.*
> *Now into the earth he has been conveyed, he*
>   *on whom we have been wont to look.*
> *Therefore in tears let us smoke together."*

Renno continued the chant in the language of his ancestors, with Ta-na-wun-da, Mist-on-the-Water, and even Little Hawk and Ma-ton-ga occasionally crying out the response, "Haih! Haih!"

> *"Now, then, we wipe away your tears so that*
>   *in peace you may look about you.*
> *And we remove the obstruction from your ears*
>   *so that you will hear the words spoken.*
> *For a solemn event has befallen us.*
> *Every day we are losing our great men.*
> *They are being borne into the earth.*
> *Also the warriors, and also our women, and*
>   *also our grandchildren, so that in the midst*
>   *of blood we are standing.*
> *Now, therefore, we wash off the blood marks*

so that this place will be clean where we
are gathered."

The chanting continued for almost an hour, Renno offering his nephew words usually reserved for a chief of their people. For Renno knew that had El-i-chi lived, he would have passed the sachem's headdress to his son Gao. Now the honor and the terrible responsibility had fallen again upon Renno—and, after him, upon his own son.

When the chant ended, Ma-ton-ga moved off to the side and continued to beat slowly upon the drum, while Mist-on-the-Water and the brothers knelt at the grave and spoke a final good-bye.

Renno moved away from the others, listening and watching as Ta-na-wun-da rose up and began a Seneca chant of mourning for the cousin who was his brother of the spirit. Hawk stood as well and joined Ma-ton-ga. Mist-on-the-Water alone knelt at the grave. She began to sob and then wail, her tears flowing down onto the birch-bark coffin, into the hard, red earth.

Other voices began to chant along with Ta-na-wun-da, and Renno glanced over to see if it was his elder son or the Creek woman. But they were silent. He nodded and smiled, recognizing now the low voice of El-i-chi and the voices of their mother and father and their father's father. Their song was a circle that embraced the funeral party and called Gao to his home.

A thin wisp of mist rose from the burial pit and gathered in the air at the edge of the grave, taking form as a young warrior. He wore a loincloth and beaded gorget, with a belt of white wampum at his waist. When he turned and smiled at Renno, his face was that of Gao, son of El-i-chi and great-great-grandson of the first white Indian.

The others were unaware of this shimmering apparition, which approached Mist-on-the-Water and rested a hand on her shoulder. Yet with his touch, a change came over her, and she stopped crying and smiled.

Renno watched transfixed as Gao shifted his hand to her belly. Though she did not seem aware of him, she placed her own hands over his and looked down at herself with an expression of sheer wonder, as if she had felt the first stirrings of life.

Gao moved away from his wife and walked up to Ta-na-wun-da, who continued to chant. Reaching down, Gao grasped his friend's forearm. Though Ta-na did not see him, his expression grew more peaceful, and he raised his arm and followed as Gao led him to where Mist-on-the-Water was kneeling—as Gao placed Ta-na's hand on her shoulder precisely where Gao had rested his own.

Mist-on-the-Water raised her eyes to Ta-na, who smiled down at her. The apparition moved away a few feet and stood looking at his friend and his wife. Lifting his hands to the two of them, he closed his eyes. In that instant, Renno realized with a start that Ta-na-wun-da and Mist-on-the-Water would one day walk the path together—that Gao was giving his blessing and that all was as it should be.

When Gao's eyes opened, Renno felt them gazing into his soul. Gao did not move his lips, but his words rang clear in Renno's mind: "Thank you, my uncle. I go ahead and will see you again when it is your time."

Turning, he walked behind Little Hawk and Ma-ton-ga and placed a hand on each of them. Ma-ton-ga responded by turning and gazing at Little Hawk. There was no mistaking the expression in her eyes.

And Renno knew that all was as it should be.

Gao started down from the hilltop. Coming toward him were Renno's father, Ghonkaba, and grandfather Jagonh. They came up on either side of the young warrior, took his arms, and led him toward the lake of the Seneca.

Renno sensed a presence behind him, and a voice whispered, "You have brought my firstborn son home, and soon you will follow. First you must look into the eyes of your son. You will see in them the same spirit that walked with Ja-gonh and Ghonkaba, and with our great-grandfather Renno before them. The spirit that now walks with you."

The apparition of El-i-chi moved past Renno and followed after the others. When he reached his son's side, the four men turned and glanced back up the hill a final time. Again El-i-chi spoke, his voice sounding within Renno's heart.

"Look upon your son. When you see in him the sachem, then we shall ride to the longhouse. Then we shall hunt at each other's side."

The spirits turned and continued their journey, down off the hill and out across the crystal-blue waters of Kanyadariyo, the Beautiful Lake, beyond. As they disappeared into the mist upon the water, the chanting and the drumming faded and were gone.

"It is finished," a voice said, and Renno turned to see Little Hawk standing behind him. Just beyond, Ma-ton-ga had lowered her drum, and Ta-na-wun-da and Mist-on-the-Water were filling the grave with dirt.

"Os-sweh-ga-da-ah Ne-wa-ah . . ." Renno whispered, using Hawk's Seneca name.

He gripped his elder son's forearms and stared deep within him, searching for that special light, that sign promised by the manitous. All that he saw were Hawk Harper's flashing blue eyes.

In time, Renno told himself and smiled. *The spirit of the white Indian shall reveal itself in time.*

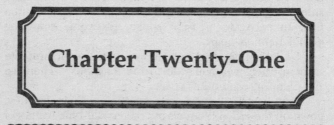

Chapter Twenty-One

 Following the burial ceremony, Renno showed Hawk, Ta-na-wun-da, Mist-on-the-Water, and Ma-ton-ga some of the places of his youth. Just north of the lake, they visited the former site of Kanadasegea, once the capital of the Seneca Nation. They walked across overgrown fields, with Renno describing how the longhouses had been laid out and showing them where the surrounding orchards and crops had once stood. Because the Seneca allied themselves with the British during the War for Independence, the American army had attacked the town in 1779, running off the inhabitants and razing all the buildings, orchards, and stores of grains and vegetables. During that campaign, more than forty villages were destroyed, until virtually no longhouses, fruit trees, fields of corn, or Indians remained in the region.

After two days exploring the former Seneca homeland, the group began the return journey to Rusog's Town, riding west through the Genesee Valley. The first leg of the trip was uneventful; however, as they approached Lake Erie, where they would turn south toward Tennessee, they decided that Ta-na-wun-da should travel ahead and serve as scout, since recently this region had been the focus of much action between the Americans and the British.

It was late on the morning of Christmas eve when the group crossed a narrow field between a series of forested hills. Renno was at the front, the two women rode side by side in the middle, and Hawk took up the rear. The winds had picked up considerably during the night and had deposited half a foot of fresh snow carried off Lakes Erie and Ontario. The wind had not abated, and snow swirled around them, slowing their progress. Furthermore, the snow deadened hoofbeats, so they did not know anyone was in the area until a detachment of six American soldiers emerged from the trees just ahead.

Renno pulled to a halt and eyed the approaching troops, gauging the danger of the situation.

"What shall we do?" Hawk asked, riding up beside his father. His eyes were on the soldiers, still a hundred yards away.

"We'll wait here."

Hawk twisted in the saddle, examining their surroundings through the haze of blowing snow. "We could make a run for those trees," he suggested, pointing to a stretch of woods to the south.

"No. If we run, we invite pursuit. You're a captain yourself, so we have nothing to fear—even with the women along."

"I just wish Ta-na were with us."

Renno shook his head. "It's better he isn't. You and I look like any of those soldiers, but your brother might raise suspicion."

As the troops slowed their horses to a walk, Renno raised his hand in greeting. He tried to determine who was the leader, but the soldiers' uniforms were encrusted with snow, their collars turned up and their hats pulled low against the wind, obscuring any rank insignia.

"Hello!" he called, kneeing his horse forward a few steps. "Are you from Fort Niagara?"

A soldier in a greatcoat pulled ahead of the others, keeping his head down as he reined in before Renno. The other five fanned out slightly so that each could see what was going on.

"Aye, from Fort Niagara," the lead soldier replied with a nod.

"Please send my regards to Major Wilson."

"Haven't you heard?" the soldier asked, lifting his head. "Fort Niagara came under attack by the British on the nineteenth. It fell, and most of the garrison was killed, the major among them. The rest were taken prisoner, except for a few of us who escaped in the confusion —much like your squaw back there did a few weeks ago."

The soldier whipped open his coat, and Renno saw a large-bore military pistol aimed at his chest. Hawk saw it as well and reached for his own weapon, but the other soldiers jerked up their pistols and rifles and trained them on the travelers.

"What is the meaning of this?" Renno demanded.

"Don't recognize me, do you?" the soldier asked, removing his hat. "I'll bet *she* does," he added, waggling the pistol at Mist-on-the-Water.

"You're that captain, aren't you?" Renno realized.

"Henry Bushnell, at your service—late of the Fort Niagara stockade, thanks to you and that squaw." He glanced at his comrades and grinned. "Fortunately, after the major went down during the British attack, other officers released me so I could add my gun to the effort. And not a moment too soon, or I might not be standing here right now."

"We've no more quarrel with you, Captain, so if you would—"

"Well, I've got a quarrel with *you*. And so do these fellows. That right?" he asked them, and they nodded in assent. "You see, we don't take kindly to a squaw sticking a blade in some of our friends and then running off to tell her British compatriots all about our defenses."

Hawk rode forward now. The others kept their guns on him, but no one moved to stop him. "Captain Bushnell," he said, "my name is Captain Hawk Harper, lately assigned to the president's staff."

"A West Pointer, eh?" Bushnell asked, eyeing him suspiciously.

"That's correct."

"You look a lot like this fellow," the captain noted, staring at Hawk and then at Renno.

"Mr. Harper is my father."

"Well, I don't much care for West Pointers. And I care even less for your father." He motioned one of the soldiers forward. "Now, if you'll be so good as to turn over your weapons. . . ."

Renno considered going for his pistol. But with six guns trained on them, several of them, the women included, probably would be killed. He turned to Hawk and motioned for him to comply.

The soldier gathered up their arms and distributed them among his comrades.

"The squaws', too," Bushnell ordered, and one of the others rode over and checked them for weapons. A pistol was taken from each.

"Now, if you will kindly accompany me . . ."

"Where are you taking us?" Hawk demanded.

"We're on our way to Albany. My report on the fall of Fort Niagara—and the treason of Major Wilson—will likely mean a promotion for me." He turned slightly in the saddle. "For all of us," he assured the others. "As for you people, I think Albany would be a bit far to take you. I'd say over there, by those trees, is far enough."

At his signal, the soldiers positioned themselves around the four prisoners. Under their guns, the travelers were forced to ride off the trail to the nearby woods. At the edge of the trees they were ordered off their horses. The soldiers dismounted as well, and one of them gathered up the reins of all ten animals and led them off to tie them to a couple of trees. The other five soldiers, meanwhile, goaded the travelers into the woods.

In the shelter of the trees, there was much less snow on the ground, and the forest provided an effective barrier against the wind. Without the swirling snow, the sun was able to break through, giving the forest a serene, almost magical quality.

"This ought to be about right," Bushnell declared, ordering them to halt about fifty yards into the woods. He looked at the ground around them. "Snow will soon cover our tracks. By the time anyone finds you, I'll be a retired general and you'll be nothing but bones."

Renno addressed one of the other soldiers. "Are you going to let this man turn you into a murderer?"

The soldier looked around a bit uncertainly.

"Go on, Corporal," Bushnell prodded. "Tell him what you think."

The man's voice wavered a bit as he replied uncertainly, "I think I lost a few good friends when that squaw set them Injuns free. But this ain't—"

"And we lost a lot more when she set the British upon us," Bushnell cut him off, and the others nodded.

"Why not tell them why she helped the Indians escape?" Renno challenged, then turned back to the corporal. "Didn't Major Wilson explain why he arrested your captain?"

"Shut up!" Bushnell raged. Taking a quick step forward, he lashed out with the pistol barrel, catching Renno on the cheek and jarring him. Hawk instantly leaped at the man, and one of the soldiers fired, the slug catching Hawk in the shoulder and knocking him to the ground. Ma-ton-ga immediately went to his side.

"Stay where you are!" Bushnell ordered Renno and Mist-on-the-Water when they started toward Hawk.

"This ain't right," the corporal muttered, looking nervously between Bushnell and the other three soldiers.

Smiling, the captain strolled over to him and

wrapped an arm around his shoulder. "You know what'll make you feel better, Milowe? That squaw over there." He nodded at Mist-on-the-Water. "I had her already, so what say you be the first one this time?" He turned to the other men. "You fellows can have that one there"—he indicated Ma-ton-ga—"just as soon as we finish with their friends."

Stepping away from Corporal Milowe, he raised his pistol and aimed it at Renno.

"Let me do it, Captain," one soldier declared, stepping forward. "I lost me some good friends back there."

Grinning, Bushnell lowered his pistol slightly. "Certainly, Private," he said, waving for the soldier to proceed.

Renno stood tall, blood dripping down his cheek as he stared into the private's eyes. The young man drew up the barrel of his rifle. For a moment he seemed unnerved and lowered the rifle; but then he shook it off and muttered, "You bastard!"

There was a moment of silence as he raised the rifle again, followed by a sharp whistle of air. The private staggered forward, his rifle firing into the ground and then slipping from his hands as he pawed at his neck. He collapsed to one knee, clutching the bloody shaft of the arrow that protruded from his throat.

As the private sprawled facedown on the ground, a piercing war cry shivered through the trees. A second arrow followed the first, catching Captain Bushnell in the side and dropping him to his knees. Thinking themselves under Indian attack, the other soldiers fired wildly in all directions.

Renno caught a glimpse of a bow being drawn back. Sensing the direction of the shot, he leaped at the young corporal, barreling into him and throwing him off his feet. The arrow sailed just overhead, thudding into a nearby tree.

Snatching the pistol from the corporal's hand, Renno swung the butt against his temple, knocking him unconscious. As Renno cocked the pistol, a stab of pain shot through his lower back, and he thought he might have been struck by a soldier's bullet. He tried to disregard it and stand, but he felt a sudden weakness and could only manage to kneel. He looked around, seeking to bring the gun into play, and spied Hawk wrestling on the ground with one of the soldiers. The other one stood nearby, furiously reloading his pistol.

Renno was about to fire when a figure came running through the trees. It was Ta-na-wun-da—chest bare, Seneca war paint on his face, tomahawk in his hand. He smashed into the soldier, driving him back against a tree trunk. Dispatching the man with a quick swing of the blade, he spun around to his brother, still struggling with his adversary.

Because of Hawk's wound, he was not faring well. The soldier had managed to draw his knife, and he was straddling Hawk, trying to ram the blade home. Hawk was gripping the man's wrist, but his shoulder was weakening, the tip of the blade dancing just above his throat.

Renno aimed his pistol, but he could not get a clear shot without the risk of hitting Hawk. Suddenly the soldier's body jerked, and he gasped, spitting up blood. His body stiffened, then went slack, and he pitched to the side, a tomahawk in his back. Some distance away, Ta-na-wun-da stood with his arm still extended, dappled sunlight glinting across his bronzed chest. Renno gazed at him, feeling he was looking upon a Seneca warrior of old —perhaps even the legendary sachem Ghonka, who had raised an orphaned white baby and named him Renno, the first white Indian.

"Father!" Hawk shouted, snapping Renno from his reverie.

Twisting around, he saw Captain Bushnell raising his pistol to fire almost point-blank at him. Before Renno could bring his own weapon into play, Mist-on-the-Water gave a chilling cry and launched herself at the officer, her fist clutching a knife she had hidden beneath her skirt when the soldiers first confronted them. She hurtled into him, and his arm was knocked to the side, the pistol firing harmlessly into the trees.

Bushnell tried to throw the woman off, but she lashed out with the knife, slicing long gashes across his hands and arms. He struck her in the face, knocking her to the side, but she was back on him in an instant, slashing at his face. He jerked his head to the side, and the first thrust took off his right ear. The second laid open his throat, and as blood gushed from his neck, she plunged the blade deep into his chest. His body quivered, the spurting blood slowing to a trickle as his heart ceased to pump.

Mist-on-the-Water stood away from the dead man, smiling with satisfaction. Coming up beside her, Ta-na-wun-da took her in his arms.

Renno turned toward Hawk and saw that Ma-ton-ga had already removed his shirt and was fashioning a bandage for his wound. With some difficulty, Renno managed to stand. Ta-na must have seen his father's struggle, for he dashed over and asked, "Are you all right?"

"Had the wind knocked out of me," Renno replied, waving off his son's concern.

He made a quick count of the five motionless bodies and suddenly remembered that a sixth soldier had remained with the horses.

"Ta-na, there was one more—"

"No longer," his son interrupted, drawing a finger across his throat.

Renno nodded. "You were following them?"

"Yes. But I confess I did not expect such a play."

Renno gestured at Captain Bushnell's corpse. "We had something of a quarrel at the fort."

"It certainly appears so," Ta-na commented, shaking his head as he took in the bodies sprawled among the trees.

Just then one of the soldiers stirred. Ta-na drew a

knife from his belt and started toward him, but Renno grabbed his arm.

"Not that one," he told his son. "He tried to stop them."

"So that's why you foiled my shot."

Renno grinned. "You were aiming at him? I thought you *wanted* to hit that tree." He jabbed a thumb at the nearby tree where Ta-na's arrow had struck.

When the corporal groggily lifted himself onto his hands and knees, Renno bent down to help him up. But Renno's legs gave way, and he fell awkwardly onto his side.

Ta-na knelt beside him. Gripping him around the shoulders, he asked, "What is the matter?"

"Nothing," Renno insisted, his face tightening from the pain in his back.

Hawk and the women came over to see what was wrong. Renno looked up at them and forced a smile, his vision clouding over as he tried to focus on the people huddled around him.

"What is it?" Hawk asked anxiously, kneeling beside Ta-na and his father.

"I think he's been shot," Ta-na declared, looking for some sign of a wound.

Renno groaned, his body arching against the pain. As Ta-na eased his father onto the ground, his hand moved down along the spine to the lower back. Gasping, he pulled his hand away and held it in front of him. His palm was covered with blood.

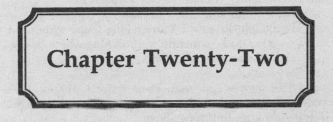

Chapter Twenty-Two

 Voices floated up to Renno through the haze, through the swirling snow. . . .

"It is the old scar. The old wound."

"Must have torn it open during the fight."

"Riding from Tennessee couldn't have helped."

"Why did he come?"

"The voices. The visions. I heard them, too."

"Will he be all right?"

"The bleeding has stopped, but if it reopens . . ."

"What can we do?"

"Find a place to winter."

"Build a travois."

"First El-i-chi, then Gao, and now—"

"Don't talk like that!"

"I won't let him die!"

The snow was brilliant, each flake a minute crystalline sun that flashed in front of Renno's eyes as it drifted past. He tried to reach out and brush them away, but they floated all around him, dancing, chanting, calling to him in the voices of his children—and in the words of a manitou that rang in his memory:

Look into his eyes. See in them the sachem. Only then can we journey. Only then. . . .

"Os-sweh-ga-da-ah Ne-wa-ah . . ." he whispered into the blinding whiteness. "My Little Hawk. . . ."

"Father!" his son called to him.

He thought he saw a figure taking shape within the snow, wearing it like a mantle, approaching where he lay.

"Father! Can you hear me?"

"My son . . ."

Other figures appeared. Ta-na-wun-da. Mist-on-the-Water. The snow drifted slowly around them, hazy light filtering through the trees above.

"Wh-what happened?" he muttered, trying to sit up.

"Rest easy, Father," Hawk urged, helping him back onto his side on the ground. He felt something soft beneath his cheek—a rolled-up blanket—and realized he was covered with a heavy deerskin robe.

"Was I . . . shot?"

Hawk shook his head. "The old wound in your back reopened. You lost blood, but Ma-ton-ga got the bleeding to stop."

Look into his eyes. . . .

"What?"

"I said you lost some blood. That's why you passed out. But the bleeding has stopped."

His eyes . . .

"Are you all right?" Ta-na-wun-da asked, kneeling beside his father in concern.

"Yes," Renno replied, his voice a bit weak as he blinked his eyes to clear them.

"You gave us quite a scare," Ta-na remarked.

"I'm fine. Really I am."

His vision continued to clear, and he noticed Hawk's arm in a sling and remembered that he had been shot.

"What about you?" he asked, gesturing at the arm.

"It's nothing," Hawk assured him. "It passed right through."

Renno looked back and forth between his sons and the two women, who stood behind them. Then he saw someone else standing off to the side. He thought it was a manitou until he recognized the uniform.

Noticing his father staring at the man, Hawk said, "Corporal Milowe is fine. He wanted to make sure you were all right before he left." Turning, he signaled the soldier to approach.

As Milowe came over, Ta-na-wun-da began hauling away the bodies. With the ground frozen, burial was unfeasible, so they would be burned on a pyre out beyond the forest.

"I, uh, want to thank you, Mr. Harper," the corporal began somewhat hesitantly, kneeling beside Renno. "And I want to apologize for what they done. I seen how it happened, and I know it weren't your fault. That's what I'll report when I get back to Albany."

"No," Renno told him. "Let their families think they died at the fort, on the field of battle."

"I agree," Hawk put in. "No one need know of their actions."

"That captain don't hardly deserve such concern."

"No," Hawk admitted. "But he's received his judgment. And if he has family who love him, they needn't suffer any more than necessary."

"I suppose you're right," the corporal said.

"When we leave, you're welcome to travel with us as far as you'd like."

"No, thank you. I'm fixing to head east. My parents are in Albany." He glanced over at the bodies. "Guess I oughta help with them first."

Hawk saw the corporal's discomfited expression and knew he had no desire to witness the cremation of his former comrades. "We won't be leaving here for a while," he said. "We can take care of the bodies, if you want to put some miles behind you before dark."

Milowe's face brightened. "I'd appreciate that, Captain Harper."

"Just Hawk."

"Thank you, sir."

"Take as many of their horses as you want," Hawk told him. "We'll use any ones left."

The corporal again thanked Hawk, then said a final good-bye to Renno. Taking up his pistol and a couple of the weapons that had belonged to the other soldiers, he headed back through the trees. A minute later they saw him riding eastward.

"I'd best help Ta-na with those bodies. We'll spend the night here, then get you moved somewhere more comfortable."

"I'm fine," Renno insisted, again trying to sit up.

"You aren't, and you'll do as we tell you," Hawk countered.

Renno lay back down, nodding in resignation. "Go on and get about your business," he grumbled with a mock frown. "The sooner you boys are finished, the sooner we can get back on the trail."

"You just rest up," Hawk told him. Rising, he walked past Mist-on-the-Water, who was building a fire and arranging the campsite, and over to where his brother was working.

Renno was watching them drag the bodies out of the forest when Ma-ton-ga came over and knelt behind him, lifting the robe to inspect his wound. He looked over his shoulder at the Creek woman. She was focused on her work as she removed and replaced the bandage.

"You keep me alive, you hear?" he said.

She stared up at him uncertainly.

"Don't let me die—not until I reach home."

"No die. You rest," she muttered in broken English.

Renno gazed at her a long moment, reading the worry in her eyes. Smiling, he said in Creek, "Please do not tell them."

"There is nothing to tell," she replied in her native tongue.

"It is not going to heal. It will kill me first."

"You cannot know this. I do not know this."

"In time you will, as I do. All I ask is that you not let them know. When the time comes, I want to tell my sons myself."

"You will die an old man," she tried to reassure him.

"I *am* an old man. Just keep me alive long enough to make it home. I want to see my wife and daughter again. I . . . I want to say good-bye."

Ma-ton-ga was about to reply but stopped abruptly and looked up. Renno followed her gaze and saw Ta-na-wun-da approaching. He had a curious expression, and Renno feared he might have overheard part of the conversation. But then he smiled and said, "The sky is clearing; there will be no more snow. We will light the pyre before we leave."

"Tomorrow," Renno said emphatically.

"We will see how you are feeling."

"I will be fine."

He glanced over his shoulder at Ma-ton-ga and repeated it in Creek. She looked nervously between the two men, then lowered her head and nodded.

"We will see," Ta-na said. "Now I suggest we have something to eat and get some rest. The sun will be down within the hour, and the night will be cold."

Renno watched him walk over to where Mist-on-the-Water was preparing supper. He noticed how comfortable they appeared to be together—how easily they fell into conversation and smiled at each other.

The sachem closed his eyes. *Just for a moment,* he told himself. Soon he was fast asleep.

When Renno awoke it was dark out, and the fire had burned down to low, glowing embers. He was still lying on his side under the robe, and he raised up on one arm and glanced around the campsite. Trees loomed tall and dark overhead, and the hint of a moon was visible through the pine branches. He noticed four other bedrolls around the fire, but only three were occupied. Undoubtedly one of his sons was standing guard, probably near where the horses were tied.

The air was quite chilly, and Renno decided to add some wood to the fire—provided he could stand and move around. It took considerable effort, but after a couple of minutes he managed to pull himself to his feet. Wrapping the robe around him, he took slow, careful steps toward the fire.

He stood warming his hands over the embers, looking from one blanket to the other, determining who was where. Not until one of them shifted and he spied blond hair did he know it was Ta-na-wun-da keeping watch.

A pile of branches had been gathered near the fire. Walking over to it, he picked out several short, sturdy ones and gingerly placed them over the coals, taking care not to stir them too much and possibly awaken the sleepers. He stood a moment longer until he had fully warmed, then returned to his own bedding.

Renno was about to lie down when he heard a horse whinny. Turning toward the sound, he headed through the forest. As he neared the edge of the trees, he halted and softly called his younger son's name, then paused and repeated it.

"Hawk?" came the reply.

"No. Renno."

"What are you doing up and about?" his son said in concern as he approached through the trees.

"Just checking to see if you're awake."

"How is your back?"

"It feels all right." He reached a hand just above the small of his back. "A bit stiff, is all."

"The plaster Ma-ton-ga made should keep the wound closed while it heals."

Renno nodded, then asked, "Mind if I join you?"

"Just for a while. Then I want you to get back to sleep."

"You sound like an old man," Renno said with a mock frown.

"Perhaps if *you* acted your age occasionally instead of pretending to be a young buck, you wouldn't be wearing that plaster right now."

"While we're standing here talking, those horses could be halfway to Canada," Renno teased, prodding his son forward.

Ta-na-wun-da led the way out of the forest and over to where the horses were tied at the edge of the field. It was quite a bit lighter in the open, and Renno was easily able to see that five army horses had been added to their own.

"The corporal took only two," Ta-na explained. "We have enough for each of us to ride one and trail another." He glanced back at his father. "Or to pull a travois."

"I don't need one," Renno declared. "It will be a lot smoother riding in a saddle than bouncing around on one of those contraptions."

"Perhaps," Ta-na acknowledged.

One of the horses was stamping nervously, and Ta-na walked over to it and patted its muzzle.

"You did well back there," Renno called to him. "You reminded me of the Seneca warriors of my youth."

Ta-na turned to face him, and even in the moonlight, Renno could see his smile.

"You made me proud to be a sachem . . . and your father," Renno added, and his son lowered his head in respect.

"My brother would have been proud of you, too," Renno continued. "You were like a son to El-i-chi."

"From what Mist-on-the-Water told me about Gao's bravery at Fort Niagara, he would have been even more proud of his own son."

"He is."

"Does he speak to you?" Ta-na asked, coming closer.

"El-i-chi?"

"And the others. Do they still speak to you?"

"When they choose."

"And what do they say?"

Hush! The sachem approaches. . . .

Renno closed his eyes, as if listening to a voice.

Look into his eyes. . . .

"Father?" someone called out, and Renno turned to see Little Hawk emerging from the trees. "Whatever are you doing out here?"

"I . . ." Renno started to reply, but the words caught in his throat.

The sachem approaches. . . .

"You really should be lying down."

"He's all right," Ta-na said, coming up beside his father.

Look into his eyes. . . .

Hawk noticed the strange way Renno was staring at him, and he came closer. "Is something wrong?" he asked, cocking his head as he examined his father.

Renno reached out and grasped his elder son's forearms. Holding him tight, he gazed deep into his soul, into his crystal-blue eyes. The moonlight danced upon them as if they were Kanyadariyo, the Beautiful Lake.

"What is it?" Hawk asked.

Deep, cool eyes. The eyes of a soldier and a lover. The eyes of a son.

Renno felt the surge of blood in Hawk's arms. He was three-quarters white, yet his blood was the same as that which coursed through Renno's veins. The very same blood that stirred within Ta-na-wun-da and within so many sachems of their people.

But was it a sachem's blood? Renno held Hawk tight, staring into those powerful eyes, searching for something he had been promised. He saw moonlight and more, yet there was no special sign, and he wondered when he would finally look into these eyes and know that the next sachem had come.

"Father, speak to me," Hawk insisted, breaking Renno's grip and moving back a few steps. "Is it the wound?"

Renno shook his head. "I . . . I was just thinking about something. It isn't important."

"Come. I'll take you back."

"Let him stay," Ta-na-wun-da declared, stepping between father and son.

"But he should be—"

"Sometimes a man heals better standing on his feet than lying on the ground."

Hawk fell silent as he looked at Ta-na, then beyond him to his father. Finally he shrugged. "Perhaps you're right. But only a little longer."

"Go back," Ta-na told his older brother. "Get some more sleep. I'll wake you when it is your turn to stand guard."

Hawk hesitated, staring between the two of them. "All right," he replied at last. "But don't stay up long, Father."

"I'll be fine."

Hawk headed back into the trees.

"Thank you," Renno said as Ta-na-wun-da turned toward him.

"Hawk was right, but I wanted you to stay."

"So did I," Renno heard himself saying. But it was as if the words were coming from another mouth. For within him, his true voice was crying, *Hush! The sachem approaches!*

No moonlight was reflected in Ta-na-wun-da's eyes; they glowed with a light of their own. It was a light Renno had seen as a child, burning in his father, Ghonkaba. The same light that blazed forth from Ja-gonh and the first Renno.

Ta-na-wun-da reached forward and took hold of his father's forearms. As Renno grasped him back, he felt the powerful rush of blood. Three-quarters Indian, Ta-na-wun-da had even more Seneca blood than Renno or any of the previous white Indians. But it was more than blood that surged so powerfully through his veins. It was a spirit that came not just from sharing the lineage of the first white Indian but from being part of a line that stretched back to Ghonka and all the full-blooded Seneca shamans before him.

It was truly the spirit of the shaman.

He is the one! Renno realized with a start as the light blazed forth from his son's eyes. *It has been Ta-na-wun-da all the time!*

"Father . . ." Ta-na whispered.

"My son," Renno breathed in reply.

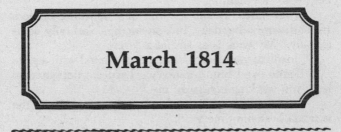

March 1814

Renno pulled his horse to a halt at the end of the tree-lined lane that led to Huntington Castle. It had been a long and tiring journey from western New York, down through Iowa and Kentucky, and across the Barrens to Rusog's Town in the Cherokee Nation. The winter had been relatively mild, yet there had been several times when the travelers had been forced to seek shelter and hole up until the passing of a storm. Fortunately the snows were never deep, and with two horses per rider they had made good time.

Renno wanted to kick his horse into a gallop and race down the lane to the house he shared with Beth Huntington Harper. But he forced himself to sit still, breathing in the aroma, imagining that the pecan trees were already in bloom and the fields were ripe with corn and grain. He could smell the smoke drifting from the cabins and longhouses of Rusog's Town, and he imagined each of his Seneca and Cherokee friends going about their daily business as they awaited the coming of spring.

Ta-na-wun-da rode his pinto up beside his father and asked, "Is it as you remembered?"

"Better," Renno replied, looking around him. "Far, far better."

Ta-na gestured toward the fields. "This year I will help with the planting."

"I am fine," Renno assured him, reaching behind. He still wore a bandage, but the wound bled only occasionally. "My back is as strong as ever."

"Just like your head," Ta-na commented with a grin.

Renno eyed him dubiously. "I will be delighted to have you working *alongside* me."

"And I will be delighted to have you rocking on the veranda, watching me work."

"And pointing out when your rows have gone crooked."

Ta-na chuckled. "I would have it no other way."

Hawk joined them now, riding up on the other side of Renno. Turning in the saddle, he looked first at his father and then Ta-na-wun-da. "Perhaps I should ride over to the village and tell Ah-wa-o about her son."

"No," Ta-na said firmly. "Gao was my brother. It is something I must do." He reined the pinto around. "I will meet you at the house after I am done."

"Take the army horses with you," Renno told him. "They rightfully belong to Gao's family."

Ta-na nodded, then rode back to where the women waited. He spoke with them briefly, and then Ma-ton-ga untied from her saddle the line that held the remuda of army horses. She handed it to Ta-na, and he and Mist-on-the-Water rode off down the road that led to Rusog's Town, the five extra horses trailing behind them.

Renno waited until Ma-ton-ga had come up beside Hawk. Then he unwound the reins from his saddle horn and exclaimed, "I'll see you at home!"

With a sharp kick, he set the horse into a gallop. Hawk and Ma-ton-ga stared at each other a moment, then took off after him down the lane.

* * *

"Father! Father!" Michael Soaring Hawk shouted, racing down the veranda steps to meet the riders.

Hawk could hardly get his foot out of the stirrup as the young boy reached up and tugged at his boot. "Just a minute," he pleaded with a grin, then dismounted and scooped his son into his arms. Michael squeezed his neck so hard that he had trouble breathing. "I'm back, just like I promised," he said while prying the boy's arms from around his neck.

"Grandpa!" Michael exclaimed as Renno climbed down off his horse. Twisting in Hawk's arms, he reached for Renno, who snatched him up and gave him a playful swing, then set him down with a hug.

"Look!" Michael blurted, tugging Renno's coat sleeve and pulling him toward the veranda.

Renno looked up to see a boy and girl standing at the top of the steps, looking a bit shy as they took in the excitement. The girl had blond hair, but her dark eyes and olive complexion were evidence of her part-Seneca blood. Her younger brother had dark hair and features but the blue eyes of his mother.

"Emily, is that you?" Renno said in wonder. "And little Louis? Why, you're all grown up."

"I'm six," Louis announced, taking a step forward. "Are you my grandpa?"

"I certainly am." Renno came up the steps and knelt in front of the boy, who gave him a tenuous hug. "And, Emily, you must be eight," he said to his granddaughter.

"My birthday was on Christmas."

"Of course it was. You don't think I'd forget my own granddaughter's birthday, do you?"

Smiling demurely, she approached and offered him a hug, as well.

"Where is your mother?" Renno asked.

"Right here," a woman declared.

He looked up to see Renna standing in the doorway. His mouth dropped open, and he could not move, so staggered was he by the sight of his daughter, home at last from France.

"Aren't you going to give me a hug, too?" she asked, coming over to him on the veranda.

He rose, and she fell into his arms. They stood there, just holding on to each other. Then he kissed her on both cheeks and pulled away slightly to look at her.

"You are . . . stunning," was all he could say.

"The latest Paris fashion." She stepped back and pirouetted, showing off her satin dress with its heavily flounced hem that flared out below the knee. Even with lace edging its plunging neckline, the dress was extremely décolleté, with Renna's modesty protected by the white cashmere shawl she wore over her shoulders.

"We've seen nothing like that in America," Renno commented, shaking his head. "But I wasn't talking about the dress. You'd be stunning in a monk's habit."

"I'm so happy to be home!" she exclaimed, hugging him again. Then she rushed over to her brother and embraced him as well.

Renno was gazing in wonder at his first- and second-born when Beth came out onto the veranda and placed her arm around his back. He turned to find her smiling up at him, and he swooped her into his arms and kissed her full on the lips.

They stared into each other's eyes a long moment, and then Beth nodded toward Renna and Hawk. "They look wonderful together, don't they?"

"They certainly do. Where's Beau?" he added, referring to Renna's husband, the comte de Beaujolais.

"He'll be in Washington a few weeks," she explained. "But Renna insisted on coming out here just as soon as their ship docked."

"I hope she won't be rushing right off again."

"To France?" Beth shook her head. "I think she and Beau are planning to be in America a long, long time." She looked around. "Where is Ta-na?"

"He'll be along presently. He went to the village first."

She gave him a squeeze. "Think of it—the whole family together again." Seeing Renno's smile fade, she asked, "Did you find Gao?"

He drew in a breath and let it out slowly. "Gao will not be coming home again. He is with his father now."

Beth's eyes welled with tears, and he held her close.

When Ta-na-wun-da brought his aunt the news of her son's death, she did not break into tears. She silently walked over to a chair beside the cabin's hearth and sat down, staring into the flames. Ta-na knelt beside her, resting his head on her lap.

"He was a great warrior, like his father," Ah-wa-o said, her voice low but steady.

"I miss him already," Ta-na replied.

"I lost him a long time ago—the day he rode off with Tecumseh. I knew then that all would end in death."

"No," Ta-na declared, lifting his head to look up at her. "All is not death. A part of Gao is still alive."

She looked down at him questioningly.

"He is alive here." Ta-na clapped his hand against his chest.

Ah-wa-o nodded, but there was little spirit in her eyes. It was apparent that to her, these were no more than words one speaks over the dead. They held truth, perhaps, but did nothing to take away the pain.

Ta-na-wun-da stood, and when she did not look up at him, he touched her cheek.

"Gao has left us. But he has sent us his wife . . . and his child."

Mist-on-the-Water came forward now, her hands resting on her midsection. As Ah-wa-o stared at her daughter-in-law, her eyes slowly lit with understanding.

"Your son—my husband—lives here as well," Mist-on-the-Water whispered.

"A . . . a child?" Ah-wa-o breathed. She reached

over to Mist-on-the-Water and gingerly touched the faint swell of her belly, feeling the new life within.

Hawk and Ta-na-wun-da walked out across the fields of Huntington Castle to a small rise that overlooked Rusog's Town. The sun was setting behind the village, spreading bands of color across the sky as it touched the horizon and slowly passed from sight. The brothers watched in silence, listening to the rushing waters of a nearby stream and the distant hoot of an owl.

"It is out there," Ta-na-wun-da commented, gesturing beyond the village.

"What is?"

"Your future."

"Where?"

"In the West. In the place where the sun sleeps."

Hawk whispered the phrase in Creek: "Ma-ton-ga . . ." He seemed momentarily disoriented, then shook his head as if to clear it and muttered, "How do you know?"

Ta-na gripped his brother's shoulder. "Because, Little Hawk, that is where my own destiny lies."

They heard voices and watched Mist-on-the-Water and Ma-ton-ga approaching from the village. Though still some distance away, they could be heard giggling and whispering to each other.

"She is a brave woman, you know," Ta-na commented.

"Ma-ton-ga?" He waved a dismissive hand. "She is more warrior than woman."

"Perhaps it will take a warrior to again capture Little Hawk's heart."

"Don't be crazy." Hawk jabbed his brother playfully.

"Let's go see what they want."

"A fatal mistake," Hawk told him. "You should never engage the enemy on their terms—especially not a woman."

"But they're coming out here onto our ground."

Hawk chuckled. "So they would have us think. Still, I suggest you keep your tomahawk close at hand."

"Come along," Ta-na said, tugging at Hawk's sleeve. "They won't hurt us."

"They don't need to. We probably already have our paws in the trap."

Ta-na grinned. "If it proves too painful, we can always gnaw them off."

"The women?"

"Our paws, big brother. Our paws."

Ta-na-wun-da wrapped his arm around Hawk's shoulder, and together they started down the hill toward the Cherokee village. Toward Mist-on-the-Water and Ma-ton-ga . . . and their future.

Author's Note

 I would like to thank editors Pamela Lappies and Dale Evva Gelfand for their excellent work on this manuscript and for their creative advice and assistance throughout the writing of this novel. A special thanks also to all my friends at Book Creations Inc. and Bantam Books, with whom it has been such a delight to work over the years.

To learn more about relations between America and the Indian nations during the time of this novel, I recommend the superb biography *A Sorrow in Our Heart: The Life of Tecumseh*, by Allan W. Eckert (New York: Bantam Books, 1992).

DONALD CLAYTON PORTER

THE SAGA OF THE FIRST AMERICANS

*The spellbinding epic of adventure
at the dawn of history*

by William Sarabande

SHADOW OF THE WATCHING STAR

___56029-8 $5.99/$7.99 Canada

___26889-9 BEYOND THE SEA OF ICE $5.99/$6.99 Canada

___27159-8 CORRIDOR OF STORMS $5.99/$6.99 Canada

___28206-9 FORBIDDEN LAND $5.99/$6.99 Canada

___28579-3 WALKERS OF THE WIND $5.99/$6.99 Canada

___29105-X THE SACRED STONES $5.99/$6.99 Canada

___29106-8 THUNDER IN THE SKY $5.99/$6.99 Canada

___56028-X THE EDGE OF THE WORLD $5.99/$6.99 Canada

And also by William Sarabande

___25802-8 WOLVES OF THE DAWN $5.99/$7.50 in Canada